PRAISE FOR SABRINA A. FISH

"*DIOMERE'S EXILE* is an enthralling story about love, betrayal, and hope. It will keep you turning the pages until the end!"

~*Tamara Grantham, award-winning author of the Fairy World MD series*

DIOMERE'S EXILE

THE GATE KEEPER CHRONICLES, BOOK 1

SABRINA A. FISH

SAF Books, LLC

CONTENTS

DIOMERE'S EXILE

The Gate Keeper Chronicles

First published in 2017. This edition published in 2024.

Copyright © 2024 by SAF Books, LLC/Sabrina A. Fish

Cover Art by Jaqueline Sweet https://www.jacqueline-sweet.com/

This edition published by SAF Books, LLC www.SabrinaAFish.com

For questions or concerns about the quality of the book, please contact us at Sabrina@SabrinaAFish.com

Digital ASIN: B0DDM8P8WQ

Paperback ISBN: 9798304644211

Published in The United States of America

Also By Sabrina A. Fish

Children of Hades Trilogy

Vampire Queen's Search

Vampire Queen's Revelation

Vampire Queen's Victory -2025

The Gate Keeper Chronicles

Diomere's Exile

Diomere's Healer

Diomere's Mercenary

Diomere's Siren –2025

Diomere's Queen –2026

Multi-Author Series Contributions

Spellbound Mail-Order Husbands

Auras, Heirs, & Witchy Affairs

Shifter Mail-Order Brides

Attracting His Mate

DEDICATION

For Larry, who believed in me
even when I didn't believe in myself.
I love you.

GLOSSARY OF NAMES

Arriana Quinones *(ahr-ee-ahna kwi-noh-nez)*: half Mer & half Light Fairy, Nadia's sister

Captain Theo: human, captain

Cilix *(cee-licks)*: human, Gregor's servant/butler

Darryn *(dahr-rin)*: human, priest of Asha

Deacon Bouras (dee-cun bor-ahs): Earl of Orangol in Thuno

Delmar de Amadeus *(del-mahr de ahmah-deh-uhs)*: Mer, King of Diomere

Doron *(dor-un)*: human, royal servant

Faina Alkaev *(fay-ee-nah ahl-kav)*: daughter of Lord Odell Alkaev

Flip *(flip)*: human, street urchin in Diomere's capitol city

Geeta de Ribera *(gee-tah de ri-ber-ah)*: Mer, Healer, Member of Vromia Guild, Nadia's cousin

Gregor Cyrene *(greh-uhr sahy-reen)*: Human, Marquess of Cyrene & Sestos

Hermios Aetos (her-mee-ohs ah-tohs): Earl of Kepoi in Thuno

Jamison *(jey-muh-suhn)*: human, member of Vromia Guild, The Shark's scholar

Jasara/Jasna *(juh-sah-rah/ jahs-nah)*: Reis' mother, Dieuroi Mavros' mistress

Jon El-Mofty Guru *(jon el mohf-tee)*: Mer, Member of Vromia Guild

Kardia Quinones *(kahr-dee-uh kwi-noh-nez)*: half Mer & half Harpy, Nadia's sister

Lareina de Quinones *(lah-rey-nah de kwi-noh-nez)*: Mer, Queen of Diomere, Nadia's sister

Luis de Quinones (loo-is de kwi-noh-nez): Mer, Nadia's father

Madame Gybris (mad-uhm gahy-bris):

Madelena de Amadeus de Quinones *(maduh-leenah de ah-mah-dee-us)*: Mer, Princess of Diomere

Maro (mah-roh): human, Prince Reis' manservant

Torin (tor-in): human, palace marshall in Thuno

Mavros Vasious *(mahv-ros vah-shus)*: human, Dieuroi (god king) of Thuno

Mondami *(mon-dah-mee)*: Magic World in habited mostly by non-humans

Martinos *(mahr-teen-ohs)*: human, Gregor's coachman

Nadia de Quinones *(nah-dee-uh de kwi-noh-nez)*: Mer, Vromia Guild leader

Odell Alkaev (Oh-del *ahl-kav* **)**: Marques of Elis & Lycia in Thuno

Paulo Krupin *(pawl-oh kruh-pin)*: human, Earl of Pella in Thuno

Pell *(pel)*: human, member of Vromia Guild, The Shark's Lieutenant

Reis Vasious *(rees vah-shus)*: Mer, bastard Prince of Thuno

Saimond *(sahy-mond)*: Non-magic world inhabited mostly by humans

Sarna (*sahr-nah***)**: human, Member of Vromia Guild

Stefan Vasious *(stef-un vah-shus)*: human, Crown-Prince of Thuno

Tiago Amadeus *(tee-ah-goh ah-mah-dee-us)*: Mer, bastard Prince of King Delmar of Diomere

Victor Pajari *(vic-tor pah-jah-ree)*: human, Earl of Juktas in Thuno

Zephyra de Quinones *(zef-eer-ah de kwi-noh-nez)*: Mer, Nadia's sister

SAIMOND MAP

NON-MAGIC HUMAN WORLD

The Gate Keeper Chronicles

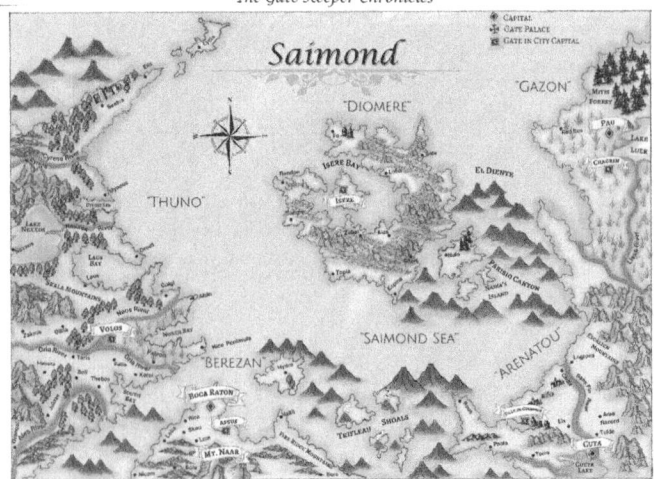

Digital version map created by Collette Carmon

AUTHOR NOTE

This book is steamy fantasy romance for readers 18+. It contains
explicit sex, violence, and sexual assault. If any of that bothers you,
don't read this book.
You've been warned.

Also, the prologue has been added as bonus content to celebrate this
2nd Edition release.
It covers the event that caused Nadia's exile.
I hope you enjoy it.

PROLOGUE (BONUS SCENE ADDED TO 2ND EDITION)

ISERE, DIOMERE-12 YEARS AGO

Nadia stifled a yawn. She glanced at the nursemaid who sang a quiet lullaby while feeding the infant prince his bottle.

The melody wrapped around her, reminding her of times as a young girl when her mother would hum the same song. Inhaling the warm island breeze coming in through the window, she sank further into the song's tightening embrace.

Her eyes fluttered shut as her memories took her back to her childhood.

Resting her head on her mother's lap, she sighed as gentle fingers combed through her long hair. Her eyelids grew heavy.

"I love you, mami."

Her mother stopped humming. "Be strong, my daughter. Strife's shadow is upon you."

She jerked awake and, cursing under her breath, glared out the open window. Getting caught sleeping on assignment wouldn't prove to her skeptical superiors that she deserved her promotion to captain at only twenty years of age. Especially when those superiors looked for any reason to overturn the queen's decision.

She ran her left hand down the braid hanging over her shoulder and glanced up to see the nursemaid's gaze following the gesture. Releasing the braid, she dropped her hand to rest on the hilt of her sword.

The corner of the nursemaid's mouth lifted.

Nadia clenched her jaw. The woman, a distant relation of the royal line, knew Nadia didn't trust her. Though she didn't doubt the woman truly cared for the young prince, her instincts told her to be wary.

Like the rest of the royal family, Jasara was more than she appeared.

Her gaze fell to the infant, heir to the island nation of Diomere, cradled in the nursemaid's arms. She couldn't help the swell of pride at being trusted with such a precious charge.

The babe opened his dual-colored eyes as if sensing her attention. She met that piercing, too aware gaze. She'd do well to appreciate the dullness of her assignment, for something told her it wouldn't always be easy keeping him from harm.

She tried to convince her sister to find another to care for the child, but the Queen just smiled. "Jasara is a distant cousin, family, and she loves my son. Between her care and your strength, my sweet boy couldn't be in safer hands." The Queen had laughed at Nadia's scowl. "If you feel that uneasy, move your things into the other nursemaid chamber. Jasara didn't want help, so it remains empty."

Nadia ran her hand along the pommel of her sword. The raised edges of the leather wrap pressed into the pads of her fingers.

She turned her gaze toward the moonlit ships anchored in the harbor outside the prince's window. They floated in the water, yellow sails furled, the royal crest hidden in the folds. Lanterns bobbed on the decks of three of the great ships, readying to sail as soon as the sun rose. Flower blooms, white petals glowing silver in the moonlight, floated in the water around the ships. The sailors' offerings to the gods in supplication for fair winds and calm seas.

She stared at the warm sea water that invited her to call her other form and dive beneath the waves. Her skin tingled as a'mi, the power that made her and her family different from most on this side of the gate, swelled inside her. She imagined she could feel the powerful fins of her shifted form tingling along the nerves of her human form.

Jasara continued to hum.

Nadia ignored the sea's call and pushed her a'mi back into the pool of power deep inside her. Shrugging her shoulders as it fought her control, she scowled at the other woman.

Why hadn't Jasara wanted the help of another nursemaid? Where had she been the year before the prince was born? And why had she felt the need to return and offer to care for the royal heir? Instinct or a'mi, Nadia wasn't sure there was a difference, told her that the older woman was hiding something. But what?

She scanned the large sitting room, her sharp gaze delving into every corner and shadow. She checked the three doors that opened up to the nursery's main sitting room and the opened windows that stretched across the remaining wall.

Nadia got up to stand guard each time the baby woke, too suspicious to allow the woman alone time with the baby. Other than annoyed glances and tight-lipped smiles, Jasara did nothing that Nadia could see wrong.

Shrugging her shoulders, she forced her gaze back to the harbor. She stepped forward, her eyes narrowing.

Jasara stopped humming. "Is all well, Capitán?"

A slow fog rolled in from the sea, spilled around the ships, and crept toward the castle like long fingers intent on squeezing the life from the island people. A prickle of unease crawled up her back.

Calling her a'mi, she reached out with her power, attempting to connect to the water making up the thick cloud of fog. She pushed, commanding the fog to recede.

It charged forward as if responding to someone else.

She narrowed her gaze, pulling from the deep well of power inside her, and stepped forward, bending the fog to her will. Slowing to a halt, the dense blanket of fog receded back toward the sea.

Nadia shrugged the tension from her shoulders.

"A heavy fog rolled in. I thought—" She darted a look at Jasara's bemused smile. "—nothing. It was nothing."

Glowering at the thick fog hovering above the water, she ignored Jasara's lifted brow. She returned to her position, shoulders back.

Jasara started to hum again.

The soft melody slowly chased the uneasy feelings to the back of Nadia's mind. It threaded through her subconscious, wrapping her mind in heavy layers. Her shoulders relaxed. She really did need to ease up on the woman. It was clear by the smile on Jasara's face that she loved the baby very much. She'd done nothing to warrant Nadia's constant scrutiny.

Drifting in a dreamlike haze, she relaxed her grip on the sword at her hip, though she didn't release it completely. Her eyelids drooped. She watched the nursemaid rock the child as if from a far distance. Her head fell back to rest against the wall, but her subconscious fought against letting her eyelids close.

Fingers of fog crept over the windowsill and slowly reached toward the sleeping infant.

Becoming louder, Jasara's song changed. The nursemaid inhaled the fog and blew it toward Nadia.

Eyes falling closed, Nadia slid down the wall.

Pain burned across her cheek, breaking the hold on her mind. Nadia's eyes snapped open.

Jasara spoke and her awareness dimmed. Her eyes drooped, but she refused to let them close again. Jasara leaned over Nadia, her bright red hair brushing softly against Nadia's chest. She touched Nadia's cheek.

The burning subsided. Unease pushed at the dream state surrounding her. Why was she on the floor?

Her unease strengthened. "Siren. You've bespelled me."

A deprecating smile softened the woman's face. "A small amount siren, a small amount seer, but only enough to be of use on occasion. Nothing compared to you and your sisters."

Her gaze sharpened and bore into Nadia's.

"Remember this, dear cousin," the woman said, her voice harsh. "Even the weakest can overtake the strongest if they are cunning. Beware treachery from those you don't consider a threat."

Nadia frowned through the haze holding her captive. "I knew—" she struggled to keep hold of her thoughts "—something off about you."

"Your instincts will serve you well as the first Sankta Hogo-sha," Jasara whispered. The woman smoothed a pale hand over Nadia's brow. "Don't be too long."

Nadia lifted her eyebrows as Jasara's words cut through the haze in her mind. "What is Sankta..." her voice faded as the haze thickened.

"It is time for the Sankta Hogo-sha to make themselves known. The gates must be opened. I'm sorry, mia sarko kuraga, but this is the only way I could save my own daughter. The gates must be opened. Come find your prince or all will be lost."

She knew she should question Jasara's words, but the haze tightened until unconsciousness swallowed her.

CHAPTER ONE

N adia sucked in the crisp morning air as her feet kicked up plumes of powdery red dirt on her early morning run. Ancient red woods towered around her, but she didn't admire their majestic beauty like she had the first time she'd run this path twelve years ago. Nor did she pay attention to the pounding of her friend, Pell's feet on the path next to her.

Her attention focused inward on the dark mental landscape where she controlled her a'mi, or power.

Dark shapes, representing the five elements of earth, air, fire, and water, appeared as shadows against the black landscape in her mind. She reached for the bisected triangle that represented the air element. The symbol lit up a dull gold and a podium holding a large gold scales of justice appeared in the center of the dark space, tiny eddies of swirling air filling the scale on each side.

She frowned, worry churning her gut at the diminished level of her a'mi, represented by those miniscule swirls of air. Only two years before the element had appeared as two twisting funnels that reached into the darkness above.

The muscles in her legs flared with pain as her agitation pushed her to run harder.

"Gods curse it, Nadia," Pell groaned next to her as she pulled ahead of him. "Not so damn fast."

Shooting him an apologetic glance, she slowed enough for him to draw even with her, then returned her focus to her a'mi. She pulled a small amount of power from the slightly higher side of the scales. Air swirled around her body, cooling her perspiring skin. Exhaling in relief that the power still heeded her command, she offered up a prayer of thanks to the gods when her foot caught on a tree root barely visible in the dim, early morning light. The breeze cooling her skin lightened. Her focus snapped back to her power center just as the gold scales began to fade.

"No," she said, firming her jaw.

She focused on her a'mi, and the scales solidified, but the element slipped through her fingers and disappeared from either side of the scales. Of the five elements at her command, this one had always given her the most trouble. With her power at such alarming lows, she could only do one or two tasks with it before she had to let it recharge for several hours.

Teeth grinding, she released the power, and the symbol faded like smoke.

They approached a familiar turn in the path. She picked up her pace, seeking to clear her mind. Pell groaned beside her but matched her stride.

The loamy smell of the forest filled her lungs with each breath. She loved their morning runs, the dampness of the fog in her face, the twitter of birds, the whistle of the wind past her ears, and the burn of muscle reminding her that she was alive and well. Only when she trained like this did her mind empty of all her worries and responsibilities, of the burning fact that she ran among the paths of a country that, though beautiful, wasn't her home, of the heart wrenching knowledge that she still lived in exile. She clenched her jaw and shoved the troubling thoughts aside, focusing on the pounding of her and Pell's feet along the dirt path.

They turned the last corner to see a row of shacks appear from among the ancient red wood trees of the forest which surrounded Volos, the capitol city of Thuno. She slowed to a jog, then a walk, a trickle of sweat dripping from her temple. Pell stopped and bent to rest his hands on his knees, sweat dripping from his nose, his head hanging between his arms.

"Keep moving," she said in a sing-song voice.

Pell raised his head and glared at her. Nadia lifted an eyebrow.

"I hate you," he said, his usual cool and controlled voice strained as he struggled to pull in a full breath.

She shrugged as she walked up the path to the hollow tree where they'd stashed their water skins and their larger weapons. "Yet here you are." She smirked and tossed him his water skin.

A smile pulled up the corners of his mouth. "I supposed I did bring it on myself," he said. "I should've just let you think I was another untrustworthy man bent on befriending you to gain your father's favor."

She scowled at him. "Can you blame me? My father tends to attract people as evil as himself."

Pell nodded. Friends since childhood, he knew exactly what her father was like and hadn't been surprised when her father turned his back on her after her exile.

Nadia lifted her water skin in salute then moved it to her lips for a drink. She closed her eyes as cool water rushed down her throat, replacing the stone's weight of sweat she'd lost on her run. Each droplet of water sang to her a'mi as it was absorbed into her body. Lowering the skin, she opened her eyes to find Pell staring at her, blue eyes dark with lust, fists clenched at his sides.

She met his heated stare, aware that he'd been interested in more than friendship since she'd developed breasts at twelve. Preferring weapons training over boys, she'd told him not to ruin their friendship by turning into an idiot male. She'd considered allowing him into her bed shortly after her exile began, but despite being lonely and homesick, she'd decided not to muddy things with sex. He'd agreed at the time, but the look in his eyes, the same he'd had many times over the last year, told her he'd changed his mind.

Pell stepped forward and brushed a sweaty strand of hair off her forehead. "We'd be so good together, you and I. We have trust, friendship, and history."

She nodded. What he said was true. They were great friends, though he sometimes annoyed her beyond reason. She trusted him as much as she'd ever trust any male. A memory forced its way out of the tightly locked box in her mind. She'd been nine when she'd heard a distressed cry come from her father's study and walked in.

Her father, bent over a crying woman, had looked up and met Nadia's shocked gaze, a cold smile on his lips. "Lieutenant Sando wishes to become a captain despite his low birth. To prove his loyalty, he offered me the use of his pretty wife. Wasn't that nice?"

Nadia hid her clenched fists behind her back. "You're hurting her, Father."

"She likes what I'm doing to her," he said, fisting her hair and pulling her head back so he could look into her face. "Don't you, my dear." The woman nodded vigorously, even as another tear trailed down her cheek.

Nadia's father patted the woman's head and looked back at Nadia. "You'll find that there isn't much people won't do in the name of greed. Remember that, daughter. Everyone has a price."

She shook her head. Her father had taught her many lessons. What was Pell's price? The memory of her ex's betrayal, the most painful of all, attempted to push into her mind. She shoved it back in its box. She'd never let another man that close, no, but perhaps she could enjoy Pell's offer. Hadn't she been feeling restless the last few days? Maybe she'd gone too long without a man. With Pell came years of trust, safety, and companionship. There were worse reasons to start a relationship.

Pell smoothed his hands down her sides to her hips and pulled her around until his erection pressed into the junction of her thighs and her breasts molded to his chest. The sensations weren't unpleasant, though they also didn't spark any real excitement in her.

He moved his hand under her shirt and up to the bands binding her breasts. She didn't bring her hands up to participate, but she didn't stop him either. His fingers loosened the knot on her bindings and slid up to cup her heavy breasts. She shivered when cool air whispered across her sweat dampened skin, feeling her nipples tighten as she let her eyes close.

Pell pulled her shirt and loose bindings over her head. She let him but felt no excitement or anticipation. Was something wrong with her? He pinched one of her sensitive nipples, yanking her attention back to the moment, and she grimaced. Maybe if she tried harder. She lifted her hands to caress Pell's chest through his shirt, but still felt no spark of desire for him. *This is wrong.* She wouldn't be her father. She wanted to feel a connection, to find the one spoken of in the old stories her mother had told her. She wanted a true heartbond like Geeta, even if such a thing most likely didn't exist for her.

She sighed. "Stop."

Pell, one hand on her bare breast, pulled her close. "Please, Nadia. You want this as much as I do."

He covered her mouth with his, licking the closed seam of her lips. Pushing against his shoulders, she opened her mouth to protest further when he thrust his tongue into her mouth, gagging her. She called on her a'mi, but she'd used up what little ability she'd managed to build up. She hooked a leg around his and shoved as hard as she could, pulling his knee out from under him. He sprawled on the ground at her feet, a surprised look on his face.

Wiping her arm across her mouth, she glared down at him. "I said stop." She grabbed her shirt from the ground and pulled it over her head. "We're friends. To be anything else is a complication I prefer to avoid."

"You were enjoying it, at first," he said, his voice hitching at the end. Nadia raised an eyebrow. Eyes flashing with hurt that caused guilt to twist her stomach, he lifted his chin. "I thought you were just playing coy."

"Next time don't think. Check to be sure," she said, shrugging. "If sex is all you're after, go visit Adrial and her nightingales."

"Fine," he said, his face smoothing into a mask as he straightened. "I apologize. I'll make sure to double check next time."

"You're forgiven." She squeezed his arm, determined to make sure it never had the chance to happen again. His friendship meant too much to her.

He clenched his jaw and nodded as he reached into the hollow tree for his sword and tied it around his waist. "I need to get back to the Emerald Mermaid."

Apparently, their training was over for the day.

Desperate to return to their usual camaraderie, she changed the subject. "Great, I'll walk with you until we reach the healer's hut. Geeta's helping me with my disguise for tomorrow's festival mission." She pulled the strap of her water skin over her head and returned her own sword to her hip. "Did you get the drawing of the necklace you're to retrieve?"

Pell stiffly turned to follow her into Volos. "It should be waiting on me when I get back."

"Perfect." Silence descended. Pell walked beside her, careful not to let their arms brush. Nadia was only too happy to see Sarna, third in command after Pell, waiting in front of the healer's hut.

The only Thunoan trusted with the truth that Nadia was the faceless guild leader known as the Shark, Sarna was a woman of few words. Standing at only five feet four inches, the guild-woman's petite build and doll- like features belied her lethal skill with a sword and her sharp intelligence.

Sarna nodded a greeting at Nadia, barely acknowledging Pell. Though she never spoke a word against him, Nadia knew that Pell annoyed her to no end with his constant need to check in with Nadia, know her location, and his need to know everything she did.

He smirked at the stoney-faced woman. "Good morning, sweet Sarna."

"We both know there isn't a single sweet thing about me," she replied, her tone flat. Turning her back to him in clear dismissal, she lifted an eyebrow at Nadia. "Shall we get on with it then?"

Pell's eyes narrowed at the woman, something hard flashing in his eyes. Realizing Nadia watched, he smoothed his expression and gave her a stiff, shallow bow. "I'll see you later."

Nadia nodded, still feeling bad that she'd hurt his feelings. He paused as if waiting on Sarna to say something. When the other woman just gave him her usual bored look, he shrugged, then turned to continue alone to the Emerald Mermaid.

"What crawled up his butt and died?" she asked in a dry voice.

Nadia stared at Pell's retreating back, heart heavy. "He's frustrated with me."

"Of course," Sarna said, lips pulling into a smirk. "Years of suppressed attraction and lust will do that to a man."

She gave the other woman a searching look.

Realizing that Sarna spoke in general terms, she defended a friend who'd earned her loyalty with his steadfast presence at her side. "That's not it." Turning, she climbed the stairs to the healer's front door. "Neither of us would chance ruining years of loyalty and friendship for sex."

She entered Geeta's home, knowing she'd made the right decision. She only hoped Pell let it go without any lingering hard feelings.

CHAPTER TWO

A hard knock on Gregor's sitting room door pulled his attention from the book in his lap. The door swung open and Stefan Vasious, crown-prince of Thuno, stalked into Gregor's sitting room, a frown on his face, his usually neat hair stuck up in all directions. Picking up a broken quill pen, Gregor closed it in the book, marking his page, and then set the book aside. He wasn't surprised his servants hadn't announced the prince. Stefan spent most of his free time here with Gregor away from the two-faced courtiers and their politics at the palace. Nodding curtly to Gregor, Stefan crossed to the sideboard and poured a drink.

Gregor lifted a brow. "You usually come back from your fishing trips in better spirits. Did your father suffer another headache?" Stefan shook his head, grabbed the bottle and his glass, and sank into the chair across from Gregor.

"Something worse?"

Stefan drained his glass and poured another. "My brother fell into the sea."

Both of Gregor's brows rose. "Is all well?"

"Reis is a..." Stefan swallowed, his ruddy face deepening into a darker red. "He changed into..." The prince lifted his glass and drained it again.

Gregor's gut clenched as he waited for Stefan to spit out whatever was wrong with the boy he treated like his own younger brother. Stefan met Gregor's gaze with bloodshot eyes. "While under the water Reis had a fish's tail and greenish gray skin." Gregor leaned forward. "He had gods-forsaken gills on the side of his neck."

"Are you sure?" Gregor asked, his heart a rapid staccato in his chest.

"I said it, didn't I?" Stefan growled, jumping back to his feet and beginning to pace, his finger jabbing into the air as he made his point. "Pulled him out of the water myself. Saw the webbing between his fingers and I'll be damned if he didn't change back human before my eyes."

Gregor's mind raced. "He's Mer." He glanced up at Stefan. "How is this possible?"

"Apparently, Father didn't learn enough about Jasna before making her his mistress."

And that oversight wouldn't be changed now either. Reis' mother had disappeared when her son was three. Dieuroi Mavros had given up looking for her long ago.

"But it doesn't change the fact that it shouldn't be possible," Gregor insisted, his mind going over all the implications.

Stefan halted and turned to glare at Gregor. "Explain."

Gregor stood and crossed over to the door of his study. He pulled a key from around his neck and unlocked the door, Stefan on his heels. After lighting a lantern, he searched the wall-to-wall shelves stuffed with glass-tube encased scrolls, leather-bound books, and small, cedar wood boxes which held those books too delicate to be crammed in with the rest. Crossing to the shelf which held everything he'd been able to collect on the Mer, he pulled a scroll from its tube on the top shelf and spread it on the long table standing in the middle of the room. Stefan, muttering to himself about scholars and their excitement over things that made normal men crazy, poured himself another drink.

Gregor pointed at the section he'd remembered. "According to this, he shouldn't be able to live without the presence of A'mi. Before the gates closed, all non- humans on the Saimond side of the gate had to live in or near the gate cities. When the Gate Keepers decided to close the gates, all A'mi were forced back onto the Mondami side of the gate. Those who managed to evade them and stay on this side slowly wasted away and died."

Stefan dropped the decanter of whiskey onto the table with a heavy thud. "Died? How long did this take?"

"It doesn't say."

Stefan growled, his fingers tugging at his hair. "First, my father and now this," he said, then paced across the room and back. "Father worsens daily. I fear I'll lose him soon." He stopped and scowled. "I won't lose my brother, too. Especially to my father's mad rambling."

"Rambling?" Gregor asked, his heart aching for his friend.

Stefan's shoulders drooped. "He suffered a massive episode after what happened to Reis." The prince turned toward Gregor, his face lined with worry. "This one worse than any so far." His brows lowered again. "He started ranting about Ashra punishing him. A bunch of Order hogwash, no doubt. Those damn priests and their nonsense are the first thing to go when I become king. Mark my words."

"And Reis?"

The prince frowned. "He heard. Kept him away from Father and made sure my father went straight to his bed when we arrived back at the palace. Reis is keeping to his rooms today, my own guards at his door."

"You really think your father would turn against a son he's loved for the past thirteen years?"

Stefan pinched the bridge of his nose. "Before the headaches, absolutely not. But they've messed with his mind to such an extent that I'm just not sure anymore. He believes the drivel fed him by the Order. I'm worried he'll tell them what happened, and they'll turn the country against my brother."

Gregor rolled the scroll back up and replaced it in its tube before returning it to its shelf. Picking up the whiskey bottle, Stefan stalked back into the sitting room. Gregor extinguished the lantern and then followed the prince out, locking the room behind him.

He went to the cabinet and poured himself a drink, then returned to his seat across from Stefan. The prince sat, eyes closed, his head resting against the chair's cushioned back, deep lines grooved between his brows and bracketing his mouth.

"The representatives from Diomere arrived today with what I can only assume is good news," Gregor said.

Stefan sighed. "Yes, a messenger waited for us when we arrived. Apparently, I'm now betrothed."

"I've heard Princess Madelena is very beautiful."

"Very beautiful and very cold. I got the impression she wasn't happy with marrying a foreigner and leaving her home," Stefan said with a shrug.

Gregor grinned. "Doubting your ability to thaw her out? Mayhap you need more practice?"

Stefan swung his hand up and gave Gregor the two-fingered salute. "Says the man who hasn't bedded a woman in months," he replied with a smirk.

Gregor shrugged. "I haven't seen anything that appeals to me."

He studied his best friend. "I'm surprised you've agreed to marry someone you've not really had a chance to know. The connection with the shipping mecca would be nice, but we don't need it."

Stefan shook his head. "I insisted that she be allowed to visit for six months so we could get to know each other. If we're both in favor after that, we'll plan a wedding. If not, then she'll return to Diomere, and I'll look elsewhere for a wife with no ill will between our countries."

"Your father agreed?"

"Not at first, but he eventually acceded to my wishes so long as we could announce the engagement at a ball he's planned for two nights from now. He seems to think that I'll give in to the people's expectations and marry her regardless of how we get along." He scowled. "I want what he had with my mother. True friendship, affection, love."

Gregor nodded. He too wanted a true partnership like that between Dieuroi Mavros and his queen. Rather than ignore her until he wished to use her body, Stefan's father had listened to his queen, asking her advice on matters of state, having her give her opinion on disputes at court, and giving her a role in ruling the kingdom alongside him. Theirs had been a real partnership, full of respect. Neither had they shied away from showing their affection for each other in public. They'd often shared secret smiles, long looks, and soft touches.

"We can only hope a woman like your mother is in both our futures."

Stefan smiled. "You can start searching for a wife at tomorrow's ball. All of the nobility will be present. There are bound to be a few women there interested in snagging the future king's advisor."

Gregor scowled. "I don't want a woman interested in me for my position. I want a family. A wife who looks at me and our children with love."

Stefan nodded, his smile dimming. "Yes, Marla taught us both to be wary, no doubt."

Gregor shoved memories of his dishonest ex aside. Was it too much to ask for an honest woman like their late queen? Surely, not all women were like his mother and ex-betrothed.

CHAPTER THREE

Nadia stood in the shade cast by one of the Earth Temple's four towers. A breeze swirled under her skirts, filling the air with the heady scent of the wisteria vines that climbed the towers. Her gaze swept across the crowded square, noting each of the three exits and the position of each guard. Mentally mapping out escape routes, she wished for the thousandth time that she'd worn her usual breeches and boots. But she knew Geeta had been right to talk her into the restricting skirts. No one would recognize her dressed in the Thunoan style, her face covered in a half mask of common cloth.

A knot formed in her stomach. Not being able to take her other form was almost worse than being exiled. She slammed the door on that thought. Things could always be worse.

A group of laughing women, eager to celebrate the Festival of the Sun, bustled past, their arms laden with flowers to set at the goddess' feet. The goddess' statue stood in the center of the square decorated in boughs of greenery and colorful flowers while water poured from her hands. Masks, worn in an array of styles for anonymity, covered the faces of those present. Musicians strummed their instruments while merchants, their booths set up between large-canopied trees, sold meat pies, sweet breads, and festival masks. The novice priests kept the wine flowing, free to all in honor of the goddess' glory. Nadia smiled. *The free wine is indeed a blessing.*

Pell appeared beside a large-bellied noble. Though the man hid his face behind a grotesque beak mask, his physique and booming voice exposed him as the nobleman her second sought.

Pell appeared to watch the jugglers in front of him before glancing her way. Bright blue irises blinked back at her from behind his own disguise. Biting back a smile, Nadia rolled her eyes. His mask, painted with a frown on the white half and a smile on the black half, fit him perfectly. She didn't see Pell move, but he disappeared into the crowd and the noble he'd been standing beside no longer wore the gold chain she'd seen around his neck.

Her people didn't normally steal from wealthy lords like common thieves, but business was business, and the noble had stolen the ring hanging from the gold chain. Its true owner, a widowed merchant woman who'd refused the noble her bed, wanted it back. When Thuno's god-king had ignored the woman's petition, she'd approached Vromia Guild.

Nadia, satisfied the job was complete, turned her attention to the second reason she'd agreed to join in the festivities. Her royal contact should have arrived by now.

She palmed a tiny, rolled parchment from the pocket of her dress and scanned the revelers, paying attention to the masks each wore. A mouthless mask of solid white with a single slash of red appeared from behind a group of laughing women in matching feathered masks. She straightened the cheap, half mask on her own face and pushed away from the wall. She turned, looked back over her shoulder as if someone chased her, then laughed and ran across the square. After a dozen steps, she collided with a wide, muscled chest and looked up into a full mask of glossy Gazon porcelain.

She inhaled and smiled. The familiar mix of honey, wood, and lemon of Geeta's frankincense soap meshed with his own unique male scent. Geeta would be thrilled to know that a noble wore one of the new soaps she'd sold to a local high-end apothecary.

Playing her part, she bit her bottom lip and looked up at him through her lashes. "Pardon, m'lord. I didn't mean to mistake you for a running path."

Striking amber irises surrounded by thick black lashes peeked from the eyes of the mask. A ripple rolled through the power inside her, like this man had reached in and touched a finger to the still surface of her a'mi. Her mind went blank as desire rolled through her, taking her breath.

"If all runners were as beautiful as you, I'd be willing to be the path more often," he said, his voice low and husky.

Ignoring the feelings he elicited in her, she barely kept from rolling her eyes. Expose a little cleavage or the hint of a curvy figure and men were all the same, the sight of a woman's face being totally unnecessary to judge beauty. Even had she not been wearing the mask, she knew there was nothing beautiful about her. Too tall and mouthy, she preferred dressing like a Diomerean nobleman rather than the noblewoman she was. Never mind the scar that bisected the left side of her face.

"Thank you, m'lord," she said, tone dry. She smiled and batted her lashes up at him.

His low chuckle sent a shiver down her spine as he stepped back and bowed. "Dance with me."

Playing along to get what she'd come for, she nodded. He rose back to his full height, his striking eyes crinkled at the corners as if he smiled under the mask. She resisted the urge to pull her hand from his, forcing herself to continue as if she were truly just another young woman intent on enjoying the lax rules of the festival. He reached the dance floor and turned to sweep her into his arms.

Their gazes locked. He pulled her body against his from chest to hip, his hand pressed firmly against the small of her back.

She smiled sweetly and dropped her gaze, then muttered though clenched teeth. "Ease off."

He loosened his hold, giving her a bit of space, then dipped his head to whisper in her ear. "Acting the coy miss isn't one of your gifts."

His lips grazed her ear, causing an arrow of desire to arc through her body.

She tilted her head, their cheeks only a breath apart, and whispered back. "Insincere flattery is obviously one of yours."

Unable to resist the swell of muscle under her palms, she caressed his chest as she pulled away, chin lifted. Her smile slipped and her conscious spoke up in reprimand. *You're acting like Father.* Her stomach flipped, threatening to eject her morning meal. A man whore who couldn't resist a pretty face, her father had five daughters with five different mothers. Refusing to allow herself to be anything like him, she jerked her hands from the masked man's chest as if she'd been burned.

He trapped her gaze in his. "Is it not said that flattery makes friends and truth makes enemies?"

Nadia scowled and shoved her a'mi deep.

"Then I'd rather be enemies," she said, then stepped back as the song ended.

She held her hand out in the traditional greeting of her people, rather than the shoulder clasping Thunoans used. She didn't worry about it helping anyone identify her. There were people from various nations here today, the celebration of Asha a popular event.

His smoldering gaze held a challenge as he slid his palm against hers. His thumb caressed the back of her hand, making her shiver, before he finally pulled his hand back toward his chest, the parchment she'd slipped him tucked between his fingers. The greeting ended with their palms over their hearts.

Nadia ignored the heat pooling in her stomach. "The gods keep you, m'lord."

"Asha's blessing on you, lady," he said.

She told herself she clenched her fist because the greeting demanded it, not to hold on to the feel of his skin against hers. Tearing her gaze away, she strode to a nearby vendor's stall.

She smiled at the merchant as she perused his selection of meat pies. Pointing to a small, stuffed pastry, she handed him her coin and glanced over her shoulder. Heated eyes studied her.

Her thighs clenched. She frowned and struggled to wrestle back control of her traitorous body. The man tilted his head in a shallow nod, then turned and disappeared into the crowd.

Nadia returned to her place near the tower as the great bell began to toll. Though her unease over the encounter made her stomach queasy, she made herself nibble on the pie as if she hadn't a care in the world. She hoped taking lead on this mission hadn't been a mistake.

Pell usually passed off the information they were paid to gather, but she'd wanted to watch the Choosing Ceremony. As she struggled to shake off the unsettling reaction to the masked man, she mentally berated herself, remembering the hard lessons she'd learned when it came to members of the opposite sex. Her frown deepened.

Pell appeared beside her, his voice muffled behind his mask. "That isn't our usual contact."

"How do you know?"

He turned his head toward her, shoulders back betraying his military background. "The usual contact is my height."

Nadia scanned the crowd. "Find out who he is."

The grating of the temple's gates interrupted Pell's response. The music faded. Six priests, straining under the weight of a golden chalice four feet high and nearly as wide, moved through the opening gate.

The signal to all that the Chosen ceremony started.

The priests lowered the chalice to its pedestal. A small tree, its leaf covered branches symmetrically pruned and reaching toward the sky, grew in holy soil within the chalice. The Chosen, ten boys and girls born in the city on the longest day of the year thirteen years before, stood in a line to one side. Though still children in her home country, new teenagers were officially declared adults in Thuno on their thirteenth birthday. While other new thirteen-year-olds in Thuno celebrated this birthday by choosing an apprenticeship or announcing a betrothal, these ten Chosen had a different choice to make first: accept or reject a'mi, or magic as Thunoans called it.

Most, if not all ten, would reject it.

The line of teenagers approached the priests, who anointed them with a smear of sacred white ash on their forehead. The crowd whispered among each other, bored with a ceremony they considered rooted in fairytale, though none dared miss it for fear of earning their goddess' displeasure.

A tall, richly dressed boy glanced over at his parents as the priest touched his forehead, nodded, then muttered something to the priest who also glanced at the boy's parents, then smiled and nodded. The priest did the same with at least three others. Then a curly haired girl stepped up to the priest, her wide eyes darting around, making the priest frown and mutter at her. She shrugged and the priest glared as he swiped a finger across her already dirty forehead. The girl ducked her head and took her place at the end of the line.

Nadia noticed the girl's poor-quality clothing and made a note to check on her and her living situation. The girl darted her gaze around the crowded square. And Nadia couldn't help but wonder if the girl just might be desperate enough to defy the teachings of the priests in order to escape whatever had her so frightened. Should she choose a'mi, the Guardian would appear and take her through the gate to Mondami, the world of the A'mi.

Before the war, which closed the gates between the worlds, families would proudly prepare for months before their chosen's coming of age ceremony.

Years ago, Nadia devoured every book she could find on the great accomplishments achieved when innovative Sa'i and A'mi minds worked together. The lightboxes still used in her home country were one of those inventions, though the knowledge of how they were made had been lost when the gates closed. Superior to oil a'mi powered the lanterns without draining the one activating them.

Nadia remembered the many Sa'i children she'd seen choose a'mi in her home country. The wonder of watching them come into their power, before the Guardian appeared to take them through the gate, left many of those watching with smiles of envy tinged with sadness. Looking around at this crowd, Nadia knew it would be much different. No child from Volos chose a'mi, not in the last hundred years. Their parents and Asha's priests taught them that to choose a'mi was to choose to become a slave of Druj, the god of death and chaos.

Nadia knew the other side of the gate simply held a world of supernaturals, some good and some bad, who worshipped their chosen gods just like the humans did on this side.

The head priest stepped forward, holding a tray covered with a silk cloth. On the cloth lay a golden mallet. One side of the hammer's head remained naked gold while the other side was padded with leather. The priest offered the mallet to the first teen. Taking the mallet, he knelt before the golden chalice. He skimmed his other hand quickly over the holy soil and then struck the chalice with the leather-covered side of the mallet's head. The teen stood, handed the mallet to the next, and returned to his smiling parents.

The gathered crowd grew restless, ready to return to the real reason they were there, the Festival of the Sun festivities. As the line of chosen grew shorter, the watching audience grew bored. Some even turned their backs to continue conversations the chosen ceremony interrupted.

Nadia shook her head at the disrespect. She doubted any would choose a'mi, but couldn't walk away at the chance to see the Guardian of the Gate. She'd seen this same ceremony thirteen times across the many lands of Saimond since she'd been banished. Though the people and patron gods were different, the ceremony was always exactly the same. Rarely did a child choose a'mi. She told herself to turn and walk away. No Thunoan child would dare make such a choice.

Feeling someone watching her, she turned her head to meet the intense scrutiny of their contact over the heads of the whispering revelers. She caught her breath.

Pell followed her gaze. "Should we leave?"

She shook her head. The man continued to watch her, his gaze dipping to caress the dress that she knew lifted and framed her breasts like a present. Her pulse raced. He moved toward her, each step slow and sensual like a large jungle cat stalking a mate. Her muscles tensed. Pale golden eyes locked on her, curious yet wary. Instinct screamed for her to run, even as her a'mi reached for him. That he already had her common sense and her a'mi at odds proved the danger he held for her. She lifted her chin and felt for the handle of the blade she usually carried on her hip.

Loud cursing rang out and the crowd quieted.

The spell broken, Nadia jerked her attention back to the ceremony. A man, his hair matted and clothes threadbare and dirty, lunged toward the last chosen, the poor, curly-haired girl as she turned the mallet in her hand so that she held it with the uncovered side toward the chalice. The side that told the gathered crowd that she chose a'mi.

The teen ignored her obviously drunken father as he tripped on the stairs and fell to his knees. The teen focused on the chalice. The man pulled himself to his feet at the bottom step leading up to the chalice.

"After everythin' I've done for you, you'd dare attempt to run off with some Druj cursed A'mi dog?" The man lost his balance and fell back. "Come down here, you ungrateful hussy."

Nadia stepped forward, hand on the handle of the dagger at her waist as memories of her own father's callous treatment superimposed the man's words in her mind. Pell's fingers curled around her wrist and squeezed. She whipped her head around, eyes narrowed on her friend.

"The guards will handle it," he said, his eyes full of pity as he nodded his head toward the unfolding drama. "Look."

Guards moved closer to the man, blocking his path up the stairs. Inhaling a deep breath, Nadia remembered herself and why she shouldn't interfere. She nodded her thanks at Pell, then turned back in time to see the girl hesitate with her hand above the chalice's soil as she darted a glance toward the man.

The head priest stepped forward. "Child, be absolutely certain. Once you do this, there is no going back." The girl glanced at the priest, and he took another step closer. "Would you risk selling your soul to Druj, simply to escape a difficult life?"

Nadia, and the rest of the wide-eyed crowd, waited with bated breath to see what she would do.

The man lunged forward into the guards, his face twisted with rage as spit flew from his lips. "You ungrateful whore. Place your hand in that dirt and I'll cut off your head and shit down your throat when the guardian fails to appear."

The crowd pulled further away from the man as the guards shoved him back.

Jaw clenched hard enough to crack a tooth, Nadia glared at the girl's father. "Find out who he is. Make sure he has no other children in his care and that he isn't able to make more of them."

"Guards, if this man interrupts the ceremony one more time, remove him," the head priest said as he glared down his nose at the man.

"She's my whore of a daughter and I didn't give 'er my blessin' to be here today," the man insisted as he climbed to his feet.

The head priest sneered. "She's officially an adult and no longer needs your permission." Turning back to the girl, his expression softened. "Cursing your soul is not an escape, girl. Even a cur for a father is better than what waits in the land of the A'mi."

Nadia leaned closer as the girl squared her shoulders and thrust her left hand into the soil as her right hand swung the mallet's head toward the chalice. Nadia inhaled as the high-pitched gong of mallet on chalice moved through her.

The girl smiled as the soil moved up her arm. Soon her entire body was encased in the swirling soil that absorbed into her skin.

The crowd backed away.

From the waist down, her legs darkened with bark, then split into a twisted collection of roots. Her curls twisted into a mottled blend of thick branches, vines, and sweeping leaves.

Nadia held her breath as the girl transformed into a race she'd only heard of in stories as a child at her mother's knee.

A line of light split the air behind the chalice and slowly widened into a door. Raising their hands to shield their eyes, the crowd squinted to see. The shadow of a large man appeared in the center of the light. Several women in the crowd fainted, while others let out wails of fear. Cowering away from the portal, the priests held up their hands, fingers curled, to ward away evil. *The fools fear one of their own goddess' most beloved creations.*

The Guardian stepped from the door, a figure in a long gold cloak, its deep hood hiding his face. An aged hand with skin so pale it appeared blue emerged from the cloak. The girl glanced toward the priests. Her father wretched his arms from the grasp of the soldiers who'd pulled him away when the girl had begun to shift.

"No. I'd rather see you dead than a child of the Druj worshiping A'mi." The man lunged toward the girl, his eating knife glinting in the sunlight.

The Guardian swept his hand out as if shooing a fly, and the man flew back into the guards. The girl smiled and without a backward glance, stepped forward to place her hand into the Guardian's. The cowled figure swept his gaze over the shocked faces of Thuno's people, moved past Nadia, stopped, and returned to rest on her. The memory of who she was and why she couldn't go home surfaced. A muscle ticked in her clenched jaw.

The Guardian's voice, speaking the language of the A'mi, rolled over her mind like a bolder crushing stone. "The boy must be found before the sands run out."

CHAPTER FOUR

N adia sucked a breath into starving lungs and pressed back into the tower's shade. "Did you hear that?"

"Hear what?" Pell asked.

She tugged at the garrote she wore on her wrist. Of course he hadn't. "Nothing," she muttered. "Nothing at all."

She turned back toward the drama unfolding in the square. Pell stared at her a moment longer, then turned back toward the glowing portal. Nadia sighed. She hated that Pell wasn't privy to all her secrets, but some things weren't hers alone to share.

As if he'd heard her thoughts, the Guardian glanced at her one last time, then pulled the newly born nymph into the light. The doorway shrank until it disappeared from sight. The people assembled in the square before the Earth Temple stood frozen.

The head priest stepped forward. "Bring the girl's father," he said, his face pale.

The soldiers, their faces twisted with disgust, grabbed the man, who stood frozen in a pool of his own piss, then dragged him forward.

"You've brought Druj's dark attention to Volos for the first time in a hundred years. For this you're to be tortured until dead to appease the god of death."

The man's ruddy face blanched white, then bloomed red. "I did nothing wrong. The whore snuck out at all times of night and day. I thought she was spreading her legs for whatever man had caught her eye. For all I know one of them coulda tempted her toward the A'mi."

"I hope that the new nymph escapes to a life full of joy and happiness, while her sorry excuse for a father suffers eternally in Druj's forge," Nadia hissed to Pell, who nodded grimly. "Check and make sure that if he has other children they're brought to Geeta's hut for the night."

The man screamed profanities at all the gods and the head priest flicked his fingers. The guards knocked him across the back of his head with a sword hilt to shut him up, then dragged him away. Turning to face the pale-faced crowd, the high priest lifted his hands.

"People of Thuno, do not let Druj's dark chaos dampen your celebration of Asha's light. To do so is to let the dark win," he said as another priest stepped up to the potted tree holding a golden pitcher and goblet, the latter which he filled with wine. "Like the sacred tree, we'll dig our roots deep and turn our faces up to the light. Our acolytes will come around with free wine to help cleanse our pallet and resurrect our joy for Asha. Musicians, play for Asha and let us celebrate her in the way she deserves."

Nadia shook her head as the musicians struck a lively tune while acolytes filed out of the temple, some pushing carts loaded with wine and others with medical supplies to tend to the women still lying prone from fainting. "I'll see you back at the Inn," she muttered to Pell, her gaze scanning for the masked man and not seeing him.

She and Pell slipped out of the square, each going a different direction. Her thoughts circled in her head as she made her way to her home. Instincts prickling, she looked back over her shoulder and picked up her pace. Deciding against the direct route, she wound her way through the city, the streets growing more crowded, dirty, and narrow the closer she got to the harbor and its smelly docks.

When the itchy feeling between her shoulder blades dissipated, she turned down a dirty street which had identical, tiny homes. She nodded to the man and woman lounging on the front porch of the last house in the row. Looking more like bored locals than guards on watch, they nodded back, their gazes sharper than any mere local. She knocked once, opened the door, and stepped into the healer's hut.

Inside, the strong aroma of the drying herbs that hung from the ceiling in the kitchen filled her nose, making her sneeze. Geeta, Nadia's cousin and closest friend, stood at the long table that separated the kitchen from the sitting room and glanced up, blowing strands of blonde hair from her face, as she mixed some concoction which undoubtedly tasted like death. The dark circles under her fever-bright eyes squeezed Nadia's heart with worry. She knew if she looked in a mirror, she'd see the same gauntness beginning to appear in her own face.

The door had no more than closed when Nadia stripped off her mask and dropped it on the table, followed quickly by her skirts and petticoats. "How you and every other woman wear these twice cursed things, I'll never understand."

Geeta's smile lit up her whole face, alleviating her sick pallor for a moment. "The mystery of what's hiding under these skirts drive men crazy. With the flash of ankle or calf, we compel men to do exactly what we wish."

Her friend's words evoked the memory of pale gold eyes staring from a solid white mask and she shook the annoying contact from her mind.

"A child chose a'mi today," she said, the memory of seeing the guardian causing her heart to beat in a completely different way than the golden-eyed stranger.

Geeta stopped her stirring and set the bowl down on the table as a knowing look lit her green eyes. "You finally saw the Guardian."

She clenched her jaw and pulled a pair of black salvar, the loose pants favored by Diomerean noblemen, over her hips. "He spoke to me." She met Geeta's surprised glance and lowered her voice. "The boy must be found before the sands run out."

"Did the queen mention anything about time running out in her last missive?" Geeta asked with a frown as she rounded the table. When Nadia just shook her head, the blonde woman continued. "Well, whatever the reason, we know he's here in Thuno. We'll find him as soon as possible. The queen obviously doesn't care so long as you find him. She's probably read your letter hundreds of times since you sent it."

"He wouldn't be lost if I'd done my job," Nadia said, her shoulders slumped as she clutched Geeta's hand. "It's been years since I've been in Diomere. What if she hates me for allowing him to be taken?"

Geeta smoothed a strand of hair from Nadia's forehead. "Lareina doesn't blame you and never has."

"My head knows you're right, but my heart throbs with guilt," she said, then rubbed her temples.

Geeta tugged on Nadia's braid and gestured for her to turn. "Aren't I always?"

"Ha," Nadia laughed, shaking her head. Her smile vanished as she used her fingers to comb out the fancy style Geeta had created to match the skirts. She held her smallest dagger's sheath while Geeta began to weave her hair around it in her usual braid. "The boy will be thirteen in six moons' time. I wonder if the guardian's warning refers to that?" She shoved her arms into the long-sleeve shirt Geeta handed her.

"Perhaps the Queen will update us about this in the next missive," Geeta said.

"I know my nephew is here. I feel it. I wasted too much time making myself the Shark."

Geeta placed her hands on either side of Nadia's face and met her gaze. "The power of the guild helped us get this far. We'll find him. He's in this city."

"We're getting weaker. If we don't figure out what's wrong soon, I'm afraid we'll be too sick to finish our search."

Geeta bustled back over to the table, their exchange seeming to give her a little of her once bubbly energy. "We can't worry over what we can't do anything about. Your sister will come and bring with her a solution to our problem."

Nadia smiled. "How would I have managed without you all these years, my friend?"

"You'd smell as bad as the rest of these foreigners, no doubt," Geeta said, her nose wrinkled.

Nadia remembered the familiar scent of frankincense and spices emanating from her mysterious new contact. Geeta made lotions and soaps to sell in the market, which were gaining in popularity, if those as well dressed as the masked man were purchasing them. That particular scent combination had always been one of her favorites that her friend made.

Frowning at the wayward direction of her thoughts, she shoved the memory aside and belted a sleeveless tunic over a long- sleeved undershirt that had been an addition to her outfit when she arrived in Thuno. A woman in pants and bare arms would have been too much for the modest people here. Not that many women wore pants in her home country. Nadia simply found the loose salvar Diomerean men wore tucked into their boots much more convenient. *Can't exactly skulk among the shadows in a skirt,* she thought to herself.

Smiling to herself, she slid daggers into the sheaths at wrist, hip, and ankle. "I've got the ball tonight to finish the Elis job, then I'm headed to Asha's Library tomorrow morning. Brother Jamison is supposed to have the list of boys in Volos between the ages eleven and thirteen for me. I'll have a copy made for you so we can start eliminating the ones you know."

The healer nodded, then picked up the bowl and started mixing again. "Jon and Sarna return soon, do they not?"

Nadia slid the last and slimmest dagger into the sheath in her braid. Feeling more comfortable with all her weapons back in their proper places, she moved to the back wall of the small house, hiding her smile. Despite her worsening condition, talk of the dark giant they'd saved from being sacrificed to the god of fire could still pull a spark from Geeta.

She reached toward the shelf built over the hearth and pressed a knot in the wood. The section of wall moved, and Nadia pushed it open into a narrow tunnel that disappeared into darkness.

"Yes, yes, but your shagging will have to wait until after I've received my report," she said as she grabbed a torch hanging on the tunnel wall and stuck it into the fire in Geeta's hearth.

Geeta hurled the spoon at her and her bark of laughter echoed down the tunnel.

"To Meren's dark depths with you, jealous harpy," Geeta yelled as Nadia walked into the darkness and the wall closed behind her.

CHAPTER FIVE

That evening, Nadia walked into the royal ballroom escorted by one of her regular patrons at The Mermaid. They stepped up to the top steps of a long curving staircase and paused to survey the highly anticipated chalk drawings swirling across the dance floor.

"Lord Paulo Krupin, Earl of Pella escorting her highness, Princess Nadia de Quinones of Diomere," the steward announced in a deep voice that echoed across the large room.

Nadia ignored those craning to get a look at the exiled princess as Lord Krupin escorted her down the stairs. She continued to admire the elegantly chalked drawings depicting the coat of arms of both the Thunoan and Diomerean royal houses surrounded by flowers native to both countries in celebration of the much-anticipated royal engagement.

Negotiations to see Prince Stefan married to Princess Madalena of Diomere had been going on for so many years that upon receipt of the Diomerean King's acceptance of the marriage contract, Dieuroi Mavros decided to hold a ball, despite the princess' absence.

Across the ballroom, Thuno's sovereign sat upon a raised dais, a goblet of wine in one frail hand and a huge smile spread across his sallow face. Rumors said the head pains and resulting mad rantings getting worse over the last months with the Dieuroi spending more time than not bedridden and Prince Stefan running the country in his father's place. *Dieuroi, indeed. If he's the son of a goddess, then I'm a monkey's uncle,* she thought to herself.

The Order had been the ones to so name him, declaring that Asha had inhabited the queen's body during conception after she'd been unable to conceive for the first five years of the royal marriage. Beside his father, Crown Prince Stefan, a younger, healthier version of the god-king, sat watching those around him, his sharp gaze telling her the goblet in his hand was for show only.

Dieuroi Mavros' sunken skin glowed with satisfaction as the orchestra started playing and dancers began to step onto the floor. He'd long had his eye on a stronger relationship with the shipping magnate that was Diomere. This marriage was a step in that direction. Things must be dire for her home country to risk its long-standing neutrality and show favor to one nation over another.

As a patriarchal society, Diomere would never allow a woman to take the throne. Since her sister, Queen Lareina, couldn't have any more children, Princess Madalena was being married off to make way for another branch of the royal family to ascend the throne if King Delmar died without Prince Areisteo being found.

Lord Krupin pulled her across the ballroom, both of them nodding at those they knew, until they reached his two closest friends, the Earls of Kepoi and Soli, both peers with lands located south of Thuno. Also regulars at The Mermaid, the two nobles often invited her to join them at their table and share what had made the rounds on the rumor mill since their last visit to the capitol city.

"Paulo, my Lady Nadia, you've finally arrived," Lord Hermios Aetos, Earl of Kepoi said with a jovial smile on his round face.

Nadia inclined her head. "Asha's light see you, Lord Aetos, Lord Bouras."

"Well met, Lady Nadia," Lord Deacon Bouras, Earl of Orangol said, his stoic expression softening.

The men soon fell into conversation about their respective lands, leaving Nadia to focus on the reason she agreed to accompany Paulo for the evening.

She tugged the belt at her waist, irritated by the way it emphasized her breasts in the chiton, or sleeveless, tunic style gown traditionally worn by the women in her home country. She longed for her usual pants and loose shirt as she scanned the groups of people in attendance. Having to wear skirts twice in as many days surely meant she'd earned the sea god's wrath somehow.

"His majesty can barely look at his bastard since he and the two princes returned from their last father/sons outing. If not for the crown prince, I think the boy would find himself on the block," Lord Aetos said, his hands smoothing down the blue silk that draped his rounded stomach as he glanced toward his king.

Nadia tilted her head to listen as she continued searching the assembled nobles.

"Has anyone discovered why his majesty has had such an abrupt change of heart after twelve years of playing the doting father?" Paulo asked.

"Rumors accuse the bastard prince of being a demon," the Lord Bouras said, his drooping mustache making his mouth appear set in a permanent frown.

Nadia tucked the information away, her mind turning to the guild-related reason for attending the evening's event. Hired as the

Shark to obtain information on a trade agreement between the Marques of Elis and the Marques of Myndus, Nadia expected to finish the job tonight thanks to the Marquess of Elis' unsuspecting daughter.

Spotting the younger woman, Nadia touched her escort's arm. "I'm going to say hello to Lady Faina Alkaev, Paulo."

Lord Krupin smiled indulgently. "Of course, my dear. Give the young lady my regards."

Resisting the urge to curl her lip at the old noble's patronizing tone, she nodded and excused herself. When she approached the group of debutantes, the young lady's eyes lit up. "Nadia, how wonderful to see you," she gushed. "You remember Ladies Pajari, Utkin, and Vasilyev?"

Nadia nodded to each of the young women in turn. "Good evening."

Once the greetings were out of the way, Faina hooked her arm. "Won't you join me in the powder room?"

Smiling her assent, she waited while the younger woman excused them from the group, then followed her to the lady's room.

Faina kept a gentle smile on her face even as she said in a low voice, "I have the most exciting news."

"It wouldn't happen to be about a certain auburn-haired noble, would it?"

The younger woman flashed a wide smile at her friend as they entered the powder room and waited for it to clear. Once she was sure they were alone, Nadia flipped the door's lock and turned just as the younger woman spun around.

"Peter officially asked my father for my hand last night. They are ironing out some details with my dowry now, but I hope to be able to announce it officially within the week," she said, her round face flushed and brown eyes dancing.

Nadia wrapped the younger woman in a hug. "I'm so happy for you." She pulled back and let her gaze wander from Faina's brunette head to her small feet.

"Why are you looking at me like that?"

"I'm looking to see all the ways becoming engaged makes one more beautiful, so I can let the others in on the secret," Nadia said with a grin.

The younger woman swatted Nadia's arm. "You tease."

They both laughed then Nadia frowned. "But why do they have to negotiate your dowry? Wasn't it set before you attended your first event?"

Faina checked her complexion in the mirror. "I told Daddy I wanted Peter and that he should make sure Peter's family sees me as a good match. Daddy met with Peter's father and then added to my dowry." The younger woman turned glowing eyes to Nadia. "Peter asked for my hand the next day."

"Your father had to add to your already sizable dowry before Peter's family would allow him to ask for you? What in all of Saimond did they want added?"

Faina waved a hand dismissively. "Half ownership of some island Daddy owns in the south."

Nadia nodded, her client's suspicions confirmed. "I'm truly happy for you, Faina. I wish you both nothing but happiness together."

The younger woman grabbed Nadia's hands. "Thank you so much. I would've still been hesitant to go to Daddy about it if you hadn't given me courage. Thank you for being such a wonderful friend."

Guilt flashed through her for using the girl, but she reminded herself she had helped the young woman land the husband she wanted. Smiling, she turned and followed Faina out of the powder room.

Bored out of her mind after nearly twenty minutes of meaningless chitchat, she bid farewell to the group of young women and started across the ballroom toward her escort only to run into a hard chest.

Large hands caught her shoulders. "Please excuse my clumsiness, m'lady."

Nadia looked up into a striking male face framed by shoulder length brown hair. Her gaze clashed with pale amber eyes. Her jaw dropped. Those eyes appeared in her dreams every night.

Heat crawled up her neck. "The fault is all mine, m'lord."

The man stepped back and bowed, but before he could officially introduce himself an older man, who'd be handsome were it not for the ornate tunic he wore in a horrid shade of murky yellow, clapped him hard on the back. "I see you've met our resident exiled Diomerean Princess, Marquess," the man said in a booming voice.

Nadia hid her balled fists in her skirts as she and her handsome contact turned toward Lord Victor Pajari, Earl of Juktas. The obnoxious noble had been trying to get her into his bed since she'd first made her appearance in Thunoan society.

For his part, the still-as-yet-unnamed noble kept a pleasant smile on his face. "We were just getting to that point, Victor." He slipped from beneath the other man's heavy hand and once again bowed toward Nadia. "As I was saying, I am Marquess Gregor Cyrene. I'm pleased to make your acquaintance, Princess."

Nadia frowned. "My sister is queen. However, my father is only a duke. So you see, I'm not a princess the way you mean it here. I am Dona Nadia de Quinones, Infanta de Diomere."

Gregor smiled. "Never-the-less, please forgive me for nearly trampling you."

"No apology necessary, Marquess. It is I who forced you to use me as a running path."

His eyes widened. "Indeed, my lady running path."

She knew she probably shouldn't reveal herself, but she couldn't resist the impulse. Her a'mi hummed in satisfaction at his obvious recognition and reached for the striking man.

She ignored the inner voice that called him hers and lifted a brow. "I prefer Lady Nadia. It reflects my personality so much better, don't you think?"

Lord Pajari stepped into Nadia's personal space, forcing her attention away from Lord Cyrene, and leered at the cleavage revealed by her gown. "An exotic name to go with an exotic and coy personality, to be sure."

Nadia bared her teeth at the noble she privately referred to as Lord Obnoxious. "Not coy, m'lord, but simply overwhelmed at the generous welcome I've received in Thuno. You've all been so very accommodating."

Lord Pajari crowded closer until his ugly yellow tunic brushed against her. "It's such a shame that you've been forced by exile to work in order to support yourself, Princess. I'm currently in need of a wife. I'd be more than willing to overlook your lack of a dowry"—he licked his lips— "for the chance to produce an heir with such superb pedigree."

Suppressing a shudder, she stepped aside, forcing herself to retreat rather than pull her dagger and stick it into the pompous lord's lecherous heart. "As much as I am humbled by your offer, m'lord, I must decline. The Emerald Mermaid is quite profitable, and I'm not nearly as destitute as you seem to believe." She glanced up at the quiet Marquess who watched their exchange with an amused expression.

His gaze held hers and she lost her breath. Her cheeks grew warmer as her a'mi buzzed inside her, heating her blood. A smile spread across his face, brightening his eyes and turning him from striking to beautiful.

Lord Cyrene reached forward and lifted her gloved hand. "It seems the lady isn't interested in your rather unromantic proposal, Victor. Do be a pal and go find someone else to produce that heir for you." His voice stayed pleasant, but neither Lord Obnoxious nor Nadia could mistake the steel underlying his words. He flicked a dismissing glance toward the fuming noble and pulled her toward the refreshment table. "You intrigue me, princess," he said, those pale eyes seeming to see through her. "I hope that once we know each other better, you'll regale me with your story."

Firmly squashing the fluttery feeling his smile created in her stomach, Nadia attempted to pull her hand from his grasp. "You presume much, m'lord." She frowned when he failed to release her. "If you'll excuse me, I have an escort to return to before he comes looking for me."

He swept his gaze over the room of assembled nobles. "Oh? And who is this escort?"

"I don't see how that's any of your business," Nadia said, both brows raised.

"I simply wish to see whether my competition will be difficult or not," Lord Cyrene purred.

Nadia's jaw dropped and he quietly chuckled. Gritting her teeth, Nadia gave him a cryptic smile.

"Don't bother. I'm not interested in anything complicated. My current escort understands this." She let her eyes drift over every delectable inch of his tall frame then back to his smoldering gaze. "Somehow, I doubt you'd be as amenable to that."

He smiled, his eyes lighting with the challenge she hadn't meant to issue. "I very much look forward to changing your mind."

"I don't like you. Your arrogance makes you no better than Lord Pig and his disgusting proposal."

Unruffled by her cold words, he lifted a hand and smoothed an escaped wisp of hair off her cheek. "I'm nothing like your Lord Pig." He leaned forward until their breaths mingled. "I look forward to proving that to you."

She sighed. Geeta always told her that her mouth would be the death of her. It might not be the death of her this time, but it hadn't helped deflect his attention. No matter how her a'mi pushed her toward him, she didn't have time for the complication that was the Marquess Gregor Cyrene.

Deciding that anything else out of her would just make the situation worse, she dipped her head in a regal nod. "My lord marquess."

His eyes burned into her back as she walked away. She reached Lord Krupin's side and, unable to help herself, darted a glance back toward Lord Cyrene. He gave her a small smile and inclined his head. She forced her attention to return to Paulo and his friends.

CHAPTER SIX

That evening, Nadia pulled off her robe and slipped between the cool sheets of her bed, exhausted. Lord Cyrene flashed across her mind, one corner of his mouth lifted in a knowing smile. Her a'mi stirred. She squeezed her eyes closed and recited the ancient A'misrian alphabet until her thoughts grew heavy. With a sigh, she drifted to sleep.

She blinked awake to see a cloudless blue sky above her. Warm sea water caressed her skin, its salty smell familiar. An island, the protruding top of a dormant volcano's crater, curved around her providing a protected cove, its steep ridges spotted with low-lying brush that thickened around a narrow strip of sandy beach. Palm trees stood along the beach's edge like sentinels guarding the array of wildlife which called the cove home. A cottage hid among the thicker foliage behind the palm trees, its thatched roof and stucco walls providing a natural camouflage.

She smiled and used her Mer tail, its green and black scales sparkling in the sunlight, to propel herself through the waters of her favorite sanctuary. A black-footed albatross flew over her and called to its mate while a family of monk seals splashed near the island's white sand shore, barking for her to come play. A solid male chest slid up behind her, his muscled arms sliding under her breasts.

She rested her head back onto his chest. "I've been floating here alone for a while, waiting for you. It seems that even in my dreams, males make me wait."

Warm laughter rumbled under her cheek. "A dream, love?" He leaned down and grazed her neck with his lips. "Let me show you how very much awake you are."

Nadia glanced up, not surprised to see her dream Mer wearing Lord Cyrene's face. She turned in his arms, smoothing her hands over his chest, and smiled. "I suppose it isn't sane to argue with one's own dream creation, but why not?" She ran her gaze down his body to the scales that started low on his hips and covered a powerful fish's tail. "If this isn't a dream, why do you have a Mer tail?"

Gregor's gaze clouded. "I've had a fascination with the Mer since I was a child." He blinked and looked down at her, his brow wrinkled, then shook his head, his expression clearing as he ran a palm up her side. "This all feels very real to me."

A knot formed in her stomach. If only this were real life. She pushed the heavy thought aside and caressed his face. His chin was too strong in a face that screamed arrogance. He had a high forehead. She suppressed a smirk. No doubt he'd go bald with old age. She rolled her eyes mentally at herself as she focused on his mouth. His lips were full and looked soft. She wanted to taste them. As if reading her mind, he leaned forward.

His lips hovered a hairbreadth from hers. "What's going on behind those beautiful eyes?"

Nadia smirked. "Wishing you could read my mind?"

"Since the moment I met you." He sighed.

Nadia laughed, liking this dream version of the infuriating Lord Gregor Cyrene. Feeling playful, she splashed him in the face and twisted out of his arms. "Maybe I just need incentive. Catch me and I'll give you that kiss I was just imagining."

She dove into the wonder of Paraiso Canyon, its coral covered volcanic ledges and murky blue water creating a secret city in the depths beneath the waves. Parrotfish, unicornfish, and ulua scattered around her as she sped through the water, dodging in and out of formations of coral reef. She darted a look over her shoulder to see Gregor on her tail, teeth bared in a predatory smile.

She pushed her voice into his mind in the way of the Mer. "Watch out for the darker caves. You never know when octopi may reach out and grab you," she teased.

He glanced toward the cave she'd purposely swam past, veering off to give it a wide berth. Taking advantage of his distraction, she swam behind a ledge of the reef and put on a burst of speed toward the island. The sea's bottom rose beneath her, until the water was shallow enough for her to stand. With just a thought, her tail became legs, and she ran across the sandy bottom toward the beach and the lush vegetation beyond. She'd gone only a couple of steps when a hand closed around her ankle and her feet were pulled from under her.

Gregor's head broke the surface of the water, his arms wrapping around her as she fell. "You'll not get away from me that easy," he said, standing on his own legs and carrying her out of the water up onto the soft, white sand of the beach.

Nadia laughed. "I almost made it."

Gregor looked down at her and stopped, his smile fading as he dropped her legs and pulled her against his chest. "I want my kiss."

She wound her arms around his neck, pressing sensitive skin against the light smattering of hair on his chest, and tunneled her fingers into his hair. "Your wish is my command," she whispered.

She trailed kisses from his chin to his mouth, teasing him, before finally pressing her mouth to his. With a groan, he took control, licking her bottom lip until she opened to the invasion of his tongue. He broke the kiss and moved down the column of her neck, nipping and sucking at the sensitive skin.

She ran her hand down his arm, threading her fingers through his, then broke the kiss and pulled him up the beach. "Come, I'll show you my cottage."

"It's yours?"

"I inherited it when my mother died. It's my sanctuary. The place I used to go when I needed to be alone."

She pulled him onto the wide, covered porch, its wood planks creaking under her feet and making her smile. She pushed the door open and stepped into a large room with a kitchen and dining table at one end and a sitting room on the other that looked exactly as she'd left it the day before her exile. Her favorite blanket lay tossed across a blue chaise. The book she'd been reading lay on the blanket, the curved edge of a flat, white, sea biscuit marking her page. Shelves stuffed with books lined an entire wall, while more stacks of books filled the seat of an overstuffed chair and the square table between the chair and chaise as well as the dining table.

Gregor stepped in behind her, and she resisted the urge to straighten up. Reaching for one of the robes hanging on hooks by the door, she pulled it on, then handed the biggest one to Gregor.

His gaze jumped to hers, but she turned away. Though he was only a figment of her imagination, of her dream, having him in her favorite of private spaces, which she'd only ever allowed her sisters to visit, unnerved her. She watched him from the corner of her eye as he pulled the robe on and move to the wall of books.

He ran a finger along one of the spines. "You read."

She lifted one brow. "Is it so unbelievable?"

She smiled as his face pinkened, but he just shook his head. "I've never met a woman who enjoyed knowledge as much as I do."

Nadia shrugged. "Don't give me too much credit. I read for pleasure more than knowledge."

"Don't we all?" Gregor said, turning to study the titles on her shelves. "You enjoy reading histories written of battles." He pulled a book from the shelf. "Obscure battles...and those of the A'mi."

"Yes." Her forehead wrinkled. "You recognize written A'misrian?"

"I collect and study anything of the A'mi I can get my hands on, especially anything to do with their language."

"You don't fear the Order and their promise to punish those who don't revere Asha above all the gods?"

He smiled, then turned back to the shelf and replaced the book. "We in the North hold to the old ways. None of the five gods are any higher than the other. We worship them all."

A hard lump formed in her throat. She wished again that this was more than a dream. She shook her head and moved into the kitchen as he continued browsing through her books. When she glanced up again, he stood beside a small square chess table sitting before the fireplace, two chairs to either side of it.

He picked up one of the carved pieces. "They're A'mi creatures."

Nadia pulled a bottle of wine from the rack on the counter. "Yes." She pulled the cork from the bottle.

"They're exquisite."

"My sister, Kardia, will appreciate the praise. She used the project to master her control of earth and fire." Nadia pulled two lumpy wine glasses, a result of Kardia's first attempts to master the two elements, from the shelf above the sink and filled them with wine. "Do you play?"

One side of his mouth lifted in a smile as if he were keeping a secret. "Some."

"Sit, then." She moved toward the table and handed him a glass of wine. "Let's see how good you are."

Gregor's amber eyes glinted, his smile becoming predatory. "Indeed."

They sat. She lifted her wine to her lips and stared at him over the rim. Lowering the glass, she set it aside and slowly ran her tongue along her bottom lip. His gaze heated. She reached out and moved a sea horse shaped pawn into the center of the board, its long mane seeming to float around its head as if her sister had captured the image floating in water. She glanced back up and lifted a brow in challenge. He narrowed his eyes and looked down at the board. Challenge accepted. She smirked.

He moved his own pawn and looked up. "How many sisters do you have?"

"There are five of us."

"And you're all Mer?"

She moved her knight, carved into the shape of a griffin, and looked up. "No, only I and my youngest sister have Mer mothers. The other three have mothers from different A'mi races."

"Your father was able to cross through Diomere's gate?"

"No." His gaze jumped from the game board to her face, and Nadia looked away. "They were Chosen who'd decided to stay in Diomere rather than cross over into Mondami."

His brow wrinkled. "Your father…"

"Took advantage of young women barely out of pig tails, yes." Gregor studied her in silence as she drained her wine glass and stood to refill it. She leaned against the counter, their game forgotten. "My father is not a good man."

Gregor crossed to stand in front of her. He took the wineglass from her hand and set it on the counter, then traced the edge of her face with his finger.

"And my mother is an evil woman. But we aren't them."

Nadia let him pull her into his arms. "I wish you were real."

"Am I not?" he asked, a smile curling the corners of his mouth.

"No. You're a dream," she said, her smile sad. "A very nice dream."

His finger trailed from her face, down her neck, and along the edge of the cleavage revealed by her robe. She shivered. His hand dropped to the robe's belt and pulled it loose. The robe opened, revealing her body. When she didn't stop him, he leaned in to follow his finger's path with his lips. He nibbled the edge of her jaw, down the curve of her neck, and along her breast. He sucked one tight bud into his mouth. An arc of desire arrowed to the pleasure pulsing between her legs. She arched into him, the evidence of his own arousal pressing into her lower stomach.

"How is it that you keep trying to take over my dream?" she asked, pushing his head away from her breasts. "I want to taste you."

He chuckled. "I'd never deny a beautiful woman her wish."

Nadia loosened his robe, then bent and closed her teeth around one hard nipple while raking her nails lightly down his back. He groaned. She bathed the sting with her tongue, then sucked the hard nub into her mouth. He arrowed his fingers into her hair as she did the same to the other nipple. She smoothed her palms over his backside and squeezed the firm globes, then smoothed a hand over his hip until her fingers wrapped around the silk covered hardness of his erection. He shuddered, his hips jerking forward. She pumped her hand over the smooth steel of him once, twice, until a bead of moisture appeared at the tip. She licked her lips and dropped to her knees.

His fists clenched in her hair. "If this is your dream, shouldn't I be pleasuring you?"

Nadia gave him a sultry look from heavy-lidded eyes. "As you said, it's my dream, and I want a taste."

She leaned forward and licked the glistening bead from his tip, closing her eyes to savor the salty drop. He jerked in her grasp, a low groan making her smile. When she opened her eyes again, she lay on her side in her bed, her fist clutching the hard spine of the book she'd been reading, and her unfulfilled desire throbbing between her legs. She threw the book to the floor and squeezed her knees together with a frustrated groan.

CHAPTER SEVEN

The morning after the ball found Gregor arriving at Asha's temple with a bounce in his step and memories of one of the best dreams he'd ever had warming his thoughts. He waited for a group of priests to leave the second level garden terrace of the three-story temple, leaving him unobserved below in the colorful oasis the priests had created for the goddess' statue.

Muted beyond the square's walls, carriages clattered and horses clomped along the busy main avenue which stretched from the palace, through the center of Volos, and down to the harbor. Thick vines climbed the stone walls and towers, stretching out from the tops of the walls several feet toward the wide-canopied trees lining the inside of the square. The vines, covered in large bunches of purple, pink, and white wisteria flowers, created a natural shaded walkway around the square's perimeter that perfumed the warm, moist air with their fragrance. Birds flitted and twittered among the branches while the water pouring from the goddess' hands created a harmonious accompaniment.

Knowing others could appear at any moment, he crossed the small bridge over the fountain's pool to Asha's statue in the square's center and laid a seedling in a tiny pot at the goddess' feet. "I offer praise to Asha, goddess of life-giving earth."

He untied a shell pouch, revealing a tiny glowing ember from his home fire and placed it next to the potted seedling. Digging a hole in the pot's dirt, he placed a dead butterfly in the hole. "I offer praise to Naar, god of heat-producing fire."

He blew on the ember. "And to Soira, goddess of the air we breathe."

He covered the butterfly's corpse with the dirt. "I offer praise to Druj, god of death and master of the afterlife."

He poured water from a flask onto the dirt. "And to mighty Meren, god of water and the deep depths of the sea. I thank you all for the care you show, for your blessings and your many gifts to the Sa'i."

Hooves clattered on the cobbled paving stones of the square's main entrance.

Gregor quickly dug another hole in the potted seedling's dirt and covered the ember. He kissed his fingers then moved past the statue toward the gates of the temple. He didn't bother looking back. Had any of his fellow Thunoans seen him praising all the gods they would have been appalled and probably would have alerted those inside the temple.

He'd been raised on his family lands in the north where the old ways weren't forgotten, despite the best efforts of the Order. The sect had come into power in Thuno when the previous king had ruled. Before that king died, the priests controlled all of Thuno's major cities with an iron grip, and Dieuroi Mavros' illness had only made it worse.

But they hadn't been so successful in the north. Though they didn't dare worship openly, northerners still worshiped all the gods. And they still passed down stories of Saimond's true history with Mondami and the A'mi. As with all peoples, Gregor knew there were good and bad.

He entered the temple into an entrance hall of the same gray stone as the outside lit by the sun shining through the circular window above the front doors. Three sets of double doors, one on each of the three other walls, led farther into the temple. Above the doors, directly across from the entrance, hung a gigantic painting of Asha's hands cupping a mound of earth from which a wide-canopied tree grew.

Crossing the echoing foyer, he pulled the doors under the painting open and entered a stone hall lined with tapestries depicting scenes of Asha's blessings. A mother bird feeding her babies a wriggling worm, a rose unfurling its petals, the sun shining down onto a field of golden wheat.

He stopped before a set of double doors halfway down and entered the Order's main library.

A priest looked up from a table near the door. "Good morn, my lord. Can I help you find something?"

"I have an appointment with Father Marco." The priest nodded and stood. "This way."

They wound through packed bookshelves and long tables surrounded by clusters of priests with their heads bent over books and scrolls. When they reached a line of office doors along the back wall, the priest stopped at Father Marco's open door. The priest looked up as they tapped on the door frame.

"Gregor. Come in, come in." The priest stood to his feet and waved Gregor to the chair in front of his desk. "Thank you, Novice Jordos."

Gregor waited for the door to close behind him. "Asha's blessing on you, Marco."

"And you, my friend." The priest resumed his seat. "I assume you've closed up the family seat and moved your things here permanently?"

Gregor nodded. "I won't open the estate again until I've a wife and children to run its halls."

"And your private collection?"

"Safely installed in the house here." Gregor regarded him with a smile. "And I'm looking forward to adding to it. What do you have for me?"

The priest Gregor had grown up with grinned and bustled to a table in the corner stacked with a box marked correspondence, an open book, and a box of broken quill tips. "I received three new texts about the A'mi in a shipment sent from Arenatou." He lifted the correspondence from the box and removed the false bottom, revealing three scrolls and a flat sheet of paper. "I made copies of all three, but I can only give you the originals of two. The third is a scroll that contains information about the gate keepers. The Voice has been notified of its existence, so it's due to be destroyed tonight."

The most senior priest, referred to as the Voice, supposedly chosen by Asha herself to be her official voice to the people, would see all knowledge of the A'mi erased from all the lands of Saimond if he had his way.

Gregor frowned, resisting the urge to snatch all three and run. "May I look at the artwork on the original? I'd like to make notes about it on the copy you made me."

"Of course."

Marco returned to his seat behind his desk and left Gregor at the table in the corner with the documents, original and copy. Gregor looked them over carefully. The Order confiscated any text on the A'mi and either locked it away from the public or burned it. After his appointment as head of acquisitions of Asha's library five years before, Marco, who loathed the destruction of knowledge, contacted Gregor, who he knew had a passion for collecting anything to do with the A'mi. They'd saved over twenty priceless texts in the last five years.

Gregor pulled his sword from its thick leather scabbard and set it aside. Then he pulled at a tab inside the scabbard, revealing a compartment. He slid the two original documents into the compartment, then turned to the remaining scroll and its plainer copy. Two ornate pillars decorated the scroll on either side of the text, while an arched beam rested across the top of the pillars decorated with words in A'misrian, the language of the A'mi.

Gregor copied the words and an outline of the pillars and beam. He couldn't copy each of the a'mi creatures decorating the pillars, a gifted artist having obviously drawn each lifelike image. A bare-breasted woman stretched her arms above her head, her hooded eyes inviting her prey closer. Her lower body, shaped like a serpent, coiled in a pile beneath her as the rattler on the end of her tail seemed to vibrate on the page. Beneath the lamia, a man creature reached toward a glowing moon, his lion's mane of hair seeming to stand on end with the power arcing between his hands, his muscles rippled in knotted masses across his chest, arms, and legs. Dragon wings stretched behind him as if he were moments away from jumping into flight, while his scorpion tail waved behind him, warning his enemies to beware.

At the top of the second pillar, a jinn floated, his eyes glowing orbs, piercing in their intensity. One hand gripped the band circling his neck while he clenched the other hand in a fist in front of hips that disappeared into a swirl of power. In the last drawing, a man and woman, both naked, stood back-to-back with matching hungry expressions on their faces. Bat-like wings sprouted from their shoulders, the male's gold, the female's black, their spiked tails entwined between them.

Having no gift for drawing, he simply noted their unique attributes and the placement of the symbols for each of the five elements, Air, Water, Fire, Earth, and Spirit. Scanning the document and checking it against the words on the copy, he made certain none had been missed, and then sat back.

"They only translated the first few sentences and stopped? And they're just going to destroy it? What if the gates are ever reopened? The information it contains could help us discover how to control who comes through." He turned to face the priest.

"The Voice is only interested in locating the gate here in Thuno. When it became clear this scroll was only about the Arenatou gate, he ordered it destroyed." Marco shook his head. "The Voice is visiting the temple in Laus or I wouldn't have been able to get you even that copy. I'll be returning it to his office as soon as you leave."

Gregor nodded and slipped his copy into the scabbard compartment, then slid his sword in and returned it to his hip. He stood and clasped Father Marco's arm.

"May the gods protect you."

Father Marco opened the door. Gregor stepped out and, at the sound of Nadia's familiar voice, had to grit his teeth against a wave of desire that arced straight to his groin. Nadia stood beside a priest, a parchment in her hand. His gaze traveled down her body, brows lifting at the sight of the loose pants encasing her legs. Remembered images of those long legs, bare on a foreign beach, nearly unmanned him. He forced his eyes back up, lingering on her breasts and waist before continuing up to her frowning face.

"This should be all of them," a priest said beside her.

Her cheeks blazed red, making the thin scar stretching from temple to mid-cheek on one side of her face a bright contrasting white, as she folded the paper and tucked it into the pouch at her waist. "Thank you, Brother. I appreciate your help."

The priest nodded and disappeared back into the office next to Father Marco's.

She quirked a brow at Gregor, then turned and left without another word.

Gregor bit back a smile, waved to Marco, and then followed her into the quiet hall outside the library. Stretching his strides, he soon fell into step beside her. She scowled. Gregor smiled.

"What do you want, Lord Cyrene?" she whispered.

He picked up his pace so that he got to the door first and could hold it for her. "Princess."

She paused, studying his face as if to see if he'd really forgotten that she didn't like that title.

He stared back, face serious. Then winked, making her scowl.

He kept his amusement from his voice. "Do you visit Asha's Library often?"

"No."

He followed her rigid back into the temple square, wondering if the real Nadia's mouth would be as talented as his dream Nadia. "Not a lover of knowledge?" he asked, grabbing her hand and tucking it into his elbow.

She yanked at her hand, but he held it in place as they passed Asha's statue and continued toward the rush of carriages, horses, and people on Volos' main thoroughfare.

She blew out a loud breath of frustration and stopped moving, pulling Gregor to a stop beside her. "Knowledge, I have no problem with, but I doubt that library has anything in it that has to do with anything other than Asha. You Thunoans' single-minded worship of one god is tragic."

"You say what's on your mind, and you don't care that we stodgy Thunoans know that you don't follow our religion." He started walking again, pulling her along with him until she reluctantly fell into step beside him. "I like it."

"I'm so glad you approve," she muttered.

Gregor suppressed a smile. The real Nadia's mouth would be even better, he decided. "I love knowledge, no matter its source. I collect literature on every subject I can get my hands on. You're welcome to peruse my private library whenever you'd like."

"I'll keep that in mind," she said dryly. She pulled him to a stop as they reached the street. "Well, this has been fun, but I have to get back to the Mermaid."

"I'll walk you."

She clenched her jaw. "It's right there." She pointed across the street at the four-story inn she called home.

He gently squeezed her hand. "I'll walk you."

She stared at him, unsure how to handle his quiet insistence. Even if he hadn't dreamed of her, he'd want her. She intrigued him. She wore so many different titles. Exiled princess, innkeeper, guild member. Adding mystery to the truth of which was really her. One or all? She was a new text in a language he'd never seen, and he couldn't help but want to decipher her.

"Fine," she muttered, pulling her hand from his. "But this changes nothing. In fact, it proves my initial assumption."

He lifted an eyebrow.

She sighed. "You're a complication. I don't have time for someone like you."

Her furrowed brow paired with her slightly pained expression was so adorable, a term he was sure she didn't associate with herself, that Gregor felt an overwhelming urge to pull her close. Knowing he'd earn himself further enmity if he dared act on the urge, he clasped his hands behind his back and refrained. Barely.

"You should know that I plan to complicate your life with my presence as much as possible." He turned and smiled. "I won't give up." He stopped at the inn's front gate and reached for her calloused fingers, then pulled them to his lips. "Until we meet again, I'll be seeing you in my dreams."

She stiffened, studying him with a sharp gaze. "You dream of me?"

"In vivid detail," he said, his eyes moving down her body and back up.

Her mouth dropped open, and it might be one of the few times she'd ever been at a loss for words. Turning toward the inn's door, she paused, gave him a pensive look, then shook her head and went inside.

Gregor finally let the smile he'd been hiding spread across his face. No, she was definitely not used to being speechless.

CHAPTER EIGHT

Nadia opened the custom door Jon had built for the cave she used as a private office and sitting room. Made of uneven and mismatched planks arranged into a contrasting pattern of light-and-dark stained squares, the door was a beautiful art piece the local carpentry guild would have been hard pressed to replicate.

Inside the small cave Nadia used as a private office and sitting room in her role as Vromia Guild's Shark, Sarna sat on a wide divan and bent over a pile of tiny scrolls on a low table made of the same planks as the door. The other woman swept the scrolls into a pouch as Nadia nodded and stepped inside the cave followed by Jon and Pell.

Nadia crossed toward her desk, passing several messily stuffed bookshelves, Sarna on the wide divan decorated with bright blue pillows, and two tufted chairs on the opposite wall from the divan. Thick carpets in various shades of blue cushioned her feet as she stopped behind her desk and sank into her chair.

Pell sat straight-backed in one of the chairs across from Sarna, while Jon moved to stand in front of her desk with his back to the other two lieutenants still dressed in the traveling gear from his latest mission.

"Killing the guard because the youngest prince tripped over his own feet and fell into the sea seems like a rather harsh punishment, even for Thuno's unstable god king," Nadia said, referring to the report Jon had started on their way to her office.

"Someding happen to de boy in dat water. De guard die because he didn't want to touch whatever it is he saw," Jon replied, his dark gaze sliding toward Sarna then back to her.

She studied Geeta's heartbonded. His dark skin absorbed the dim lantern light so that he appeared a towering shadow in the cramped space.

Nodding, she glanced to the side and met Pell's gaze. "If you two don't mind, I'd like to speak with Jon alone," she said, knowing her friend would understand.

Sarna stood and headed for the door. Pell glanced between her and Jon, then nodded and followed after the other woman.

As soon as Pell pulled the door closed, Nadia returned her attention to her cousin's gentle giant of a mate. "What did you see, Jon?"

His eyes, so dark brown as to almost be black, bore into hers as his voice rumbled out of his thick chest. "When Prince Stefan and Dieuroi Mavros pull Prince Reis from de water, de skin on his arms was blue-gray."

"Did you see his tail?"

Jon shook his head. "As soon as his head broke de water, he turned back to de familiar pale skin."

She closed her eyes. She'd found him. Her heart pounded hard in her chest. She could finally return to her sisters and give up the charade of her exile. Shoving the rising hope to the back of her mind, she inhaled deeply and opened her eyes.

"We need to find out more about Prince Reis' mother. I want to know who she was, where she came from, and when she and Dieuroi Mavros became involved. Find this information for me. Tell no one, save Geeta, about what you saw." He nodded and she waved toward the door, giving him permission to leave.

Pell entered, took a look at what was no doubt a stunned expression on her face, and closed the door behind him.

She jumped to her feet, too excited to sit still. "We may have found him."

Pell leaned a hip against her desk, his skepticism clear in his voice. "You're sure?"

She scowled. "About as sure as I am the Guardian takes the newly turned A'mi to Mondami, I'd wager." She studied his clenched jaw. "Don't you want to go home?"

Emotions chased through his eyes faster than she could identify them before they settled into an earnest plea. "We're finally reaping the rewards of all the work we've put into building up the Shark's reputation. I must admit I enjoy our position. I'll do whatever I must to keep it. You can't seriously want to return to a people who forced you into exile, can you?"

She pictured the faces of her four sisters. So different in looks, having been born of different mothers due to their father's unfaithfulness, the five sisters had all been born within three years of each other and had been raised together. She rubbed her chest, trying and failing to rub away the pain of being separated from them.

"I'd give anything for a chance to return to Diomere," she said, imagining the reunion with her sisters.

"Then for your sake, I hope this lead pans out," he said, his expression sympathetic. Resting his hands on his hips, he furrowed his brow. "You think Thuno's bastard prince is really our lost prince?"

Inhaling a deep breath, she released it in slow increments. Like her friend, she was afraid to let the kernel of hope grow. Their search took them all over Saimond in the last twelve years. And so many times they followed a promising lead only to end up disappointed.

"Maybe. I'll have to find out more about him first to be sure," she said, heat pulsing in waves through her body as her power responded to her suddenly pounding heart. "While my gut tells me this is a solid lead, let's continue scouring the archives as planned until we know for sure."

Pell nodded, then handed her a tiny glass vial and a rolled parchment, both sealed with wax. He turned to leave, pausing at the door to look back over his shoulder.

"What happens if your sisters like the lives they've created away from Diomere?" he asked in a quiet voice.

She sat the messages on her desk as a chill moved down her spine and premonition formed a tight knot in her stomach. Her sisters missed each other, true, but they also seemed happy with their lives. She knew they'd return when their nephew was found, but would they stay? What would she do if they all wished to return to the lives they'd created outside of Diomere?

And what about her? Would she return here to her place as the Shark? Would she stay in Diomere with Lareina?

Her power pulsed and her skin prickled as Marquess Cyrene's face appeared in her mind's eye, reminding her of the troubling dreams and her suspicions that they weren't mere dreams. Her a'mi buzzed, pricking her skin harder as if to say, stay. She squeezed her eyes closed.

Could she chance trusting another man only to have her heart broken yet again? Did she even want to?

The door closed quietly as Pell left her to the mess of thoughts his question had evoked. She looked down at the missives he'd handed her. Her heart lurched as she saw the familiar seal for the queen of Diomere pressed into the wax holding the scroll closed. Reaching for the scroll, she slid her finger along the parchment's edge and broke the wax seal. She read the note written in the made-up language she and her sisters created as children.

Greetings sister,

I write in hopes this finds you in good health, and I pray your search goes well. I wish I were writing for a simple update, but I'm afraid a knowing necessitates otherwise. Arri leaves in two days time to help you; however, that is not the only reason she comes. With her will be a sketch of a person essential to the future of Saimond. Find this person. His life depends on you both. In this, we must not fail.

With love, L

Excitement warred with worry inside her. Lareina, Queen of Diomere and youngest of the five Quinones sisters, had experienced visions since she was a small child. Nadia shuddered to think what Lareina had seen that was so important she'd mentioned it in the short note. She closed her eyes and held the scroll to her chest. Arriana was coming. She looked wildly around her office. So much to do.

She set her sister's scroll down. The clink of glass hitting the desk's wood surface reminded her of the other missive in its glass tube.

She peeled the wax from the vial's opening and retrieved the rolled parchment from inside. Forcing her thoughts away from her soon-to-arrive sister, she focused on decoding the message beneath the senseless arrangement of letters and numbers.

I48O99M69 Q48Y 49L18 W19V77I48R 68V59 G48N48I18L57
M19T29G

ROLAND JOB FOR DIEUROI MEET TOMORROW
NIGHT

Her brow furrowed. The Dieuroi sought the services of her rival? Prime Guild, filled only with native Thunoans, and their leader, Roland, had defected from Vromia Guild after the Shark overthrew the old leader. Certain that Pell was the Shark, Roland had quickly established his own guild and taken in any who resented taking orders from a foreigner or who'd been thrown out for breaking her guild's few rules. Roland would have stayed and attempted to gain control if he'd known the Shark was a woman.

As it was, Roland grew bolder in his moves against her. He was known for taking any job, especially if the Shark had turned it down.

That the Dieuroi had bypassed her guild altogether told her the job he wanted done would be against an innocent. Vromia Guild's few hard limits were well known.

She scowled at the piece of paper and threw it on the small brazier standing beside her desk. This was why the Shark was needed. To keep Volos' citizens, rich and poor, safe from senseless violence.

Pell's words echoed in her mind. They'd, indeed, built a life here, but was it what she wanted for her future?

Her blood rushed in her ears. She fisted her hands on the desk as all her uncertainties blasted to the forefront of her mind. Air began to swirl around her, matching her agitation.

What if her friends didn't want to return to Diomere with her? Would she leave them behind?

Her palms heated. She pushed away from the desk and began to pace.

But if she stayed, it would mean living permanently without her sisters close by.

Amber eyes flashed across her memory.

Her power swelled, orbs of fire bursting from her palms to slam into the bare stone wall next to her divan.

Would she be happy returning to the life she'd lived before the kidnapping? To being the Captain of her nephew's personal guard? Would they even want her in that position since she'd already lost him once?

A rumbling sound filled the cave. Pulled from her rioting thoughts, her eyes widened, and she frantically reached to calm her power as stone split under her feet, creating a chasm that stretched toward the scorched section of wall. Before she could pull her power back, a loud boom sounded. A chunk of the wall fell into the room.

Dust mushroomed into the air. Coughing, she waved her hands before her face. Her eyes widened when the dust cleared, focusing on a hole the size of her head which now marred what had once been the back wall of her chamber.

CHAPTER NINE

Nadia inhaled the cool, stale air coming from the darkness beyond the hole. Her heart pounded as she grabbed a hammer from one of her desk drawers and chipped away more of the wall, stopping when she made a hole big enough to climb through, revealing the back of some type of heavy wood furniture.

She closed her eyes and reached for her a'mi, praying it wouldn't fail her after such a powerful outburst. A trickle of power came at her beckoning. Remembering all the times she'd taken the former strength of her power for granted, she sent up a prayer of thanks to the gods.

She pushed her a'mi into the hole, using her connection to the water in the air to check for life. Her power shied away from something which seemed to give off a low hum, and she paused. When no heartbeat or pulse vibrated the water drops, she continued pushing her power into the space. Then her connection vanished as her a'mi failed her again, leaving her deaf and blind to what else lay beyond.

As she tried again to connect to her power, she swallowed the growing lump in her throat. This slow loss of her a'mi, of a part of herself, ached like a festering wound. Inhaling, she clenched her jaw and blinked away the burning in her eyes. She would not wallow in self-pity. Lifting the hammer, she knocked in more of the cavern wall, revealing the back of a chair.

When she'd cleared a hole large enough, she shoved the chair aside and grabbed a lantern, then stepped through. The light revealed a chamber twice the height of the one she'd just left.

She stood between two high-backed chairs, covered in a thick layer of dust. A carpet cushioned her feet, a cloud of dust billowing up with each step as she stepped farther into the room. To either side of the chairs, light boxes hung on the walls.

She pictured the symbols for all five of the elements in her mind's eye: water, air, earth, fire, and spirit. She pulled on fire, allowing the other symbols to fade. Inside her mind, two tiny sputtering flames appeared on either side of a scale. She blew on the slightly larger flame, its weight causing the scale's arm to sink slightly lower than the other side.

She reached into that larger flame and formed a glowing ball, an orb that now floated above her palm in the physical world. Moving toward the closest glass box, she pushed the orb inside of it. Instantly, the power pulsed, and five other light boxes lit up and revealed the rest of the chamber.

She whirled around to hunt for other treasures. Each of the adjacent walls on the left and the right held a set of golden doors, one set barred and the other slightly ajar, and she wondered if the barred set led to the outside. But it was a familiar sight at the back of the cave that beckoned her deeper into the cavern. Carved from the stone wall itself, towering twin columns held a stone arch with words carved deep into its surface.

She crossed to the gate and laid a hand against one of the pillars. Her a'mi jolted awake as recognition washed over her. *Thuno's Gate.*

Etched down both columns were the triangular symbols for the elements Earth, Air, Fire, and Water, while the circle symbolizing spirit was centered on the cave wall between the columns where one would walk through if a Gate Keeper were here.

Blue light burst from the columns, spreading warmth up her arm until her entire body vibrated. She focused on her mind's eye and the gold scales where her power waited for her call. She called fire to her and her scales appeared, a raging inferno of power where the tiny flickering flames had been before. Her power circulated through her body, strengthening muscles, organs, and mind until, for the first time in years, she felt whole.

She opened her eyes, having closed them during the rush of power, and focused on the gate as a'mi spread from the columns and into the rock of the cave floor and walls.

"The first of the Sankta Hogo-sha has arrived. To complete the joining, we must have the one bonded to the key," a voice whispered.

She jerked her fingers from the column and swung around, looking for the source of the voice. The gate hummed and pulsed a soft blue-white. She stepped back, resisting the pull of her a'mi toward the gate.

She'd been the captain of her nephew's guard the last time she'd seen a gate like this. She'd watched as King Delmar and her queen sister took the newborn prince to the Gate chamber in the abandoned Gate Keeper's palace. There the king had pricked the baby's finger and smeared a drop of blood on a column, causing the gate to glow from within. A voice, male and loud, filled their heads, welcoming the newest guardian. The royal family of Diomere had been the gate's guardians since the magic and non-magic worlds were closed to each other. Did King Delmar know that other gates hadn't been destroyed?

The columns stretched up so high she couldn't even reach the bottom edge of the arch with her fingertips. Etched into the stone were words in the language of the a'mi. *Geto Inter Sokai.*

"The Gate Between the Worlds," she read aloud.

Something tugged at her a'mi, and she turned away from the gate to face the barred set of golden doors on her left. Crossing the room, she strained to lift the heavy beam, but it wouldn't budge.

She reached for her power, using the tiny particles of water in the air as her eyes and ears to slip beneath the door and explore what lay behind it. Her consciousness flowed from molecule to molecule down a wide, dark hall. She paused at a beam of light that filtered through a tumbled pile of rocks and boulders, but the vibration of rushing water pulled her farther down the tunnel.

Ignoring another dark opening, she moved between water molecules toward the growing roar of cascading water until she flowed into a large cavern filled with an underground lake. Water fell from a hole in the roof which allowed a few shafts of sunlight to glitter across the calm surface.

Her consciousness returned to her with a snap.

A smile stretched across her face, but as she turned to go find Jon and Geeta, the other doors caught her attention. She crossed the cave, her eyes resting on the water symbol etched deep into the gold. Rather than door handles, a large hand impression marked each door.

She placed a hand in each of the large handprints. The door warmed under her palms, then clicked open with a sigh of stale air. She pushed the doors open and froze in awe.

She'd found Thuno's Gate Keeper palace.

Numerous glowing lightboxes, as well as gold chandeliers draped in webs, lit a large entrance hall. Slabs of blue-veined marble covered the floor. Blue tiles formed the symbol for water in the center.

Across from her, open doors revealed a much larger room lit by a skylight and more lightboxes. Long tables led up to a raised dais holding another long table. Five tapestries hung behind the head table, each decorated with one of the five elements, the one denoting water holding the center position. She returned to the entrance hall and spun around. Twin staircases framed the opening to the hall and wound up to a balcony and hallways leading to the private wings of the palace.

She spun around and ran back to the hole that led to her room. She couldn't wait to show this treasure to the others.

CHAPTER TEN

N adia pressed her eye to the hole in the tunnel's stone wall to make sure the healer didn't have a patient. Geeta sat before the hearth, her head resting back against her chair, while Jon knelt beside her, his face lined with worry. Nadia hesitated then knocked before pulling the lever to hurry into the healer's home.

"Just wait until you see what I've discovered," she said, striding to stand before the couple.

Geeta smiled, though it didn't reach her eyes. "Do tell."

"No, you have to see this for yourself."

Jon placed a hand on Geeta's shoulder. "You should rest, dhana."

Nadia met his hard gaze. "I think I've found something that will help her." She glanced at Geeta's tired face. "I hope."

Geeta placed her hand over Jon's and squeezed. "Let me change—"

"Don't bother. Where we're going, they'll just get dirty anyway."

Geeta's brows lifted.

Nadia plucked a fresh bloom from the potted plant hanging near the window, then waited as Jon helped Geeta stand. She turned away before they could see the concern on her face and led the way back into the tunnel and the caves hidden in the mountain around which the city was built.

Voices and laughter greeted her as she stepped into the main cave hidden behind the Emerald Mermaid Inn. Lanterns hung from hooks they'd embedded in the cavern ceiling, lighting the space used for meetings, meals, and the general revelry of the guild's members.

She nodded as she passed a group of men and women lounging around long tables near the side of the cave they used as the kitchen. Others sprawled in a sitting area near a large fireplace which had been carved into the cave's wall.

Pell separated from a conversation with another guild member and stepped in front of her, his back ramrod straight. Nadia stopped.

"Where have you been?" he asked, voice clipped. "I've been looking for you."

She bit back the invitation to join them she'd been about to issue, his surly tone prompting her not to include him in her newest discovery just yet. "I wasn't aware I had to notify you of my every movement."

His frown deepened. "The Nightingales sent word that Prime had an important meeting tonight."

Nadia smiled. "Excellent." Pell continued to stand in her path, and Nadia lifted a brow. "Was there something else?"

He exhaled loudly through his nose. "I'll send someone to attend the meeting."

"No need." She moved forward, forcing Pell to move out of their way. "It's already taken care of. Have a good evening."

Waving off anyone else's attempts to stop her, she moved across the cave, stopping at a storage cave for several lengths of rope, before leading the way to her office. Closing the door behind Jon, she crossed to the tapestry she hung before going to fetch her cousin, then pulled it aside.

Geeta gasped. "You found another one."

"I found more than another cave. Come." Nadia ushered them both through.

Geeta's eyes widened, a tiny spark lighting her dull green gaze. "Lightboxes!" Her cousin's smile stretched across her face. "I never thought to see them outside Diomere's royal palace."

"That's not even the best part," Nadia said, then moved toward the gate at the back of the cavern, her jaw dropping.

Where the stone had been bare when she left, now thick vines heavy with purple bunches of wisteria flowers climbed the pillars and draped the gate's arch, their heady scent filling the air.

Her cousin looked over at the gate. "What is this?" Moving to stand in the gate's glow, Geeta tilted her head back and closed her eyes. "It feels like home. I can breathe again without pain."

The healer inhaled and the deep lines around her mouth smoothed out while they watched. Nadia and Jon exchanged an astonished glance. Geeta's face glowed with health. She opened eyes no longer dulled by the fever of the past few days.

Nadia touched Geeta's cheek. "I believe it's Thuno's lost gate to Mondami. And it has somehow cured us of whatever was making us sick."

Geeta's gaze unfocused. "I don't think I'm cured. It feels more like I received a dose of the medicine I need. The weakness is still there." She turned to her heartbonded. "Jon?"

"I feel de same."

"This gate pulses with a'mi," Geeta said as she stood basking in its glow. "If we could only figure out how to make it give more to us."

"I don't feel any of that," Nadia said, then checked her a'mi levels again. "I'm back to full strength."

She knew she was completely healed, with no lingering effects of the illness. Was she missing something? Could it be because her two friends had been sick longer? Nadia shook her head, unsure. Hopefully, Arriana would know.

"I'll send a note to Lareina asking her to find out everything she can about how they work," she muttered, then pulled Geeta away from the gate. "But that's only part of what I brought you to see. Come, you can study the gate later."

She opened the doors to the underground palace. "Needs a good dusting and the spider webs" —she shuddered— "need to be pulled down. Other than that, it's as if it's only sat here untouched weeks rather than hundreds of years."

"What is dis place?" Jon asked.

"I believe it is the Gate Keeper's Palace," Nadia said. She allowed them to look around a moment, then led them back into the gate cave toward the set of doors on the opposite side of the gate. "Jon, I need your assistance. This beam is too heavy for me to lift myself."

They each took one end of the beam. Counting to three, they heaved, sending a heavy cloud of dust into the air as the beam lifted free, revealing another set of hand indentions. They sat the beam aside, then Nadia placed her hands in the spaces for them and, with a click, the doors cracked open. Jon pulled the doors open, revealing a tunnel lit with more lightboxes.

Entering the tunnel, Nadia pushed cobwebs from her hair and face with a shudder, as tiny spiders scuttled away as fast as their creepy legs would carry them. She rolled her eyes at herself.

Geeta burst out with her old full-bellied laugh, and Jon's glistening gaze met Nadia's. "The Guild would roar with laughter to see their tough guild boss fear a few harmless spiders."

Nadia blinked away the moisture and mock scowled at the older woman, then quickly checked that no creepy crawlers decided to try to make a meal of her.

Her gaze snagged on elaborate drawings decorating the passage's walls. On her right, black silhouettes of the A'mi creatures she'd seen on the pillars walked in single file away from the cave. On her left, the painted silhouettes of the non-magic Sa'i walked in single file toward the cave.

Geeta traced the image of a large jungle cat. "This really is one of the Gates between the worlds."

Nadia nodded. Making a mental note to sketch the drawings for her sister, she moved farther down the long hall.

Jon and Geeta, who'd been close on her heels, fell behind as Geeta stopped to trace a finger along the twisted limbs of a tree nymph's silhouette and the edge of one of the lightboxes that lined either side of the tunnel. The drawings ended at a pile of tumbled stones and boulders, a ray of sunlight shining through a small hole near the top.

Jon stepped forward to look through the hole. "Leads outside. De backside of de mountain, from de looks of it."

"Those who wished to travel through the gate would have had to trek around the mountain to get here," Nadia said. "Thunoans obviously didn't have an open relationship with the A'mi even before the gates were closed."

Past the stone pile stood another set of golden doors with hand indentions and the water symbol. Nadia placed her hands in the indentions. On the other side, more lightboxes revealed an intersecting hall. One direction descended deeper into the mountain. And the other led to a stone stairway which climbed farther up.

"This cave system is a gift that keeps on giving," she said, smiling.

Jon looked up the stairs. "Do you think de lead to Thuno's royal palace?"

"I wouldn't be surprised." Her a'mi pulsed inside her, pushing toward the tunnel that led deeper into the mountain. "But I'd like to see what's down here first."

Jon nodded and they continued down the descending tunnel. She'd gone another five hundred paces when the sound of running water echoed from down the tunnel. For the first time in two years, she felt her true form waiting to be released. Geeta grabbed Nadia's arm, her face stretched into a wide smile.

She picked up her pace as they descended toward the last bend.

Geeta gasped behind her. Stretched out before them, a large lake spread across a cave lit along its entire perimeter with more lightboxes. Water poured from a hole the size of her head in the cave's ceiling, creating a musical accompaniment to the peaceful lake which lapped gently against the stone shore. Sunlight speared through the hole, reflecting from the pool's calm surface.

Basking in the tranquil scene, she forgot about the tunnel she'd seen with her a'mi until Jon tapped her shoulder and pointed at it and the river of water which disappeared into its dark depths.

"Do you dink it merges into one of de twin rivers or even de sea?" John asked.

"That's why I brought the rope." They knelt by the underground lake, and Nadia gently set the bloom upon the water's surface. "Thank you, merciful Meren, for this gift."

Her skin, dry and tight over her muscles, yearned to feel the water slide against it. She gave Geeta and Jon a wide smile and laughed as they began to yank their clothes off and toss them into a careless pile.

Nadia threw herself into the pool's cool embrace first, the other two right behind her. Closing her eyes, she called to her a'mi and surrendered to a surge of power stronger than she'd felt since before she'd left home.

The power shimmered around her. Heat flashed in waves until it became just short of unbearable. When it subsided, a fish's tail and gauzy green fins replaced her hips, legs, and feet, all covered in iridescent scales of emerald green shot through with black. Her long black hair swirled in the water around her, each shimmery strand visible to the enhanced vision of her Mer eyes.

CHAPTER ELEVEN

Nadia opened her mouth and sang a musical, high-pitched song in a series of short, joy-filled notes and turned as Geeta and Jon responded, both in their own Mer forms.

Geeta dove under the water, then jumped up in an elegant arc, a radiant smile lighting her face, her skin now the same milky gray-green as Nadia's. As she arced through the air, sunlight reflected off the green and gray scales that swirled across the lower half of her body.

Nadia smiled, happy to see her friend so energetic. Geeta surfaced after her dive, the gill slits on either side of her neck and ribs fluttering, her eyes shining.

"So beautiful," Jon whispered.

Geeta's full lips lifted in a small, secretive smile. "As are you, husband."

Nadia glanced back to see Jon staring, eyes hungry. She was still amazed that the heartbond had changed Jon into one of her people. The blue and gray of his scales were a dramatic contrast to his dark skin.

Swallowing past the lump in her throat as the couple got lost in each other, she dove into the lake, its crystal-clear depths embracing her like a lover. She cut through the water propelled by the back-and-forth thrusts of her powerful tail, a transparent third eyelid snapping protectively over each eye.

Opening her mouth, she sucked in water which rushed down her throat and out of the gills in her neck and ribs. She zipped through the water faster than a marlin, darting between the separate shafts of sunlight. Surging toward the surface, she jumped out of the water and back in a graceful dive, her arms stretched above her head.

She surfaced as Jon and Geeta swam past, locked in each other's embrace. Grinning, she ignored a twinge of envy for their bond. When she returned to Diomere, she hoped to find her own heartbonded mate. She couldn't help but remember Lord Cyrene and his insistence that she allow him to escort her home. She ignored the soft ache surrounding her heart. No a'mi-fearing Thunoan would ever accept a partner who wielded a power they believed to be evil.

A quiet voice, deep in her heart, insisted Gregor was different.

Seeking to distract herself from her useless musings, she grabbed the rope from their messy pile of clothing and moved toward the river that disappeared into a dark tunnel across the lake.

It made sense that the Gate Keeper of the water element would have a way to get to the sea. The alternate escape route could be very useful as long as their ability to call their Mer form didn't desert them again.

Why had they lost the ability in the first place? How could they keep it from happening again? Frustration tightened her stomach. Geeta had been hit by it the hardest. Nadia and Jon had watched helplessly as Geeta lost the ability to call her Mer form followed by her healing abilities. Jon had also lost the ability to change forms, but not having been born with the ability, he hadn't seemed to suffer the same loss of self. Geeta, by comparison, seemed to lose a little more of her zest for life. First her robust laugh, then her ready smile, until she appeared a mere shell of the vivacious person she'd always been.

What had the gate done? Was it the presence of a'mi?

Her palm burned. She glanced down and realized she'd been squeezing the rope so hard that the rough material had cut into her hands. Easing her grip, she tied the rope together and looped it around a stalagmite protruding from the cave floor near the river tunnel opening.

Jon and Geeta, both flushed and bright eyed, surfaced beside her. Their delicate nose slits fluttered wide open.

"If you're done pawing at each other, I'd like to investigate this tunnel," she said, voice dry.

Geeta gave her a knowing smile. "Loving, not pawing. Don't be jealous."

Nadia rolled her eyes, though a small part of her did envy her friends their bond. "Take the rope as far as it'll reach, then try to swim back against the current. If it isn't too strong, we'll join you and explore the entire length of the river together."

Jon nodded, both of them aware that he had the upper body strength to pull himself against the current along the rope better than she or Geeta. She tossed him the rope, and he tied it around his waist. He gave Geeta a smoldering kiss and disappeared into the hole.

His voice soon echoed in her mind. *"De tunnel too straight. Man-made."* After minutes of silence, he continued. *"De current strong, but no difficult. Reached end of rope and still very dark."*

Thinking of the drawings on the walls between the cave with the gate and the collapsed opening, Nadia wondered if her ancestors had carved out the caves and the river exit before the closing of the gates.

"I'm on my way."

Geeta nodded. "I'll come, too."

Nadia waved her toward the surface, but Geeta dove for the dark hole. *"Geeta!"* Nadia's heart pounded in her chest as she followed her friend, catching her just as the current sucked them both through the hole into the underground river.

Clasping Geeta's hand tightly, Nadia met her older cousin's stubborn gaze. *"You're tired. I won't risk your a'mi failing and returning you to your human form."*

"I'm fine." The other woman gave Nadia a reassuring smile. *"I promise."*

Nadia swallowed, fear knotting her stomach.

"Fine, but stay behind me. We don't know what kinds of sea life have made their home down here."

Nadia swam ahead of her friend, letting the current pull them both. She trailed a hand along the smooth walls. The absolute darkness made it impossible to distinguish anything as they moved along with the current. Only her grip on Geeta's hand kept her from losing the other woman in the wide river.

Just as she was sure they must've accidentally passed by Jon, she plowed into his hard chest, Geeta right behind her.

Jon wrapped his arms around them both. For the first time, she was just able to separate the tunnel's walls and the outline of her friends from the darkness. A pinprick of light marked the tunnel's end.

Pulling away from Jon, she took the lead toward the light, picking up speed. Her heart pounded harder in her chest. She'd missed the euphoria of swimming at high speed through the water. The pinprick of light grew, lighting the tunnel.

She glanced back over her shoulder to see Jon and Geeta holding hands behind her, wide smiles stretched across their faces.

Nadia turned and lashed her tail harder, increasing her speed. Just as they were approaching the tunnel's seaweed draped exit, Geeta's panicked voice broke into Nadia's thoughts.

"Nadia!"

Nadia looked back to see Jon and Geeta far behind her, Jon's legs kicking while Geeta pulled him frantically toward the light.

Nadia whipped around and raced toward him. *"The surface. Go! I can't help you both if you revert to your Sa'i form, too."*

Geeta shot Jon an agonized look, then turned and raced for the end of the tunnel. Nadia looped Jon's arms around her neck and signaled for him to hold on. He nodded, his face strained with the need to breathe. She turned and raced with every ounce of strength in her tail.

Finally, they burst through the river's exit into the Saimond Sea. Jon's arms tightened around her neck, nearly choking her, then his arms loosened as he lost consciousness. She clutched his arms to keep him from sliding off her back. Nadia's heart jumped in her chest as she caught his hands and surged toward the surface. As soon as her head broke the water, she pulled Jon's limp body in front of her, wrapped her arms around his wide chest and yanked her fists up to force the water from his lungs.

"Jon," Geeta wailed behind her.

Nadia turned him to face her and pinched his nose to breathe air into his lungs, then moved behind him to pull her fists against his chest again.

"Come on, Jon. Wake up," Geeta cried, then placed her hands against his chest and shoved her healing power into him.

Jon coughed, choking as water spewed from his blue lips. Tears poured down Geeta's cheeks as she held her heartbonded while he struggled to breathe.

Keeping her arms wrapped around his chest from behind, Nadia leaned her head against his shoulder, letting her heartbeat slow. Once her breathing returned to normal, she studied their surroundings.

The coast of Thuno stretched out behind them, dotted with cliffs and dirty beaches. She could see the Port of Volos in the distance. She smiled. They couldn't have asked for a better emergency escape route.

CHAPTER TWELVE

The next night, Nadia approached the tavern Prime Guild called their headquarters, using her power to blur her body into the shadows as she crept between nearby buildings.

A soft breeze off the river moved through the leaves of the trees, making a swishing sound, while insects sang their nighttime song. A full moon filled the sky.

She scowled up at the bright orb, knowing it would make her job tonight that much more difficult to remain undetected.

Two Prime guards rounded the tavern's corner, clearly visible in the moon's bright glow.

She sank back into the deepest shadows, praying her power didn't crap out on her again. After the incident with Jon and the underwater tunnel, she trusted her a'mi abilities even less than before.

The guards walked along the tavern's side, only occasionally looking up to squint into the dark past their torches.

"Druj take 'em if they take all the big-breasted whore's time before I get a chance to pay for an hour," the taller of the two guards muttered to his shorter partner.

"I paid her to come to my room when our shift ends," the short guy boasted, a smirk on his face.

The taller guard narrowed beady eyes at the shorter man.

The short guard shrugged and continued, "Give me the dagger you stole off that prick you killed yesterday, and I'll share her with you." The short guard's lust-filled leer sickened Nadia as he added, "You can have her mouth while I take her ass. A pint to the one who lasts longest."

Shaking her head as the two guards rounded the corner out of sight, she reminded herself of her reason for invading her rival's territory and loosened her tight grip on the dagger at her waist. She slipped across the narrow alley, which separated the tavern from the edge of the slums, and peeked into a side window.

The rest of Prime Guild filled the rickety tables as harried barmaids balanced trays of ale and skimpily-dressed Nightingale's draped over the laps of those who'd paid their fee. A minstrel strummed the strings of a lyre in a lively tune which had the tavern's occupants roaring with laughter and singing along.

Roland's two lieutenants sat at a corner table near the stairs. One held a pale-faced young woman on his lap. Eyes wide with fear, she pulled away as he leaned forward and squeezed her breast.

Nadia clenched her fists as Roland's lieutenant, Thad, shoved the young woman onto her knees before him and opened his trousers.

An older woman with the same brown hair as the girl burst through the door of the kitchen, but was caught by the balding tavern keeper who shook his head. The older woman glared at him, sent an agonized look at the young woman, and then retreated back through the doors to the kitchen. The tavern keeper turned away from the scene, his shoulders hunched.

Nadia's heart ached for the tavern keeper she knew would lose his livelihood if he were to interfere.

The girl shook her head as Thad freed his dick.

Altair, Roland's other lieutenant, taunted his comrade at the young woman's rejection.

Thad's face flushed and his small eyes narrowed on the girl. He surged to his feet and cleared the table in front of him with a sweep of an arm. Grabbing the girl by her hair, he yanked her to her feet and slammed her face down across the table. As he reached to rip her skirts away, the tavern's door opened.

Altair pulled Thad's attention away from the struggling girl toward the hooded man in the King's colors.

Thad scowled and jerked the girl from the table. He whispered something that caused her face to blanch, then shoved her away and turned toward the visitor.

Nadia relaxed her tight grip on the dagger sheathed at her waist as the girl scrambled away from the men and disappeared through the kitchen door.

The tavern keeper glared at Roland's lieutenants until a man further down the bar called for another beer.

Nadia ignored the twinge of sympathy she felt for the tavern keeper. Had he not racked up gambling debts, Roland wouldn't have had a debt to call in when he needed a new headquarters location for his band of assholes.

She swung her gaze toward the doors where the girl had disappeared. But the man's family shouldn't have to suffer for his mistakes though. Determined to set Pell on it when she returned to her own guild headquarters, she watched the two lieutenants lead the king's man toward the stairs.

She pushed away from the window and climbed the protruding stones that made up the building's exterior until she reached the second-floor's narrow catwalk. Wrapping around the entire tavern, it allowed guests a more private way to enter and exit the second-floor rooms via a set of stairs at the front.

Pulling herself up, she crouched, listening for the guards. When no sound came, she pressed herself into the shadows against the wall and crept along the narrow walk, checking each of the windows to the guest rooms and the single door leading to the second-floor hall where the doors to the rooms were located. Finding none of the windows or the hall door unlocked, she resumed climbing the stone walls until she reached the roof's lip.

She caught movement from the corner of her eye and froze, commanding her power to blend her body into the side of the tavern. Clinging to the stones, she stared hard into the darkness. She strained to hear past the pounding of her heart and the nearby river's gurgling.

When nothing amiss appeared, she pulled her upper body up over the roof's edge.

The sound of the two guards bickering as they walked around the corner froze her in place. Pressing her legs against the underside of the eave, muscles quivering in protest, she used her power to create a glamour that made her appear a part of the roof.

The two guards, still haggling over the anticipated night with the whore, rounded the next corner out of sight.

Breathing a sigh of relief, Nadia scrambled onto the steep surface, the rough wood shingles scraping her knuckles. She rested, flat on her stomach, while her heart slowed its pounding.

Easing across the roof to the single window that opened to the tavern's third floor, she was careful to avoid the light spilling through. She inched up to the side of the window, where the pitch of the roof created a deep shadow in the moon's light.

The window was lifted to allow the breeze inside. It would definitely make eavesdropping easier.

She peered around the edge into the dark-paneled room. Near the window, a large, scarred table holding worn cards and dice, and chairs waited empty.

A low moan pulled her attention to a desk at the opposite end of the room.

The Prime Guild leader sat in the chair behind it, his face buried in the deep cleavage of a familiar, scantily clad Nightingale. The woman, a lady-of-the-night she'd hired to spy on Roland and his guild, leaned one elbow on the desk, her bored gaze on the ceiling as she rocked her hips and gave the expected moan. Her fingers clenched Roland's thick auburn hair to hold his head to her breasts.

Nadia settled more comfortably against the window's edge, praying Roland's lieutenants would arrive with the Dieuroi's man soon.

The scrape of fabric against the wooden tiles of the room behind her pulled her attention from the room's door. She slid a dagger from its sheath and melted back into the shadows, wrapping her power around her.

Peering across the roof, she scanned it and the shadows created by the roof's peaks. Large eyes glowed from the branches of the ancient redwood trees that hid the river from sight.

She scowled. Only an owl.

Telling herself to stop jumping at shadows, she turned back to the window as loud banging interrupted the two at the desk.

"Enter," Roland growled as he pushed the whore from his lap and stood to button his pants.

His lieutenants entered, followed by the King's man.

"Out," Roland ordered.

The nightingale scrambled to her feet and hurried out of the room, both of Roland's lieutenants following her naked breasts with their leering gazes.

The Dieuroi's man lowered his hood and scanned the room, paused at the window, and then settled on Roland's smirking face. "You told no one, except those present?"

Roland's brows lowered and his voice held a note of derision as he said, "I kept the meeting between myself and my lieutenants." He crossed thick arms over his wide chest. "What is it our dear Dieuroi needs done that he demands such secrecy?"

The man remained silent, measuring Prime Guild's leader with hard eyes and finding him lacking, strolled over to the window.

Nadia slid deeper into the shadows, while pulling her power tighter around her body.

The king's man leaned forward to squint through the window, then reached forward and slammed it closed.

Nadia sent a tendril of her power out, catching the window before it could close completely, so that a tiny gap remained for her to listen through.

The king's man moved away from the window and finished his search of the room, then returned to his place near the door.

Nadia moved closer to the window's ledge as Roland frowned and shifted his attention to his men.

"You told no one?" he asked his lieutenants.

Both men glanced at each other and shook their heads.

The king's man, his voice low, cold, sent shivers down Nadia's back. "You're to eliminate a problem for us before the crown prince discovers what you're about. If you succeed, you'll be handsomely rewarded."

Greed filled Roland's whisky-brown gaze. "Handsomely rewarded? As in, if I want control of Vromia Guild, or to own the Emerald Mermaid, you'd make it happen?"

His expression giving nothing away, the Dieuroi's man pulled a rolled parchment from the folds of his cloak. "Princess Nadia is an exiled royal. Thuno can't risk starting a war by taking her property from her" —he held the scroll out to Roland— "but Vromia Guild will be yours if you succeed."

Roland scowled. "That exiled royal is rumored to be the Shark's bitch."

The Dieuroi's man shrugged, his gaze traveling down Roland's body and then back up. "You're a handsome man and she a mere woman. Find a way to make her your bitch, then you'll control her property."

Roland's smile stretched across his face. He snatched the scroll from the other man's hand and broke what Nadia knew would be the Dieuroi's seal pressed into wax. The Prime Guild leader scanned the words, and his smile melted.

His forehead wrinkled, he looked up at the man. "I thought Dieuroi Mavros, the Heir, and the Bastard Prince were thick as the sands of an Arenatou duster, even despite the Dieuroi's illness. What'd the bastard do to warrant a death sentence?"

Nadia gasped and clutched at the window's ledge. She replayed Jon's report from the royal fishing expedition. Thunoans hated all things A'mi. If the bastard prince had shifted into Mer form, this change of attitude for the boy didn't surprise her in the least. She knew the young prince wouldn't see another fortnight. Her heart thundered in her chest. She'd use every resource at her disposal to get him away from Thuno even if he didn't turn out to be her nephew.

The Dieuroi's man gave Roland a hard look. "It's not your place to ask questions. You have a fortnight to complete the job if you want Vromia Guild." The man lifted the hood of his cloak and settled it back around his face, then turned. Pausing at the door, he looked back over his shoulder at a silent Roland. "Burn that. Should Prince Stefan learn of this job, you'll never get near the bastard prince."

The man gestured toward the door and the two lieutenants tripped over each other in their haste to let him out. Nadia sat back on her heels as the door was closed behind the man.

Roland sank into a chair, his lips stretched in a greedy, close-lipped smile. "Boys, we have a job to do. I want to be living it up at the Emerald Mermaid with the princess' lips locked around my cock before the fortnight ends."

Nadia rolled her eyes and turned from the window. No way would Roland be able to keep quiet about his future prospects. One of the Nightingales she'd paid to spy for her would have the details of the plan to her by the morning.

Easing her soft-soled boots down the steep pitch of the roof, she reached the edge and listened for sound of the patrolling guards while inspecting each shadow cast by the sliver of moon in the black sky. Satisfied she was alone, she lowered her body over the ledge and dropped onto the catwalk.

She froze as the guards, a different set than before, turned the corner and moved slowly along the side of the inn, both stifling bored yawns. She moved quickly toward the back of the tavern, avoiding the light spilling from the windows of the occupied rooms. From the sounds of the moans and grunts, business was good for the nightingales.

Following the catwalk toward the back of the tavern, she stopped to peer around the corner just as a hooded figure dropped down from the roof. She pulled her glamour around her just as they looked her way, and she caught a glimpse of a familiar handsome face lit by moonlight.

Lord Cyrene darted toward the catwalk's edge and climbed over, then dropped to the ground and headed for the river and the trees hiding it from sight.

Intrigued, she followed, waiting until he disappeared into the trees before climbing over the catwalk's edge and dropping down to the ground. She darted after him, checking her power to make sure it still hid her among the shadows.

Catching movement ahead, she crept deeper into the forest, the croak of frogs and chirps of crickets growing louder. She stepped around another tree, then stopped to look around, unsure which direction he went.

The hairs on her neck stood, and movement from the corner of her eye had her reaching for the dagger at her belt.

A hand grabbed her wrist.

She reacted, reaching with her other hand to pull the arm connected to the hand toward her, while dipping her shoulder and kicking a foot out to kick her assailant's knee. She threw him over her shoulder.

The assailant grunted as they hit the ground but instead of releasing her, pulled her down on top of them, then rolled, and reached for her other arm to pin her to the ground.

Arching her back, she thrust her hips into the air to unbalance them and hit the release mechanism on her wrist sheath.

A dagger slid into her hand.

She swiped at them.

They jerked backward.

Using her other hand, she grabbed the front of her assailant's cloak, got a foot under her, and kicked them over into a roll that put them on their back instead.

She straddled them, pressing the dagger to their throat with a cold smile.

They froze.

Face no longer hidden by his cloak, moonlight lit his features. She met a familiar amber stare, inhaled his honey lemon scent.

Her a'mi buzzed inside her pushing her toward him, and she frowned. It was still working, but somehow the man had seen her. Her stomach churned. Would she never be able to rely on her power again?

"Princess Nadia?" Gregor Cyrene asked, distracting her from the negative spiral of thoughts.

"Hello, Lord Cyrene," she replied, her eyes darting up to his when she felt the hardening of his cock through his pants.

She let her weight settle heavier on him, making them both gasp.

Her gaze caressed his face, and she couldn't help her wandering thoughts. Would he taste as good as she'd dreamed?

Yanking her eyes from his lips, she lifted a single brow. "Why are you here?"

"It's apparent we've both been sent to spy on Roland. Are you going to use that weapon or let me go?" he asked, his smile making things low in her stomach clench.

Nadia resisted the urge to punch his smile off his face. She was too susceptible to his charms and somehow, he knew it. She lifted the dagger from his neck, and he grabbed her wrist, rolling until he pinned her beneath him, her wrists held above her head. She bucked and yanked at her arms, cursing him under her breath in every language of Saimond, but only succeeded in making his smile widen and the bulge in his pants harder.

His gaze roamed her face, caressing the scar on her cheek, lingering on her lips. He lifted his smoldering eyes and lowered his head. A deep throbbing started between her legs and she squeezed her thighs together.

"I've been wondering what you taste like outside my dreams since the festival," he said, his lips hovering over hers.

He nibbled at her lips, but she held them pressed together. A swipe of his tongue along her bottom lip made her gasp and he was in. His taste burst over her tongue while his scent invaded every breath. Tingles burst across her body. He tasted better than any dream. The world narrowed to just the two of them. He clamped his arms around her and rolled so that she now rested on top, her breasts pressed tightly against his chest, her legs straddling his hips. The unmistakable bulge of his erection pressed against her most sensitive spot.

She yanked her head back, her chest heaving. His eyes glowed in satisfaction. Heat spread from her throbbing core through her belly to bloom in her cheeks. Her eyes lowered to his full lips, still wet from their kiss.

He laid frozen as if waiting for her to decide what would happen next. Would the second kiss be as devastating as the first? She glanced up, but his gaze was shuttered. Waiting for her. She lowered her gaze again. She had to know. She swallowed and leaned forward.

Their lips met. A thrill of a'mi darted from their joined mouths through her body. She ran her tongue over his bottom lip and shuddered at the softness. His mouth opened as he groaned and rolled them over again, nestled between her thighs, his hardness into her through the barrier of their clothes.

His mouth devoured hers while his hands trailed fire everywhere they touched.

She was drunk on a'mi and desire. Her blood rushed through her body, on fire, overwhelming, yet it felt so damn good. He deftly undid the buttons of her tunic and yanked her undershirt up over her bound, aching breasts. Nadia jerked the tail of his shirt from his pants, desperate to feel his warm skin under her fingers. She raked her fingernails over the smooth skin of his back, forcing a groan from deep in his chest. She could feel his fingers brush her stomach as he loosened the ties of her salvar, and she arched into the caress, needing more. She'd never experienced an ache as intense as that of the throbbing nub nestled at the top of her slit. The kiss of cool air on her swollen nipples jolted her from her sensual haze. They were practically having sex where anyone could come upon them at any moment.

A different kind of heat warmed her cheeks, and she shoved at his chest. "Stop."

He groaned and rested his forehead on hers. Their eyes locked and Nadia fought his pull.

"You must see this is worth the complication," he said, voice hoarse with desire.

Her eyes narrowed and she shoved again.

Reluctantly, he moved off her.

She straightened her clothing. Humiliation burned her cheeks and turned to anger. She'd practically thrown herself at him. She was no better than her father.

Gregor stepped toward her, but she backpedaled several steps away.

"I have to go," she said, shaking her head.

He stood frozen as she continued backing away, his face in shadow. She yanked her cloak close around her face and turned to go.

"Wait," he called.

She paused but didn't turn around.

"I know you were exiled with only the coin you could carry."

"It's common knowledge."

"Is this why you lower yourself to work for the Shark? Did he agree to loan you the amount needed to purchase the Emerald Mermaid? I would help if you'd let me," he whispered.

She clenched her jaw, shooting him a dark look that made his eyes widen.

"I return to Diomere after I locate my nephew, and you will one day be Thuno's royal advisor. We have no future, and I'm not the type of woman who would ever enjoy a fling," she said, her tone arctic.

She turned and darted into the shadows as silent as a wraith.

CHAPTER THIRTEEN

Nadia tapped her foot while Pell droned on about missing tithes. Normally, she'd be more concerned. Missing tithes could mean a traitor within the ranks or that a rival was luring away members. And while she *was* concerned, she wanted to meet her nephew more. She'd been preparing to use the passage up to the palace to do just that when Pell knocked.

"At least pretend to listen, Nadia," Pell snapped, then dropped the Vromia Guild's financial records on her desk.

"I'm listening," she said, meeting his irritated glare.

He lifted an eyebrow, his frown deepening. "There is a difference between hearing and listening. You've had your head in the clouds for two days. Really listen or I'll let you figure out where the missing tithes are yourself."

Nadia narrowed her eyes at one of her oldest friends. He knew she hated being given an ultimatum.

"I have a better idea," she said, her voice saccharin sweet. "Why don't you take that sour tongue you've been sharpening on me and everyone else in Vromia Guild and go figure out how to sweeten it back up."

He stiffened, his pale face flushing red.

"I'm sorry my feelings make you uncomfortable," he muttered, his expression turning sullen in a way that always annoyed her to no end.

She closed her eyes and inhaled a deep breath, reminding herself of all the reasons she didn't actually want to choke him.

"Was there anything else besides the missing tithes?" she asked.

Pell pressed his lips together as he gathered up the financial records back into a neat pile, then nodded and replied, "Lord Gregor Cyrene, Commander of Prince Stefan's personal guard and newly returned from his family lands in the north, has been inquiring about you."

Nadia, who'd been tapping her foot impatiently, froze. "Inquiring? In what way?"

Pell looked over at her, and she knew he saw through her forced nonchalance. He always did.

"I believe he's the contact for the prince you met during the festival of the sun" —his brow rose as heat crawled up her face, and she knew it'd be staining her cheeks a faint pink— "but you already knew that, didn't you."

Nadia shrugged. "I met him at the betrothal ball and suspected."

"Is this who you've been daydreaming about?" Pell asked, his brow lowering. "Is he why you aren't interested in a relationship with me?"

She suppressed a sigh and ran a hand down the braid hanging over her shoulder. Gods, she hated talking about feelings. Confusing and overwhelming, feelings were meant to be buried deep and ignored as much as possible.

"One has nothing to do with the other, Pell." Frustration and an emotion she couldn't name flashed across his face, before settling into a sad frown. She reached out to squeeze his arm. "You're one of my best friends," she said, softening her voice. "I refuse to let sex ruin that for us."

She held his gaze, letting him see how serious she was. His pale gaze studied her resolute expression, then dropped.

"You're right," he whispered, his shoulders slumping. "Ignore me. My pride didn't like the rejection."

She studied his downturned face. "Why did you push it? I know you don't love me like that either."

He reached a hand up to rub the back of his neck, then lifted his head to meet her gaze, his expression earnest.

"I'm happy in Thuno. I like what we've built here," he said with a shrug. "I'm ready to settle down and find a woman I can trust to put down roots. Choosing you for that was safe."

She stood and pulled a guard's uniform from her armoire. Pulling the jacket on over the plain white tunic she wore, she glanced over at him with a wry smile.

"Thanks," she said, tone dry. "I think."

His eyes widened. "What? It's true! You're the most loyal person I know. Once you commit to someone, they never have to worry that you'll change your mind. And you're almost cruelly honest."

"I think you forgot one important thing," she said, nose wrinkling. "Roots means children and I'd be a horrible choice for mother of your child."

Pell shook his head, then slid his papers back into his bag.

"You forget I've known you your whole life," he said, his brow raised. "I saw the way you cared for your sisters when your mother was too sick to do it. You'd make an amazing mom."

Shaking her head, her heart warming in her chest at his praise, she finished buttoning up the jacket.

He studied her uniform, his brow furrowed. "Shouldn't you wait until you've breached the palace walls before you don the royal guards' uniform?"

"Had I not needed to avoid you and your temper the last few days, you'd know why I no longer need worry," she said, side-eyeing him.

He snorted as he slid the strap of his bag onto his shoulder.

"Yeah, yeah," he mocked, then eyed the uniform. "Now tell me why you aren't worried about being seen in this uniform outside of the palace."

She turned and strode across the room.

"Because I found another way," she said and pulled back the tapestry which now hid the new wooden door Jon only finished installing that morning.

"Another cave?" he asked, crossing toward her.

"More than that." She pulled the new key hanging from the chain of keys at her neck. "Come."

They entered the gate cave, and Pell stared in awe.

"What is this place?" he asked, his eyes flashing with glee before he spun in a circle to take in the entire cavern.

"I found the Thuno Gate Cave," she told him.

His gaze darted back to the glowing gate.

"It's active?" he asked in a hushed whisper. "I thought the others were destroyed when the gate keepers left."

"Apparently not," Nadia said with a shrug.

He pointed at one set of the golden doors. "Where do those lead?"

"This one leads to the Gate Keeper palace," she said as she crossed over to the other gold door. "And the other one leads to a secret entrance to the castle, among other things."

"This is quite a discovery." He eyed her uniform again. "And why are you sneaking into the palace this time?"

"I'm going to introduce myself to my nephew," she replied as she followed him back through the door into her office.

Pell's brows rose high on his forehead. "And you think that's wise? What if he isn't really our prince? Or if he is, what if he doesn't believe you and calls for his guards?"

"I'll be careful."

"You chance our safety?" he insisted.

"I'll be careful."

His gaze darkened. "I think this is a bad idea."

"Your opinion is noted," she said, her voice hardening.

Pell frowned in disapproval and turned to leave, pausing at the door.

"Just be careful," he said, then pulled the door open and left.

The door clicked closed, and Nadia slumped forward. Sometimes she wished Pell hadn't volunteered to go into exile with her. He'd been the one to tell her about her ex spreading rumors about her inadequacies in bed. Her sister, Arriana, swore he'd only told her in hopes that her broken heart would push her into his arms and that he'd followed her into exile for the same reason.

Nadia snorted. His ability to ferret out information was an invaluable asset. And it was nice having someone she could trust handle their finances for them. She'd have been hard-pressed to stay so close on her nephew's trail all these years without him. No, she shook her head, Arriana was wrong. Pell had told her about her ex-betrothed's betrayal out of loyalty as her friend, nothing else.

She finished buttoning the jacket, careful to tuck her braid into the jacket's neck, then grabbed a lantern and started through the hidden caves. Jon had cleared the cobwebs from the steep stairway, so she started up the stairs without hesitation. Her quick pace soon slowed as her leg muscles began to burn. Each step carved higher than the average stair made her wonder about the ones responsible for carving them. She knew, on average, that the peoples of Mondami were typically taller than the humans of Saimond.

The few A'mi descendants remaining in Diomere, with the exception of her sister, Arriana, were much taller than those of their sex among the Sa'i. Unbidden, an image of Gregor flashed before her eyes. She'd been even with men in height or taller her entire life. Looking up into Gregor's face had been a vulnerable, yet arousing experience. Her body warmed.

Blushing at what she'd almost done with him and where, she shoved the infuriating man from her thoughts and concentrated on the seemingly never-ending stairs. Finally, feet sore in the boots she'd borrowed from another guard, she reached the top and a seeming dead end.

She pressed her ear to the wall, listening for any sounds. Hearing nothing, she reached for the seam along the top of the wall. A shallow indention, exactly where Jon said he'd found it, had a notch she slid her fingernail under. A panel pulled forward, revealing a lever, which she pulled. The door slid back an inch with a soft click.

Holding her breath, she pulled the door open a crack. Peeking through, she saw that the door opened into another dark chamber. She stood frozen in place, listening for any sound in the silence. When she was sure no one waited on the other side, she pulled the door all the way open so the light from the nearest lightbox lit the room.

She stepped into a storage room which held a variety of broken furniture covered in a thick layer of dust. The dirty debris covered every inch of the floor.

Sighing, she cleared a path. She moved aside chairs that looked to have been crushed in a brawl, lanterns with missing glass, tables cracked across their tops, and rolled up carpets that smelled like urine.

She reached the door and looked down at her jacket in dismay. The once pristine fabric was dull with dirt and grime. Pulling it off, she shook the dust from the material until it was once again its original bright green and gold.

Satisfied that she'd be able to walk the halls of the palace without calling attention to herself, she pushed the passage door most of the way closed and set a chair in front of it. Using a broken broom, she swept away her dusty footprints then crossed to the door leading farther into the palace. She pulled on the latch, but it didn't budge. Locked. She fished her lock-picking tools from her pocket.

The lock released with a click. She stood and cracked the door open, revealing the castle's cellar hall. Marshall Torin, the royal steward, stood next to the butler watching his men roll barrels of ale through the door to the palace buttery. She waited for them to finish up and leave, then slipped into the hallway and quickly moved toward the stairs.

She peeked into the palace's busy kitchens. As a group of servants weighed down with platters passed the cellar opening, she slipped out and followed the group out of the kitchen.

She split off from the group at the first intersecting hall, then straightened her shoulders and moved through the palace at a pace quick enough to discourage interruption, but not so fast as to invite curiosity.

She passed nobles and courtiers headed to the great hall to take the evening meal with the king, having chosen the time when she'd be able to traipse the halls without calling suspicion. She'd intercepted a report from one of the priests who ran Prince Reis' school for the city's street urchins. The bastard prince had a soft spot for outcasts like himself, it seemed.

Though confined to his rooms by his brother for his own safety, Prince Reis still kept in constant contact with the charitable organizations he'd helped establish. If the boy was truly her missing nephew, his care for the poorest citizens would bode well for his rule in Diomere. It would be a vast improvement to his father's more hands-off approach which helped those like her father get richer while the poor struggled to get by.

Nadia climbed the stairs to Prince Stefan's wing of the palace where the bastard prince had been given rooms as soon as he was old enough to leave the nursery. The crown prince's personal guard, dressed in navy blue and gold uniforms, stepped into her path.

She raised the report. "I have a missive for Prince Reis from Father Darryn."

The guard held out a gloved hand. "I'll see that he gets it."

Nadia bit her lip and shuffled from foot to foot. "But I was ordered to give it to Prince Reis and Prince Reis only," she said, letting her voice go high with worry.

The guard scowled down at her. "No one not on my list of approved visitors is allowed in this wing of the palace. Those are my orders."

Nadia let her eyes widen, and she shrank back. "If I could just stand within viewing distance of you as you hand the report to the prince, I can say with all truthfulness that I made sure the prince personally received it."

The guard's face turned red, and he crossed his arms across his chest. "No one not on the approved list goes into this wing of the palace. Either give it to me or leave. Otherwise, I'm tempted to throw your scrawny ass down the stairs, corporal."

Disappointment heavy in her stomach, Nadia shifted from foot to foot as if unsure while she was putting together a different plan.

"Is all well down there, Sergeant Zaan?" Gregor's voice called from deeper in the prince's wing of the palace.

Remembering how her glamour had failed the night before, Nadia shoved the missive into the guard's hand. "Make sure Prince Reis gets this."

She turned and all but ran down the stairs.

****

Gregor stepped out onto the landing which led from the stairs into Stefan's wing of the palace, his heart pounding in his chest. He'd recognized Nadia's voice, even in that whiny tone, and had come to investigate.

He looked at the back of the rapidly retreating figure in the king's colors. "I thought I heard raised voices."

Sergeant Zaan scowled at the king's soldier who turned the corner without looking back. "One of the king's corporals had a delivery for Prince Reis from Father Darryn. Wanted to argue with me about delivering it personally," the big man growled.

Gregor raised his brows. "Tell me exactly what sh" —he shook his head— "what he said. Every word. Prince Stefan wants no chances taken with his brother's life."

"There's really not much to tell. Said he was ordered to deliver this missive" —Sergeant Zaan held up the envelope sealed with the seal of the holy order of Asha— "to Prince Reis, and only Prince Reis. I told him that wasn't going to happen, and he got a nervous, scared look on his pretty little face and asked if he could just stand within viewing distance as I handed it to Prince Reis. That's all."

"What did he look like? Any easily recognizable features or scars that we can add to our list of suspicious people to keep an eye out for?" Gregor asked as he reached for the envelope the sergeant held out to him.

"He was a right pretty one, he was," Sergeant Zaan said. "If he had any scars or identifying marks, I didn't see 'em. He kept trying to see past me into the prince's wing, so I didn't get a good look at the left side of his face."

Gregor nodded, processing what he'd been told and what he thought he'd heard. "Good job, Sergeant. Remember, no matter how trivial it seems, I want to know about anyone who wants access to this wing, especially when it concerns Prince Reis."

"Yes, my lord Commander."

Gregor glanced down the stairs thoughtfully. The description fit the woman. It was too bad Zaan hadn't seen the left side of her face. And if it had been Lady Nadia, why? Did she wish Prince Reis ill? Was she testing Gregor's efforts to keep the prince safe? Unsure what to think, he turned to take Father Darryn's report to Prince Reis.

Mayhap it was time he arranged a meeting with his pretty little spy.

CHAPTER FOURTEEN

Voices rang out across Volos' harbor as ships departed, while others docked, their sailors throwing ropes out to those waiting to tie them down.

Nadia, one hand fisted around the hilt of the short sword at her waist and the other holding a freshly cut rose, watched a sleek merchant ship glide into the harbor, its white sails furled. Though smaller than its counterparts, the Diomerean merchant ship was a long, slim vessel known for its beauty, grace, and speed, with a projecting bow and streamlined hull.

She just wanted it to release her sister from its bowels.

Geeta leaned heavily on Jon beside her, a scented cloth held over her nose. "Tap that toe any harder on this sorry excuse for a dock and we'll all be swimming with the ships and shit."

Nadia gave the other woman a hard look, then peered at an amused Jon. "How do you put up with that mouth?"

Geeta gave her best cat-got-the-cream smile. "Because this mouth has many talents which make overlooking its flaws easy."

Jon's bark of laughter rang out over the docks, causing heads to turn.

Nadia shook her head and returned to watching her sister's ship as its crew scrambled to get it tied down and lower the gangplank.

"Cheeky heifer," she muttered, biting back a smile.

Her friend's laugh turned into a wheezing cough. The amusement leaked from Jon's gaze as he pulled her close to his side.

"I had thought you were finally taking a turn for the better," Pell said from his place on Nadia's other side as he looked at Geeta with concern, while pulling out a clean handkerchief, then passing it to her. "Nadia seems to be completely cured and Jon only a bit pale and shaky."

Geeta, tears leaking down her cheeks, took the cloth with a wobbly smile and wiped her face. "The gate needs to be open before we'll be completely healed."

"Why?" Pell asked, his brow furrowed. "You said it was producing a'mi. So shouldn't you just need to sit soaking it in longer?"

"You would think so," Nadia muttered. "Hopefully, Arriana can help us figure out why."

The ship's crew called among each other, and the passengers began to disembark. Nadia forced herself to wait in place after her sister's dark red hair caught her attention. As soon as Arriana stepped off the gangplank, Nadia strode forward and swept the smaller woman up in her arms. She swallowed past the lump in her throat, her eyes burning, as she simply reveled in having one of her sisters with her at last. When she was sure her emotions were once again under control, she pulled back and looked down into her sister's beloved face.

"I can't believe you're really here," she said in a choked voice.

Arriana stared up at her with wide green eyes, shiny with the tears trailing silently down her pale cheeks. Everything about Arriana was small. Her tiny nose dusted with a sprinkle of tiny freckles, her small, pointed chin on a small face, and her head that barely reached Nadia's chin. However, her smile was wide as she hugged her eldest sister.

"I've missed you so much, Carina," she said in a musical voice which perfectly matched her lively nature, using her childhood nickname for her oldest sister.

Nadia pulled a wrinkled handkerchief from her sister's hand and gently wiped the tears away. "I've missed you too, Sprite."

Arriana plucked the rose from Nadia's hand and knelt at the edge of the dock. "Thank you, Meren, for allowing me safe travel on your great waters. Thank you, Soira, for fair winds which allowed us to arrive quickly. Thank you, Asha, for allowing me to step safely onto your shores, and Naar for the strength of the ship on which I traveled. Thank you, Druj, for the impulse to return to Diomere so I would be there when my sister's letter arrived. Please accept this rose as proof of my heartfelt gratitude." She placed the rose upon the water's surface and watched it float away.

Nadia kissed the tips of her fingers and blew it toward the sea in silent agreement with her sister's gift.

Escorting her sister up the dock, she ignored the look of astonishment from a passing merchant that she knew was a result of including Druj, the god of chaos, impulsiveness, and the underworld, in the prayer.

Arriana threw her arms around Geeta and gave Nadia a concerned look over their cousin's shoulder.

"Thank you so much for taking such good care of my sister," she said as she released Geeta and stepped back.

The older woman blushed.

"Of course, my lady. She doesn't make it easy, but I do my best," Geeta said, then turned her body and looked up at her mate. "Lady Arriana, this is my heartbonded, Jon."

Arriana took Jon's hand and squeezed it between both of hers. "I'm happy to finally meet you, Jon. I've heard so many good things about you."

Jon nodded his head, a small smile on his face. "Dese two have done nothing but prattle on about you and your arrival since we receive word you were coming. Dey told me you had a smile dat lights up de world around you. I see dey were right."

Arriana's tinkling laughter filled the air, making heads around them turn. Nadia met each curious gaze with a hard stare and the onlookers quickly went about their business.

Pell stepped forward and took Arriana's hand. "Lady Quinones, it is a pleasure to see a familiar face from home. I trust your voyage was uneventful?"

"Thank you, Teniente de Argustanos. It was," Arriana said, her smile stiff as she addressed Pell by his formal title.

Nadia, having hoped time would ease her sister's dislike of Pell, suppressed a sigh and pulled her sister's hand from Pell's before things could get awkward, and tucked it into the crook of her own elbow.

"Come, the carriage waits," she said, pulling her sister toward the conveyance.

Pell helped load Arriana's trunks onto the back of the coach, the Emerald Mermaid's name emblazoned on its side in gold, then rode up front with the driver while the rest of them climbed inside.

Nadia settled in beside her sister. "I don't think you've changed a bit since I last saw you," she teased. "You still look fourteen."

Her sister scowled. "I'm a successful healer. I traveled to Arenatou and even earned the respect of the logic-minded medics."

Nadia raised her brows, biting back laughter at her sister's indignant look. "You're just so cute and tiny."

Her sister's lips twitched. "Mouthy shrew."

Geeta coughed and all humor faded. Arriana turned and touched Geeta's knee. "Tell me everything about this illness you've been unable to heal."

Geeta closed her eyes and leaned against Jon. "It's slowly killing me. Before last week, I had only a fortnight left."

Jon pulled Geeta tighter against his side while Nadia gasped.

"You didn't tell me that," she hissed at her cousin, her stomach twisting with nausea.

"I didn't want to worry you," Geeta said, her voice barely a whisper.

Arriana held up a hand. "What changed?"

Nadia glanced out the carriage window at the tall guild halls lining the avenue leading from Volos' North Bay, looking for any way to distract herself from how close she came to losing her best friend. Her stomach tried to crawl up her throat.

She swallowed, then focused on aproned workers loading rolls of fabric into a covered carriage in front of the textile guild building, then a clockmaker working on the large clock which stood in the center of Time Hall's courtyard. Finally, her stomach stopped trying to eject her morning meal as she continued to study the city she'd called home for the last few years.

She walked these streets often and visited many of these halls when setting up the Emerald Mermaid, yet never had she suspected that Thuno's gate hid under the mountain which towered over the city and on which Thuno's main palace perched.

She glanced over at her sister.

"Did you know other gates still survive outside Diomere?" she asked Arriana as the carriage slowed and turned onto Palace Highway.

"I mean, I assumed since Diomere's gate still exists, that the others probably did as well," her sister said, then her eyes widened and her voice dropped low. "Wait, have you found Thuno's gate?"

Nadia nodded.

"I can't believe it either," she said as the carriage pulled up to the Emerald Mermaid. "We'll show you now while your trunks are taken to your rooms."

Her sister let Pell help her out of the carriage, then stopped to stare wide-eyed at her inn. "Oh, Nadia, it's beautiful. It feels more like a large home than a public inn."

"Exactly what I was going for," she said with a swell of pride. "Come on, you'll love the inside."

Pell left them to get reacquainted, while Nadia gave her sister a tour of the inn, ending in her suite of rooms and the hidden entrance into the caves. Nadia led her sister into the caverns Vromia Guild used as a base, then into her office cave where Geeta and Jon waited.

"This rat's nest must be where you spend all your time," her sister said, gesturing toward the stacks of books and papers on the low table and floor.

Nadia raised her brows. "Yet, I know where each book and paper is when I need to find it."

"I call it the cave of controlled chaos," Geeta said, a tired grin on her face. "So far as I've seen, no vermin have crawled from under anything."

"Thank the gods for small mercies," Arriana muttered with a shudder.

Nadia ignored their jabs and pulled the tapestry from the opening to the gate's cave.

Jon assisted Geeta into the cave. The sick healer stopped before the gate, her eyes closed. The pillars glowed with an inner light that hadn't faded since the first time she'd touched them.

Her sister stepped through last and gasped. "Lightboxes in Thuno?"

They left Geeta soaking in the Gate's glow while Nadia showed her sister the palace and the lake before returning to the Gate cave. Nadia crossed the chamber and caressed the closest pillar as she did each time she passed through on her way to her hidden pool.

The glow grew brighter, and the gate warmed under Nadia's hand as if welcoming her. "Thuno's Gate."

"It looks very similar to the one in Diomere," her sister said.

Arriana moved up next to Nadia and ran her fingers over the pillar's carvings.

The pillar flashed, and Arriana jerked her hand back.

"Ow," her sister cried.

To complete the joining, we must have the one bonded to the key. This Sankta Hogo-sha belongs to another.

Arriana's startled gaze jumped to Nadia. "It spoke to me in the language of the A'mi."

Geeta stepped away from the pillars. "I heard it too."

Jon just nodded when they all looked at him as he eyed the gate warily.

"That word," Nadia said. "Sankta Hogo-sha. Jasara called me that the night she took Areisteo." She shook her head and met Arri's wide-eyed stare.

"We need to ask Lareina if she can tell us what it means," Arriana said. "What joining is it talking about?"

"The gate said the first part to me when I first touched it. I figured it is talking about the heartbond ceremony, but I don't remember

Mother mentioning the gate's role in any of the stories she told me about it," Nadia replied.

"I don't either," her sister murmured, her gaze narrowing as she eyed the doorway. "You said the gate only mentioned the joining before?"

Nadia nodded, her mind wandering along the same path as her sister's. She stepped closer to the columns and examined the markings before pressing her hand to the column.

The pillar flashed a blinding light and the voice boomed out again. *To complete the joining, we must have the one bonded to the key.*

Arriana stepped up next to her.

"I think we can safely assume it means the heartbond," her sister said. "The question now is, where do we find the one meant to be your mate? Because Geeta needs this gate completely opened sooner rather than later."

"So it is an a'mi illness then." Geeta sighed.

Arriana nodded, then took a seat on one of the cushions Jon scattered near the gate for his mate.

"The effect it has on you confirms the information Lareina found on a'mi sickness right before I left," the younger woman said as she gestured for them to join her. "Apparently, when the A'mi and Sa'i passed freely through the gates, they were careful not to stray too far from the city that housed the gate without coming back for a recharge. To do otherwise caused a'mi starvation for those from Mondami and poisoning for those from Saimond." She turned to Geeta. "Diomere has an active gate. The island is saturated by the a'mi it leaks. So those of A'mi blood allowed to live on the Saimond side, can do so without repercussion. But you've been away from Diomere for over twelve years. Your body is starving for the a'mi it needs."

"If that's true, then why haven't Jon or I been affected as strongly?" Nadia asked.

"You're both bigger. Think of two people starving for food. The one with more fat stores on his body will live longer than the one with less. Geeta's declining health is affecting Jon, because they're heart-bonded. If she had died, he would have soon followed. The heartbond allows Geeta to borrow some of his strength. He is most likely the reason she is still alive."

The bottom dropped from Nadia's stomach as she realized how close she'd come to losing her closest friend. She shot Jon a look of gratitude, realizing she owed him more than she could ever repay. She reached out and squeezed Geeta's hand, needing the reassuring warmth of her skin to ease the sick churning in her gut.

"But why does being around this gate only slightly alleviate her problem instead of healing her completely as it did me?" Nadia asked.

"This gate hasn't been opened for a very long time," Arriana said. "And isn't yet fully active, if what it said about the bond and the key is any indication. It would seem that it's chosen you as that key and therefore, you have a direct link to the a'mi which powers it." She looked from Nadia to the gate. "Until you find your heartbond and activate the key, Geeta only gets a trickle of power when near the gate."

"And if the gate isn't activated?" Nadia whispered, a lump in her throat. "What happens to Geeta?"

Arriana leaned forward, placing a hand on Geeta's head and heart, then closed her eyes. For an instant her pale skin seemed to shimmer and gossamer wings appeared to extend from her back, revealing the light fairy blood she'd inherited from her mother.

After a few moments, she opened green eyes that seemed to glow from within, her gaze stricken. "What she's getting from the gate is keeping her alive. Barely."

Jon pulled Geeta tight against him and buried his face in her hair.

Nadia surged to her feet. "We'll put her on the next ship leaving for Diomere."

A tear spilled down Arriana's cheek. "The gate is the only thing keeping her alive. If she gets too far away from it…"

"But what happens if the gate stops leaking a'mi? Or if the Order discovers that it's here and convinces Dieuroi Mavros to destroy it?" Nadia asked, then started to pace. "The only alternative is to find my heartbonded and activate this gate as soon as possible." Nadia kicked the pillow she'd been sitting on across the cave, ignoring the flash of amber eyes in her mind. "You might as well tell me to sprout wings and fly or turn water into wine," she said, her voice breaking on the last word.

All three of them stared at the gate, each lost in her own thoughts until a knock sounded on the door of her chamber. Nadia stood and passed through the opening, followed by the other three. After pulling the tapestry over the hole, she crossed to the door.

Sarna's gaze jumped directly to a seemingly healthy Geeta and widened. "Jorgan's wife has gone into labor."

Geeta nodded. "I'm on my way."

Sarna turned without further word and left.

Arriana raised an eyebrow but remained silent.

"I've got to go. I'll be back for my nightly pick- me-up," Geeta said, then stood and pulled Nadia's sister into a hug in her motherly way. "I'm so happy to have you here, dear."

The sisters watched Jon escort Geeta out, their hearts heavy. They returned to Nadia's suite in the Emerald Mermaid, where Arriana would be sleeping. They chose to take dinner privately and catch up. After the food had been consumed in companionable silence, they curled up before the fire with steaming cups of tea and a plate of cookies.

Nadia caught and held her sister's gaze, determined to shake the gloom of Geeta's impending death. "I think I've found Areisteo."

Arriana's eyes widened. "He lives?"

Nadia rubbed her forehead, remembering her close call with Gregor the day before.

"I haven't been able to confirm with my own eyes yet, but I'm optimistic it's him," she said, still able to feel the weight of Gregor's gaze on her back. "He believes he is the bastard prince to Dieuroi Mavros and the Dieuroi hired a rival guild to eliminate him after witnessing him change into his true form."

Color drained from Arriana's face. "Is he safe?"

"The assassins were hired two nights ago," Nadia assured her sister. "He's been surrounded by the crown prince's personal guard since." Nadia rubbed her neck. "He takes the leavings from the Dieuroi's table every seventh day to Thuno's poor district." Nadia met her sister's worried gaze. "If he's allowed to do that, the assassin will try to take him out then. I would."

Arriana covered Nadia's hand with her smaller one and squeezed. "I was with Lareina when I received your summons about the illness. As soon as I finished reading aloud to her, she had one of her visions. She saw someone attack a boy. A man stepped between him and the poisoned knife, then died from the poison. The sky darkened until only five stars remained. The first star wept and burned out, followed by the other four stars. The darkness suffocated the world."

"What in the dark abyss does it mean?"

Arriana shrugged. "Lareina believes the five stars represent five people important to our world. The man's death hurts the person represented by the first star. She sent me to keep him from dying."

Nadia leaned back and closed her eyes. Her sister's visions were often peppered with riddles, but they were always important. At five years old, Lareina, the youngest of the five Quinones sisters, had come running into Nadia's chamber, tears pouring down her face. She'd had a dream that her mother died. Quick to reassure the younger child, Nadia took her by the hand and led her to her stepmother's room only to find the lady laying in a puddle of her own blood, the commander of her father's personal guard dead beside her.

Nadia found out later her father had killed them both in a fit of rage. It was even more complicated than that because the commander had just been helping the woman. Some whispered they were having an affair but the lieutenant on duty that night had a different story.

He and the commander were making their rounds when they heard Dona de Quinones cry out. She'd tripped on the step leading from her balcony into her chamber, twisting her ankle. Lifting the lady from the floor, the commander was placing her on the chase when Don de Quinones walked into the room.

Their father was a plague on all five of the Quinones sisters' lives and always had been.

She inhaled, shoving the painful memory away. "She believes it's prophetic?"

"Yes."

Nadia leaned forward and banged her head against the edge of the table. "First, our nephew's kidnapping, now this." She sighed. "If we're going to keep this mystery man alive, you'd better tell me what he looks like."

"Lareina said he's tall with shoulder length brown hair and oddly pale brown eyes. His looks are memorable rather than handsome in the traditional sense."

Nadia tensed, her eyes narrowed as Arriana pulled out a small square of parchment and rolled it out on the table. Gregor's face had been painted in startling detail in her sister's hand. She'd caught the distinct amber shade of his eyes perfectly.

"The dark rings encircling the amber iris are thicker," she said in a low voice.

Her sister leaned forward. "You know him?"

Nadia traced a finger along his square jaw. "You're right, he isn't handsome so much as striking" —she traced her finger over his full bottom lip— "until he smiles."

Realizing she caressed the picture, Nadia yanked her hand away and glanced up to see her sister's brows raised and her mouth hanging open. Heat crawled up her neck to her face. She scowled and rolled up the painting.

"You have feelings for him. You, who swore off all men and sneers at the notion of love, are falling for a man." A delighted smile flushed her sister's face. "He could be your mate, the one who could help us save Geeta's life. I want to know all about him. Now."

"Me noticing that a man is handsome does not make him my heart-bonded mate," Nadia said, then rolled her eyes. "I want to save Geeta, but a heartbond requires a level of trust I don't think I'll ever feel for any man."

Arriana just stared at her, fingers tapping impatiently on the table, until Nadia sighed.

"He is Lord Gregor Cyrene, Marquess of Cyrene and Sestos, and Prince Stefan's closest ally, confidante, and Commander of the Crown Prince's personal guard," Nadia muttered, picturing the man she hadn't been able to get out her mind since the first moment she laid eyes on him at the Sun Festival. "He's being groomed as the crown prince's personal advisor." She lowered her voice and begrudgingly admitted. "And I find his smile beautiful."

Her sister clapped her hands, her excitement making her bounce in her seat. "Just wait until I tell the others. Zephyra, especially, won't believe it. She was sure you'd grow old and die alone, a sexually frustrated spinster."

Nadia scowled. "Zephyra can mind her own damn business. I've had sex. It's completely overrated."

Reminded of Nadia's past, Arriana's smile faded. "Not all men are like our father or your ex-betrothed, Carina. Would you miss the chance to find your heartbonded, especially now? Will you allow Geete to fade away until she finally succumbs to the a'mi sickness without even trying?"

Pressing her lips together, Nadia stood.

"It's not that I don't want to, sister," she said, her voice raspy with the emotions trying to choke her. "It's that I believe I'll fail."

Arriana's eyes shimmered with empathy as she whispered, "You've already failed if you don't try."

Nadia exhaled loudly through her nose, then moved toward a pair of crossed swords hanging on a stone wall across from the fireplace. She pulled the hilts of the swords toward each other. The wall pulled forward with a quiet sigh, revealing a steel banded door. Inserting her key, she waved for her sister to follow.

"Geeta will have returned to the gate's cave by now," she said, then paused before walking through the door and looked back at her sister. "I hear you. Just let me sort out my head first."

Arriana nodded and gave her sister a sympathetic smile.

Nadia shoved her fear and uncertainty into a compartment in the back of her mind. "Come. I want to show you the rest of what I found."

CHAPTER FIFTEEN

N adia entered the gate cave to find Geeta and Jon lounging on pillows at the gate's base. The couple sat up at the sisters' appearance.

Geeta let Jon help her to her feet. "Are you going to visit the lake?"

Nadia nodded, but before she could take more than a step in that direction, Arriana pulled her to a stop. "You found the gate after you met Lord Cyrene, right?" She studied the gate. "I don't think it's talking about the heartbond ceremony. It said it needs the one bonded to the key, as if it needs an already bonded pair for some type of joining."

Nadia crossed her arms over her chest, resisting the urge to roll her eyes. "I know what you're thinking. Don't. Gregor Cyrene is Thunoan. The people of this country have been brainwashed to hate anything, or anyone, connected to the A'mi people and our power."

"Hear me out, Mistress Sunshine," Arriana said dryly.

"You can talk while we walk," Nadia said as she moved out of the cave and into the tunnel which led to the underground lake, her sister following doggedly at her heels.

"What if you're the key to opening this gate, and the joining is you and your heartbonded connecting to the gate the way King Delmar is linked to Diomere's gate?" Arriana grabbed Nadia's arm with a gasp. "I see it now. You're the first star in Lareina's vision, and Lord Cyrene is your heartbonded. Heartbonded cannot live without their other half. If he dies, then so do you." Nadia shook her head.

"Sounds like another reason against heartbonding anyone," Nadia said, shooting her sister an incredulous side-eye. "I don't want to find the man who's supposedly perfect for me only to cause his death with my bond."

"We just need to make sure he doesn't die saving the boy from Lareina's vision," Arriana said with a shrug. "Then you can complete your bond, opened the gate, and save Geeta from death."

"Do you hear yourself?" Naida said, shaking her head. "If I'm the first star, are the other four you, Lareina, Kardia, and Zephyra? Should I also believe that all the other gates still exist as well?" She scowled and walked faster. "I am not the first star. Gregor will not die. Our world is not dependent on him and me to keep this darkness which we aren't even sure exists from consuming us all."

"You didn't deny that Lord Cyrene is your heartbonded." Arri grabbed her arm, forcing her to stop and face her.

"Gregor Cyrene is not my heartbonded," she said, avoiding her sister's sharp gaze. And her voice was so weak that even she couldn't believe herself.

A part of her had known who he was to her from the moment they'd met and her a'mi surged toward him. The moment he mentioned dreaming of her, she realized they weren't merely dreams she'd been having of him. When an a'mi wielder met their potential heart-bond, their power linked their dreams to help facilitate the bond.

She whirled around and stomped down the tunnel, stopping only when the tunnels split. She faced her sister, Geeta, and Jon.

"How can I trust any man with my secrets and my heart? How can I show him my A'mi side, ask him to accept the heartbond, without taking the time to let him get to know me?" she asked them, brows raised. "He'll turn and run as fast as possible in the opposite direction. And I wouldn't blame him."

Arriana wrapped her arms around her elder sister.

"You don't know he'll react like that," her sister said, peering up at her with wide beseeching eyes. "Will you let your past keep you from your future? Is your fear such that you'd willingly let your heartbond-ed slip through your fingers? Is Geeta not worth taking that chance? The big sister I remember wasn't a coward."

Nadia stiffened and pulled from her sister's embrace. "Don't throw Geeta's plight in my face, Arri. That's cruel, even for you."

Her sister dropped her gaze. "Sorry."

"Do you think it's as easy as a simple decision?" Nadia asked, her frustration making her voice elevate. "The heartbond happens only when both people willingly bare their souls. Then, as if that's not bad enough, both have to accept the other, flaws and all."

Pacing across the tunnel, she kicked at loose gravel in her path, then turned and paced back to her sister and jabbed a finger at Geeta and Jon.

"I saw how hard it was for Jon to allow Geeta to see what he was forced to do to survive in Berezan," Nadia said, her voice echoing off the tunnel's stone walls. "Until he was able to forgive himself, he couldn't accept that Geeta could forgive him. His initial rejection of the heartbond nearly destroyed them both."

She squeezed the bridge of her nose.

"And Jon wasn't raised to fear and hate a'mi users. How much harder will it be for Gregor? Never mind my own trust issues and secrets," she said, then sucked in a ragged breath. "What if Gregor does the same?"

Shoulders slumped, she turned her back to them.

"You think I'm quick to throw this chance away, but you're wrong," she said, her voice ragged with the emotion forming a lump in her throat. "I want it more than anything else in my life."

Silence pressed in on them, the faint sound of the hidden lake's waterfall barely discernible.

Arriana laid a hand on her shoulder. "I'm sorry. I was thinking like a human. I ignored the fact that the heartbond is rare even among the A'mi people."

Nadia glanced over her shoulder and forced a smile. "Come, I have something to show you." She pointed toward the stairs cut into the stone. "Jon only recently discovered that those stairs lead up to Dieuroi Mavros' palace, which I've already made good use of to reach our nephew."

Passing the stairs, she headed further down the passage.

"This way, however, leads to the real treasure," she said, her body tingling in anticipation. "A way out of Thuno altogether."

CHAPTER SIXTEEN

The next day, Nadia huddled near the edge of Volos's market square disguised as a homeless woman. She scratched her head as if bugs crawled through her ratty hair and held tight to the rope collar of the mangy mutt she'd borrowed from her friend, Gordon's collection of stray hounds.

Mistress Raptis, a stern old woman wearing a gray dress, moved down the street toward Nadia, a basket hooked on one arm. The wife of the local apothecary, Mistress Raptis walked to the market square the third day of each week, claiming the fresh air and sunshine kept her in good health far better than any of her husband's potions.

The older woman paused by Nadia's huddled form, her frown deepening as she dropped a cloth wrapped bundle at Nadia's feet. "There's something for the dog in there too, Madame. See that you share."

Nadia cackled and nodded, showing a mouth missing several teeth. She pulled the bundle close to her chest with one hand, while the other patted the dog's head.

A trio of young women, followed by their matronly escorts, eyed her warily and crossed the street, afraid of catching her particular brand of crazy.

The old woman ignored them and swept by to finish her morning errand.

Nadia pulled the bundle open and passed a strip of dried meat to the dog. Beneath a partial loaf of hard bread sat three cloth wrapped vials. One had the crown prince's mark pressed into its wax seal. Nadia shoved a hunk of the bread into her mouth as she slipped the vials into the pouch hidden beneath her dirty rags.

She finished the bread before scrambling to her feet and ambling toward the poorest section of Volos. At the edge of the city, a winding path veered off into an overgrown section of forest and over a crumbling bridge. At the path's end, a thatched roof cottage hid among a tangled mess of thickets and climbing vines. Chickens pecked at the dirt in front of the house, their soft clucking adding to the music of chirping birds and gently swaying tree limbs.

A tall, lean man with graying black hair, a wild beard, and a blade of grass clenched between his teeth tossed feed to the chickens. Fifteen years her senior and a retired guild man, Gordon looked up at her from piercing blue-gray eyes. The dog at her heels trotted past her and greeted his master.

She handed him the food she'd collected. "Mistress Raptis spoiled that one with a whole meat stick again."

The older man scratched the dog's mangy fur. "I reckon Sofos appreciated it."

She walked into the tidy shack. "The city folk were feeling generous today. I've got nearly a whole loaf of bread, two apples, three carrots, and half a burnt sweet roll from the baker's boy. Geeta sent along an onion, some dried herbs, and a roasted chicken."

She set the sack of food on the table then crossed to a chest in the corner hidden behind a curtain and opened the heavy lid revealing her boots, clean over tunic, and the weapons she couldn't conceal under her costume.

Gordon closed the shack's front door and began unloading the sack. "Give Geeta my thanks."

Nadia pulled off her dirty rags and stuffed them into the chest, then stepped from behind the curtain. "She worries about you all alone out here, Gordon." She met the gaze of the man who'd been more of a father in the five years she'd known him than her own father had ever been. "To tell you the truth, so do I."

Gordon raised chickens for eggs and collected mushrooms and sticks from the woods to sell or trade for food to feed his collection of stray animals. It wasn't enough to make sure he ate as well, so she and Geeta made sure to supplement his food stores.

"I get along, Lady Shark." A smile creased his face. "Our healer makes a fine mother hen."

Nadia laughed and plopped down in a chair at the table. "That she does."

"I hear you've a sister visiting," Gordon said, as he set a dented copper tea pot on the table between them.

Nadia lifted a brow. "Participating in the gossip ring now, are you?"

"One of the joys of retired life, my girl." The older man winked. "I also hear that a certain recently returned marquess was seen walking you from the library."

Nadia blew out a breath. "The man drives me crazy, G. His arrogance knows no bounds. Did he ask me if I wanted him to walk me home? Oh no. Just squeezed my hand and insisted in that firm, but quiet way he has. I would've seemed a mannerless harpy had I refused."

Gordon's brows were high on his forehead. "You like him."

"No. Yes." She rolled her eyes. "Maybe." Then she lowered her voice. "I'm afraid."

Gordon patted her hand. "The ones with the potential to hurt us most are always terrifying. They matter," he said, his gaze far away. "The question is, are you going to let that fear get in the way?"

Nadia shook her head. "He's Prince Stefan's commander. Sworn to uphold his crazy king's laws. If I were to tell him my secrets, he'd run or arrest me. Maybe both."

Gordon opened his mouth to reply, but Nadia just shook her head, ready to change the subject, and pulled the glass vials she'd collected while acting the beggar. Hidden inside food donations, the wax sealed glass tubes made sure the messages weren't damaged by the juices of whatever food she was given.

She handed the vial marked with the image of a nightingale to Gordon. "Let's see what our contacts have for us today."

He patted her hand, then took the vial, broke the seal, and unrolled the tiny scroll inside.

"Adrial is threatening to poison Roland's lieutenants again," he said after squinting at the coded message. "They sent another of her Nightingales back unconscious."

The Shark and Vromia Guild dealt with anyone who took advantage of Adrial and her Nightingales, and in turn the women gathered information which Adrial passed on to Gordon. The retired guild man had been the one to coin the moniker, nightingale, after catching Adrial singing to herself. Gordon, with his unkempt appearance and long silences, drove the most notorious, beautiful and poised of Volos' prostitutes absolutely batty. Nadia often wondered if there wasn't more to the relationship than they let on, but chose not to pry.

"If she feels that her girls are in danger, have her pull them. We need any information they can gather, but not at the cost of anyone's life," Nadia said with a frown.

Gordon shook his head. "She said you'd say that and to tell you that she had an idea for how to make them behave without losing the ability to gather information for you."

Nadia nodded, trusting Adrial to take care of her own. She picked up a vial with Prince Stefan's crest pressed into its waxy seal. She unrolled the tiny message and butterflies filled her stomach. She memorized the time and place, then walked over to the shack's small hearth and tossed the small strip of paper into the fire.

She had a date with her possible heartbonded.

CHAPTER SEVENTEEN

Nadia pulled her dark cloak tight around her shoulders and became one of the shadows. Like a stray cat, she perched atop the high wall surrounding a two-story house, its windows lit in a cheerful welcome. She'd come early to scope the location where she'd be meeting Lord Cyrene, leery of a trap. Muscles low in her stomach clenched as she remembered their last encounter.

She should kill the man for making her feel this way. She'd thought the dreams left her frustrated, but they paled in comparison to real life. The man's kisses were dangerously addicting. But she wouldn't succumb to them until she knew he felt the same.

Heat crawled up her neck to inflame her face. She shook her head.

Her sisters would laugh and call her a prude. Sex was a natural part of life, nothing to feel shame about, but they weren't affected as she was by their father's infidelity. They hadn't seen it with their own eyes as she had. She'd sworn she wouldn't bed someone just to slake her lust, which made what she'd almost done with Pell even worse.

Despite this chastisement, lust burned through her body as she remembered Gregor's mouth on hers. Her shoulders sagged. She didn't want to end up like her mother and trust the wrong man only to have her heart broken.

She'd been so young when her mother gave her the truth to try to protect her. Eight years old and confused by the animosity between her parents, she'd asked her mother why she married her father.

Her mother gently stroked Nadia's head and gave her a sad smile. "I let your father's handsome face distract me from his roaming eye and cruelty to those beneath his class. I ignored my own misgivings, thinking that it would all change when we were married." Her mother lifted Nadia's chin and stared into her eyes. "Never lie to yourself as I did. In the end, no matter what your father may claim, the choice is yours. Don't marry someone who doesn't earn your respect and trust with his actions. Someone that has all the qualities of a true heartbonded."

Now here she was faced with something she hadn't even believed existed, and she was standing in her own way. Did being her potential heartbonded mean he could be trusted as her mother had inferred? She had no idea, and that unknown was what made her wary.

Realizing she'd sat on the wall for much longer than she'd intended, she shoved the painful memory aside. She jumped down into the home's back garden, onto a stone path surrounded by tall trees and lush flowers. A fountain gurgled to her right. Moving silently over the path, she drew closer to a large window with light pouring from it. A servant set the table for two, while another lit candles. Ignoring the stairs that led up to an elaborate deck, Nadia reached for the handle to the servant's door.

A sigh of air was her only warning before a strong arm looped around her waist. On instinct, she dropped her wrist dagger into her hand and turned it to shove backward into her attacker's stomach while stomping down toward his foot.

A hand clamped onto her jabbing wrist and she inhaled a familiar scent. She jerked her foot to the side, clipping the side of Gregor's boot instead of crushing it as she'd intended.

His breath on her neck shot a bolt of desire through her body. She leaned back into his embrace, basking in the feelings he pulled from her body.

"The sister of a queen does not enter through the servant's entrance, m'lady," Gregor whispered, holding her against his hard chest.

She resisted the desire to lean back into him again. "No, but the Shark's emissary does."

He released her. She returned her dagger to its place and turned to look up at him. He stared down at her, an indecipherable look on his face.

She lifted an eyebrow. "Your prince has a proposition for the Shark?"

One corner of his mouth lifted and humor lit his pale gaze. "Indeed." He gestured toward the stairs that led up the back deck. "Dinner will soon be served."

Nadia frowned. "This isn't a social call, Lord Cyrene. If you wanted dinner with Lady Nadia de Quinones, you should have called at the Emerald Mermaid." She let her face settle into the cold mask of the Shark and watched his gaze sharpen as he studied her face. "The prince said he had need of the Shark's services."

He lifted a finger and traced the scar that bisected her cheek. "Are you honestly going to deny that you feel the same burn for me that I do for you?"

Desire unfurled low in her stomach. She struggled to remain detached. She'd never wanted someone's hands on her flesh like she did his. That he felt the pull toward the heartbond only added to the fire. His penetrating stare held hers as he slowly pulled her against his hard body.

She held onto her mask by the tiniest thread. "You know nothing about me. For all you know I could be some A'mi witch intent on stealing your soul as your priests preach."

He smoothed his thumb across her bottom lip, his gaze softening. "Then it's yours to steal, love." He locked his eyes with hers. "I do know you."

"I know you're beautiful, deadly with a dagger, and move as silent as a sigh. I know you smell like apples with a hint of vanilla, taste like fresh mint and lime, and your skin feels like the finest satin. I know that I can't get you out of my mind, that I'm supposed to be using you to solicit the Shark's services, and that I could care less about the prince, the Shark, or any of my responsibilities." He leaned down so that their breath mingled. "I know you're dangerous to me." His breath released on a sigh. "And I don't care."

His words razed her defenses as her body flushed with heat.

"You don't know what you're saying," she said, wishing with everything in her that he was serious.

Gregor picked up her hand and pressed it against his chest, over his heart. "I'm aware of exactly what I'm saying. We're connected somehow, you and I. I know you feel it, too."

She surged up to kiss him, her toes straining, and wound her arms around his neck. She unleashed all of the desire that had been churning inside her since their last encounter. Their tongues dueled. Her fingers threaded into his hair.

His hands smoothed over her hips, pulling her into his hardness.

They stood there lost in each other until he swung her up into his arms and moved away toward the stairs.

She pulled back and met his smoldering gaze. "Wait."

He stopped and lifted one brow. Unease pushed past the delicious feelings moving through her. She had time to get to know him before just jumping in bed with him like a harlot. *What if Gregor is just like your father? Do you really want that for yourself?*

Nadia closed her eyes and leaned her forehead on his shoulder. Geeta was worth taking a risk, but she still had time to appease the part of her which wanted a friend in her partner. She'd let desire lead her once before and that had been a disaster.

She simply couldn't repeat that mistake, no matter the stakes. "Put me down."

His arms tightened, then he released her legs and let them drop back to the ground. She glanced up, startled that he'd so easily done as she'd asked.

He lowered his head and looked deep into her eyes. "Come inside. Have dinner with me," he said and smiled as she lifted both brows. "Just dinner." His smile faded, and he leaned forward until their noses were only a hairbreadth apart. "I. Want. You." He punctuated each word with a light brush of his lips, then pinned her with his gaze. "But I'm not interested in a fling either."

She closed her eyes and exhaled, her heart pounding a rapid staccato in her chest. "I can't. I'm here in the capacity as the Shark's emissary. The two parts of my life must remain separate. There are spies everywhere. The servants are the worst."

She opened her eyes and pinned him with a hard stare.

"Can you say with absolute certainty that none of your staff would speak about Lady Nadia de Quinones arriving here by the back door, dressed like this, and leaving the same way?" she asked, brows raised.

His gaze traveled down to her soft-soled boots, up the pants encasing her legs to the blackened and padded metal of her belt and weapons and her dark cloak. Her body tingled as he lingered on her hips and breasts before returning to her face.

He nodded, glanced over her shoulder at the dark garden, then bent his arm and held out his elbow. "A moonlit stroll around the garden then."

When Nadia simply stared at him, he bent and rested his forehead against hers. "Please. I'm not ready for you to leave just yet."

She slowly shook her head, unable to resist the temptation that was her heartbonded.

Gregor smiled, wrapping her hand around his elbow, and led her deeper into the moonlit garden.

They walked the garden for hours, trading stories about their childhood antics and laughing at the other's inventive ways of getting out of mischief. Stories punctuated by his soft kiss to her knuckles or the caress of her fingers along his arm. They eventually ended up together on the bench near where she'd come over the wall, his hand enveloping hers and her head on his shoulder.

"I can say with all honesty that this is one of the best nights I've spent in a very long time, Gregor. Thank you," she said, tilting her head to look up at him.

He brushed a finger along the side of her cheek.

She shivered, the small touch sending arrows of desire across her body. A pulse low in her body throbbed and she clenched her thighs against the ache.

"Let me call on you tomorrow. No Shark business," Gregor asked, his eyes guarded as if he expected her to refuse his request.

"I'd like that," she replied, her lips twitching when his eyes flared, then filled with pleasure. "Come for the evening meal. My sister, Arriana, is visiting from Diomere and will threaten me with bodily harm if I don't allow her to meet you."

"We can't have that," he whispered, before leaning down to brush his lips against hers in a kiss so tender it had the breath leaving her in a soft sigh. Her arms wound around his neck as he sucked her bottom lip into his mouth, deepening the kiss with a sensual slide of his tongue.

Reluctantly, she pulled back, brushing his mouth with hers one last time. "It's late." She pulled against his hold and reluctantly remembered her initial reason for coming. "What does your prince need from the Shark?"

Gregor smiled sadly, then nodded, his gaze hardening as he became Prince Stefan's man, though he didn't release her hand. "Stefan needs the Shark and Vromia to distract Prime from any attempts to take Reis' life. We're hoping a turf war will buy us enough time to hide Reis until the Dieuroi can be persuaded to remove the price he's put on his son's head."

Nadia frowned, feeling her own face settle into her Shark persona. "You're asking the Shark to start a guild war for the life of a single bastard prince."

She would do anything to bring her nephew safely to his mother in Diomere, but she'd prefer to do so without harming so many innocents in the process. She'd have to discuss with Pell the ways in which they could minimize the threat to those who trusted the Shark to protect them.

"Only a distraction," Gregor said as he shook his head. "We're hiring you to take Prime Guild's attention away from Prince Reis. The Heir is willing to pay for the Shark's services in gold."

Nadia shook her head. "Keep your gold. Payment will be a favor owed and cashed in upon request whenever I choose." Gregor's brows climbed his forehead, but Nadia kept her face blank. "How loyal are you to your prince?" She stood, pulling her hood back over her hair, and moved to the section of wall she'd climbed earlier.

Gregor followed. "I won't agree to any favor that will cause me to betray Stefan."

She turned and lifted a hand to caress his jaw. "I wouldn't ask you to. This is a favor owed between you and me. Think about it. I'll expect your answer tomorrow."

She turned to climb to the top of the wall. Gregor's hands settled on her waist, and she paused. He kissed her neck, then lifted her up. Nadia, ignoring the tingles spreading over her neck, turned her head as movement flickered out of the corner of her eye. Though she didn't see anything, she kept her eyes peeled as she climbed over the wall and disappeared into the shadows without looking back.

CHAPTER EIGHTEEN

T he next evening, Gregor arrived at the Emerald Mermaid Inn at the exact time noted on the invitation he'd received. The note, penned in a neat and confident hand, was tucked into his breast pocket, directly over his heart. He'd read it more times than he'd ever reveal.

The woman had him twisted around her little finger. He knew Stefan would look askance at him for such behavior, but he couldn't seem to help himself.

In an attempt not to repeat past mistakes, he'd penned a note to a cousin who'd married a Diomerean noble woman and moved to the island nation several years before. He wouldn't receive a response for several weeks, but his instincts told him Nadia wasn't playing him.

But he had to be sure. When he was around her, he lost himself to her pull.

He'd tried telling himself she was just a woman, and noble born at that. The nobility taught from a young age to always have an agenda.

But after last night, he knew them for the excuses they were. She touched something in him no one else ever had.

At the inn's entrance, a finely tailored butler held the door for him as he called out, "Welcome to the Emerald Mermaid, m'lord. Lady de Quinones and her sister are right this way."

"Thank you."

He followed the man through a welcoming tavern with low ceilings, dark wood paneled walls, and carpets of plush emerald green. The smells alone were divine, but even he could see the signs of pleasure from the patrons. All finely dressed members of the nobility and merchant class in private booths or the fully stocked bar. A stained-glass portrait of a mermaid hauling a drowning sailor through dark waves hung above the bar. It was lit from behind by flickering candlelight, giving the impression that the waves moved. It had clearly been done by a master.

The butler turned down a long hallway, forcing Gregor to tear his attention away from the scene as they approached a set of double doors, carved with images of frolicking mermaids. The nautical theme brought to mind his dreams of swimming with Nadia.

The man pulled open the doors and bowed. "Enjoy your evening, m'lord."

He entered a large room that opened to an even bigger atrium bursting with trees and flowers. His gaze focused on the angst-filled face of a stone mermaid fountain which held the place of honor in the atrium's center, its bubbling water pouring from her eyes in never-ending tears that belied the happiness of the chirping birds and fluttering butterflies. The mermaid looked so much like his dream Nadia in her Mer form that Gregor had to fight down the desire setting his body on fire.

A discreet cough brought his attention back in the room where two women rose from pillows around a low table. Gregor drank Nadia in, wanton need tightening his body. Her knowing ebony eyes were the only evidence of the assassin he'd kissed the night before.

His heart pounded as he perused her from her carefully coiffed hair to her golden-sandaled feet. If he'd ever considered doubting her claims to royalty before, he would have given up such folly upon seeing her in the Diomerean noble dress. The deep ruby red silk, wrapped around her body under one arm and clasped over the shoulder of the other, contrasted dramatically with her black hair and pale skin. His fingers twitched, begging to caress the exposed skin of her bare shoulder. The cut and style of the cloth accentuated each curve as it draped her tall frame, teasing him with what lay beneath. He longed to unclasp the single gold broach keeping the dress from baring her body to his gaze.

His eyes lifted, skimming over her high cheekbones until they clashed with hers. "I don't know how Diomerean men handle letting their women out among other men dressed so alluringly."

She raised a single dark brow. "Trust, confidence, and respect."

"They've mastered jealously and possessiveness?" Gregor asked, lips curving.

She glanced at the woman standing beside her. "Some better than others," she said, and though her words were playful, her smile was sad. She reached for the hand of the smaller woman beside her. "Lord Gregor Cyrene, please meet my sister, Lady Arriana Quinones of Diomere."

Gregor looked at the much shorter woman next to Nadia. The shape of her eyes and face resembled Nadia's, but the likeness ended there. Everything about the woman was small except her eyes, which smiled before her lips lifted. She was opposite in every way to her sister, except in beauty. Both of them had that in abundance.

He bowed and lifted her hand to his lips. "Welcome to Thuno, Lady de Quinones."

Nadia grimaced, but Arriana only smiled serenely. "I am a Quinones de Nullo. The de before Quinones is reserved only for those legitimately born into the Quinones line, my lord." The woman glanced at Nadia before continuing, "Though my sister refuses to use it, my name has the de Nullo title on the end as do all bastards within Diomere."

Gregor glanced at Nadia who simply shook her head. "I'd say that I hope you've had a pleasant stay so far, but since you're related to my Lady Trouble, I'll assume you've managed to find some sort of quandary. Instead, I offer my unconditional assistance if ever you find yourself in need of it."

Arriana's musical laugh filled the room. "You know my sister well." She shot Nadia an impish smile. "I cannot wait to tell our other sisters about you, Lady Trouble."

Nadia smiled. "Stop it, Arri."

The sister just laughed and waved Gregor toward the table where servants waited to serve them. "Come, Lord Cyrene. Sit. Tell me about yourself. Aside from her comment about some rather steamy dreams and your beautiful smile" —she winked at Nadia— "my sister has been tight-lipped about you."

He smiled at the pink tinge spreading across Nadia's face. "You've dreamed about me, too, love? And you think my smile beautiful?"

She gave him a bland look and turned to walk back to the sunken dining table where she lowered herself to the pillow at the head of the table and picked up her wine. "Don't let it go to your head, Lord Cyrene. I'm sure you've had no end of women telling you that."

He hadn't, but he wouldn't tell her that. "Your words give me hope, Lady Quinones," he said to Arriana as he lowered himself to Nadia's right and picked up her hand to brush a kiss across her knuckles.

Their gazes locked and a pink flush colored Nadia's cheekbones, filling him with satisfaction.

Arriana lifted a decanter of wine and poured them each a glass.

Nadia looked away, and Gregor noticed the amused grin stretched across her sister's face.

"Please, call me Arri. You're the first man I've known to catch my sister's attention since—"

"Arriana," Nadia warned.

Arri met her sister's wintry glare without flinching, a sympathetic smile on her face. "—we were very young women."

Gregor watched the battle of wills between the two sisters. He hid a smile as Arriana looked away first, even as he wondered who had broken Nadia's trust in men.

They fell silent as servants refilled his wine glass and served the first course.

Once they were alone, Arriana pinned him with a sharp gaze. "Nadia mentioned you were close to the Thunoan heir, Prince Stefan."

Gregor took a drink of his wine and nodded. "Stefan saved me from drowning when we were boys. We've been close ever since."

Arriana's brows lifted. "Yes, I imagine that would create quite a bond."

"Yes."

The two women's gazes met, then Nadia's sister continued her interrogation. "Nadia and I are two of five sisters, all with different mothers. We tolerate our father, at best. Please tell us you come from a healthier sort of family?"

Nadia grimaced. "Meren save us, Arri. Just put it all out there, why don't you," she said before drinking deeply of her wine.

Gregor bit back a smile. "My childhood was perfect until the year I turned ten when my father lost his battle against a wasting illness. My mother took a lover who disliked me immediately because I wasn't as easy to manipulate as my elder brother. They encouraged my brother toward a life of drink and gambling which ended up taking his life two years ago and leaving my family estate in shambles. I've spent the last two years away from the prince's side attempting to rebuild the family reputation. I banished my mother and her lover to our smallest country home near Sestos. As you can imagine, we aren't close."

Nadia's troubled gaze met his. "I'm truly sorry for my sister's nosiness, Gregor. Please accept our condolences for the loss of both your father and brother."

Gregor's gaze softened. "No need to apologize, love. Your sister has just pointed out what we have in common aside from dreams and the ability to drive each other to distraction." He liked that he seemed to have an ally in Nadia's sister.

Nadia's throat bobbed as she swallowed. Jerking her eyes away from him, she caught her sister watching them with hands clasped under her chin and a wide smile on her face.

"So what do you like to do for fun, Gregor," Arri asked, before scooping up a bite of the grilled fish on her plate.

Aware of every move Naida made, he watched her lift her wine glass to her mouth as he replied to her sister. "I'm a bit of a bibliophile, but my real passion is collecting old texts."

"A bibliophile," she exclaimed, her round eyes glancing toward Nadia, then back as her smile widened. "You two have that in common as well."

Arri's voice, excitedly going on about the books Nadia enjoyed, faded into the background as Nadia's dark eyes studied him over the rim of her glass. Her gaze dropped to his lips as she ran her tongue along her bottom lip. Was she remembering the taste of him like he was her? Her eyes lifted back to his as he brought his own glass to his mouth.

Servants came in to light the lanterns hung around the room as dusk bathed the atrium and dining room in a soft orange glow.

Arriana cleared her throat to get their attention, then stood. "I'm going to retire. I'm supposed to be joining Geeta at first light to make her rounds." Nadia glared at her sister, but Arri ignored her and smiled at Gregor. "It was very nice to meet you, Lord Cyrene. I do hope you'll grace us with your presence once or twice more before I return to Diomere."

Gregor stood and took Arriana's hand. "It was a pleasure meeting you, Arri." His gaze caught and held Nadia's. "I promise to do everything in my power to convince your sister to see me again."

Arri grinned. "Careful, my lord. She's been known to stab first and ask questions later." Nadia glared at her sister, who just blew her a kiss. "You two need time to get to know each other. Do play nice, Nadia," her sister said and turned to leave.

Gregor held the door for Arri, then returned to the table, a smile on his face. "She's small, but feisty. I like her."

"She reminds me of my mother, though she was born of another woman. Kind, yet fierce. I'm happy to have her in Thuno with me." She lowered her voice. "Even if she is a meddlesome shrew."

"All the best siblings are." Gregor laughed. Leaning forward, he traced the outline of her hand with one finger, his smile fading. "It must have been difficult to leave them."

"I managed," she said with a tight smile, lifting her glass to her lips. When Gregor lifted an eyebrow at her abrupt tone, she sighed and toyed with the stem of her glass as she continued her story, "Leaving home with only the possessions I could fit in a couple of trunks and the gold I had in my home safe was no big deal. It's just stuff. But leaving my sisters? That was the second hardest thing I've ever had to do."

"The second hardest?"

She took another drink of wine. "The first was telling my sister that I allowed her son to be taken."

Gregor studied her face, understanding that this tough as iron princess tended to take responsibility for things outside her control. "I very much doubt you simply stepped aside the night the young prince was taken."

"His nursemaid used a'mi to make me sleep," she admitted, then lifted an unsteady hand to the scar marring her cheek. "I fell, slicing my face on a wall sconce. I fought the spell, but couldn't shake it enough to stop her from taking my nephew." Gregor leaned forward to inspect the scar. "Before she left, she actually apologized for my face and used a'mi to stop the bleeding."

"You're sure it was a'mi and not something she put in your wine?" he asked, raising a brow, even as his heart pounded with excitement at learning something new about a subject for which he'd always held an unhealthy interest.

Nadia pulled her hands from his grasp. "Ah, you Thunoans and your skepticism when it comes to all things a'mi." She rolled the stem of her wine glass between her fingers. "While I can concede that something could be slipped into drink or food, how do I explain away the scar? I didn't have it before that night. I felt the impact with the sconce, the blood dripping down my face. When I was finally able to break the hold of the spell, dried blood still marred the jacket of my uniform, yet a freshly healed scar stretched across my face."

Gregor leaned back and folded his arms across his chest. "We are taught that the closing of the gates between the worlds made it impossible for a'mi to be used in all of Saimond. Is this not true?"

"You saw for yourself the girl that chose a'mi and changed into her form," she replied. "The portal, which brought the Keeper to Thuno to collect the tree nymph, was made of a'mi as well." Her sharp gaze studied his expression as if she could see into his mind as she continued, "It's known that each of the five kingdoms of Saimond once held a gate to Mondami. These gates make using a'mi possible."

Gregor shook his head. "We're taught that Thuno's gate was one of the first destroyed so that our people could be freed from slavery. Though I don't believe all A'mi peoples were evil, I also don't trust that the power hungry among them wouldn't once again use their power to enslave humans. If the gate here does still exist, I wouldn't want the gate opened without some way to control who comes through."

Nadia pushed to her feet, refilled her glass, and then moved into the atrium.

Gregor followed and found her staring at the mermaid statue that was lit by the candles floating in its basin. He followed her gaze to the statue's face, twisted with sorrow as it seemed to beseech the heavens, while water poured down its face in a river of never-ending tears.

He stepped up behind her and rested his hands on her shoulders. "So much sadness. You can feel her despair as if the artist sculpted her from a living subject."

He held his breath as she leaned back into his chest and sipped from her glass. "In a way, he did. I sketched it myself. The face is that of my sister, Larcina, Queen of Diomere, the moment she was told of her son's abduction."

"Why would you commission such a thing?" Gregor asked, dropping his gaze to hers.

Nadia clenched her jaw and twisted away from him. "So I don't forget why I'm here."

Her expression so full of guilt that he couldn't not try to comfort her, he took her glass and set it on the fountain's ledge, then slid his hands around her waist and pulled her into his body, until she rested enveloped in his arms, surrounded by his growing devotion for her.

"Maybe you need to forget," he said as he stared into her eyes. "Leave the past in the past."

Her eyes flared, then narrowed and she opened her mouth to no doubt argue, but he dipped his head and sucked her bottom lip between his teeth, biting down gently.

Her eyes darkened to almost black as heat filled them.

"Perhaps forget only while I have you in my arms," he amended, smirking when she just snorted, before his lips lowered back to her luscious mouth.

He leaned down and slid his tongue across her lower lip, then sucked it into his mouth. His heart raced. His blood rushed to his lower body.

Turning, she pressed her body to his from hip to chest, then opened her mouth as he slid his tongue between her lips.

His arms locked around her body, grinding his arousal into her stomach. Clutching his shoulders, she arched into him. He vibrated with a need so strong it threatened to consume him. He longed to devour her, his body urging him to plunder before she inevitably pulled away, but he forced himself to show her gentleness. She was a strong, independent woman, but he would show her that with him she would always be cherished.

His lips fed from her mouth while he ran his hands up her sides, cupping her breasts through the silk of her dress.

Her nipples tightened.

He broke the kiss to trail his lips down the sensitive skin of her neck. When he reached the curve between neck and shoulder, he bit down. Her hips jerked toward him, pressing her heat into his erection.

They both moaned.

"I dream of you every night," he whispered as he kissed the slight indention of his teeth on her skin. "We belong together. You know it's true."

He stared down into her eyes and pinched one of her sensitive peaks between his fingers. Her resulting moan was so sensual that her eyes widened in shock.

Gregor growled in approval and released the gold clasp holding her dress up. She watched, dazed, as the dress pooled at her waist, baring her breasts to his hungry gaze. He bent her back, his lips latching onto one taunt nipple and lashing it with his tongue until her cries filled the room. Her legs buckled and he swung her up into his arms.

He nibbled at her lips as he carried her back toward the table where he laid her on a pile of pillows and pulled her sexy red dress down her hips so that she lay completely naked before him.

He sat back, his molten gold gaze moving over her body. "You're mine, Nadia," he whispered in a low, firm voice.

She reached up to trace one finger along the swollen erection straining the front of his pants. "Then this belongs to me. Only me. I'll kill any woman who thinks to touch what's mine."

His shaft swelled painfully in his pants, and he reached down to loosen them as he replied, "I believe you, love."

Nadia propped herself on her elbows, her dark gaze following his hands as he lowered his pants over his hips, revealing his heavy erection, its tip glistening. She licked her lips and he groaned, pulling her gaze back up to his. He knelt and ran his hands up the inside of her legs, skimming her mound, then up over her stomach to cup her breasts.

"So beautiful," he whispered.

Nadia arched, thrusting her breasts toward him as he pinched and rolled her aching nipples. When his mouth clamped onto one breast, her fingers speared through his hair, holding him in place.

He released her breast, making her whimper, his mouth and teeth trailing down the center of her body to her bellybutton, where he paused to swirl his tongue before continuing the journey. His teeth bit, his tongue soothed.

Her body writhed as he claimed every smooth inch until she lay before him trembling and dazed.

He pulled her legs over his shoulders and blew over the glistening curls protecting her throbbing center, continuing his sensual assault. His tongue swept up her slit, pulling a low, keening cry from her. He alternated flicking hard and swirling softly across the sensitive gem hidden by her curls until her cries of pleasure filled the room. Then he sucked her clit into his mouth while his tongue continued to flick until she was thrashing wildly.

Gregor was relentless, taking over her body, giving her no time to breathe. He inserted a finger into her throbbing channel, curling and finding that spot he knew would send her to the stars.

Her hands lifted to cup her own breasts, squeezing and twisting her nipples.

He watched as he continued to suck and lash her with his tongue. She twisted her nipples harder and her inner muscles fluttered around his fingers. His mouth sucked harder.

He inserted a second finger right as his teeth gently bit down on her clit. She screamed, her hips bucking as she erupted under him.

His eyes glowed with satisfaction as he rested his cheek on her thigh while he continued to stroke her through her orgasm. When she whimpered and tried to close her legs, he dipped his head to kiss her glistening curls, then moved up her body, leaving a trail of wet kisses. Then he covered her mouth, giving her a taste of herself, causing another groan to rip from her throat.

"We belong together, love, and you're going to have no doubts about that by the time I'm done," Gregor whispered in her ear, then he rubbed the head of his erection over her sensitive lips.

She shivered and her hips arched up into him, attempting to impale herself on his aching shaft.

Gregor lifted her thighs and slid, inch by inch, into her slick channel, prolonging the moment, committing it to memory to be pulled out later when she undoubtedly attempted to once again push him away. He could feel every heartbeat, every pulse of her inner muscles as they milked him, making him struggle for control.

He loved watching this tough as nails woman melt for him, her eyes widening as he pushed deep into her scorching heat. She was so tight around him, but they fit perfectly.

She gasped and wrapped her legs around his hips, her arms around his neck. "So good," she sighed.

Gregor shuddered at her words, nearly losing control right there.

He rocked slowly into her, and out, clenching his teeth as her muscles squeezed around him.

She fisted her hand in his hair and, meeting his gaze, lifted a brow. "Harder, Gregor."

He groaned, shoved deep, pulled out and thrust back in, in a rough pounding which had her clawing at his back as her body exploded again and again. Then he was pulsing inside her, hot and wet. He collapsed on her, his muscles quivering as if he'd just finished a particularly difficult training session with his men.

Only, no training session had ever left him so satisfied.

****

Nadia's chest heaved as she attempted to catch her breath, her fingers lazily tracing circles on Gregor's still quivering back. She'd never been treated with such tenderness, never had anyone look at her like he did. The patience he'd shown her spoke of an inner strength of character. She knew he felt their connection, the potential for the heartbond, but the fact that he didn't know of such a thing and still trusted the pull he felt for her was astounding.

She blushed. He hadn't hesitated to give her exactly what she demanded when she needed more. Her heart throbbed in her chest. He was nothing like the men she'd known in the past, which made him so much more dangerous. She studied his face, the long lashes resting on his cheeks as he came down from his orgasm. Somehow, in only a short time, she'd begun to have real feelings for him.

Her heart started to pound for a much less pleasurable reason as fear and guild battled for dominance inside her. She wanted to let him in so badly, but did she have any right to find happiness before her nephew was returned to Diomere? And what happened if she completed the bond she could feel pushing at her, only to die in her attempts to keep assassins from Reis?

Once heartbonded their lives would be forever linked. And so would their deaths.

Her entire being rejected the idea of a world without him in it. Though it might end any possibility of him ever accepting the heartbond if she did survive efforts to return her nephew to Diomere, she couldn't tell him. She had to push him away. She had to protect him.

Gregor opened his eyes and studied her face, his expression morphing from relaxed to resigned.

He opened his mouth, and Nadia looked away, pushing him off her. "Don't."

She sat up and reached for her dress, ignoring his sigh. Standing, she pulled her dress back on. "We can't do this. I can't do this. I have to focus on the search for my nephew."

She stood and stalked over to the gold clasp lying discarded on the floor near the fountain. When she was once again properly covered, she turned back toward him, avoiding his gaze. "The Shark has accepted your Prince's proposition."

Gregor rose and pulled on his pants, tightening the strings with short jerks of his fingers. He let the silence lengthen as he studied the closed expression on her face. "You've given so many years to a country that turned you away for something you couldn't have stopped. The child is most likely dead. Is it really worth it?"

Nadia crossed her arms over her chest. "I won't stop looking until I've found him, dead or alive."

Gregor's eyes drifted over her face, and she tilted her chin up. "You're a stubborn woman, Nadia de Quinones, but I'm not giving up," he vowed, his pale eyes locked on hers. "You could still look for your nephew while we're together, but you know that. Which means there's some other reason you're hell bent on pushing me away."

When she didn't say anything, he continued. "Fine. I've got to get back to the palace anyway and prepare for Prince Reis' foray into Volos in the morning."

Nadia's heart lurched into her throat. "You're allowing him to risk his life?"

"He's a royal, even if an illegitimate one. I've advised him of my concerns, but he wishes to proceed with his plans. He's beginning to carve out a niche for himself with the people and doesn't want to disappoint them. Like all young men, he believes himself invincible and wouldn't agree to my counsel."

Nadia turned as Gregor stalked to the table and picked up his forgotten glass of wine, taking a deep pull from the glass. He gave her a hard look.

"He'll be surrounded by so many guards that he won't be able to do much more than wave to the populace," he said, voice flat as he watched her finish adjusting her clothes.

Nadia nodded. She would send Jon and a team of her people out to provide extra support to the prince's guard.

"What do you know about Prince Reis' mother?" she asked.

Gregor's gaze sharpened on her. "What does Jasna have to do with any of this?"

She let amusement lift the corners of her mouth. "You didn't think the Shark was going to just blindly accept the job without more information, did you?"

His eyes heated at her flirty challenge, and her smile faded.

"Jasna was an exotic courtesan," he said, as he ran a hand through his hair. "She appeared seemingly from nowhere and was in the Dieuroi's bed almost immediately. She announced she was pregnant a few months later, then disappeared."

He remembered the frantic search that had followed, and how the king raged for months after. Stefan dropped by his family's city residence nearly every day back then so he could avoid the palace and what they hadn't realized was the first signs of the king's illness.

"Dieuroi Mavros was incensed. He sent out search parties, but it was as though she'd never existed. A year later, she reappeared with Prince Reis, claiming he was the Dieuroi's bastard. She disappeared again when the boy was three and hasn't been heard from since. That was nearly ten years ago."

"What did she look like?"

Gregor's brows lifted. "She had long red hair and pale green eyes. Why?"

"She stayed long enough to make sure the boy would be protected and cared for as a prince should be until I arrived," Nadia muttered to herself, remembering Jasara's last words to her that fateful night.

It is time for the Sankta Hogo-sha to make themselves known. The gates must be opened. I'm sorry, mia sarko kuraga, but this is the only way. Come find him or all will be lost.

The gates. Of course. It all made sense now. But how had Jasara known?

"What do mean, "Until you arrived?"" Gregor asked.

Nadia jerked her head up and met his suspicious glare, forcing herself to think through her sex-hazed brain. "It's fate," she said, shrugging her shoulders in feigned nonchalance. "I couldn't save my nephew twelve years ago, so now I'm being given a second chance by saving your Prince Reis."

Gregor searched her face. "You're just the Shark's emissary. How exactly is it that you'll be saving Prince Reis?"

Nadia met his probing gaze, forcing herself to keep her emotions from her face and remain silent.

"Roland was right," Gregor said, eyes narrowing. "You're warming the Shark's bed, giving you the power to influence the guild boss and therefore absolve yourself of the guilt over losing your nephew."

Nadia flinched under the chilling calm of his voice, but pulled on her Shark persona to hide her emotions.

When she continued to sit in silence, Gregor stiffened. "I'm right," he said, his voice hollow. He turned away from her. "You haven't been playing hard to get at all. You've been fighting this thing between us in some misguided need for power."

Nadia shook her head, stunned at just how far off the mark he was. She needed time to think.

Gregor jerked back around to face her and by the stricken look on his face, she knew he'd taken her silence as confirmation that he was correct. A fist closed around her heart. It was for the best, wasn't it?

He moved to the door and stopped with his hand on the door's latch. "The logical part of me knows that I should be on guard against you, that you can't be trusted. And yet, I still want you." His shoulders lifted as he inhaled. "Gods help us both."

Without looking back, he pulled the door open and left.

Nadia sat in stunned silence, her heart pounding hard in her chest. Too late, she remembered Geeta's failing health. But more painful was the ache in the deepest recesses of her heart for the pain she'd seen reflected in Gregor's gaze. All to protect her secrets.

She lowered her head into her hands. What had she done?

CHAPTER NINETEEN

That night, she lay awake for hours remembering the feeling of Gregor's mouth on her body while simultaneously regretting how the evening ended. When she finally fell asleep, she wasn't surprised that their bond pulled her into their dream world.

She opened her eyes to the star-filled night sky of her youth. She lay on a bed of fallen palm fronds covered by a blanket, just as she so often had as a girl.

Except this time she wore nothing under the blanket.

A gentle breeze rustled heavy leaves of the palm trees clustered around her, while waves crashed against the shore. Gregor, equally as naked, sat next to her, the blanket draped over his lap and his arm draped over one bent knee.

His eyes followed his finger as it traced circles on the bare skin of her stomach.

"I didn't think you'd come tonight," she said, the feel of his finger sliding across her skin making her body heat despite the tense atmosphere.

Gregor's gaze jumped to her face. "It seems I'm a glutton for punishment."

She reached out to smooth her hand up his bare shoulder, unable to resist the temptation in this place.

"I'm sorry," she whispered, swallowing the lump of guilt lodged in her throat.

Emotions flashed across his face. Surprise, longing, frustration, resignation. The last had her sitting up and taking his face in her hands.

She pressed her lips together, resisting the urge to blurt the truth. The intimacy of this place made it too easy to give in to her true desires. Reminding herself that his life was at stake, she swallowed down

"I don't wish to be a bitch, Gregor, but there's so much you don't understand."

"Then explain it to me," he begged.

She dropped her hands and pulled her knees to her chest, then rested her cheek on her knees. "The frustrating part is that you already know, but as soon as you wake, you'll just think this all a dream." His gaze clouded with confusion, but she pressed on. "When you wake up, I need you to trust me, no matter how it looks. Please don't give up on us."

His brow furrowed. "I don't understand."

He shook his head, and she knew that reality and the dream were fighting for dominance, but she wasn't ready to lose him to the real world yet.

She lifted her hand to cup his cheek, determined to make up for the evening in this way at least. "Never mind." She pulled him down until his mouth hovered over hers. "In this place, there is only pleasure."

The confusion disappeared from his gaze as desire turned his eyes golden and a smile curled the corners of his mouth. "Then let's see how much pleasure you can take." He pushed her onto her back and slipped his thigh between her legs, pressing hard against her sensitive pearl.

Nadia gasped. "More."

He covered her mouth with his, his tongue sliding between her lips, while his leg moved in a steady rhythm between her thighs.

Desire heated her blood, flowing through her body like a river of lava. Her nipples grew hard, begging for his touch.

Breaking the kiss, he nipped and sucked his way down her neck. She arched her back, offering herself to him, feeling as though she would come out of her skin.

His hands shaped her breasts, their size perfect for cupping the sensitive mounds. He slid his tongue down the swollen flesh, then flicked one hard nub with the tip of his tongue and her body jerked as every nerve in her body responded.

She slid her fingers into his hair, clutching his face to her breasts as he sucked a throbbing peak into his hot mouth, tearing a moan from her throat.

Kissing his way back up her neck to her ear, he sucked her earlobe, then bit down on it. She cried out, a fresh wave of moisture drenching his thigh.

"Gods, Gregor," she whimpered. "You're killing me."

"Then let's die happy," he said, his fingers fluttering over the curls covering her mound, then sinking in to play her body as if she were an instrument and he the musician intent on creating a masterpiece.

Her stomach tightened as his fingers slid in and out of her channel, curling to stroke that special place deep inside with each thrust. The heel of his hand ground against the swollen pearl at the top of her slit, pushing her ever closer to the edge of a sensual cliff. Her blood rushed in her veins while Gregor's pulse pounded under her fingertips.

The crest of her climax washed over her, fracturing her into tiny pieces as she arched up off the ground.

Needing him inside her, Nadia opened her eyes to urge him closer only to find herself alone in her bed. Again. She slammed her hands down on the sheets, her satisfaction turning into frustration.

Gods-cursed dreamsharing.

CHAPTER TWENTY

G regor swirled the whiskey in his glass, uncaring that it was much too early in the day for hard spirits. The scrolls lay, partially translated, on the oversized desk in front of him. He'd woken after the dream, hard as a rock. Now here he sat, drink in hand, brooding. He could still taste her, feel the soft curves of her body.

He lifted the glass and finished off his drink in one swallow. He wished for nothing more than for his dream Nadia to be the true Nadia. In reality, though, she was just like every other woman he'd ever met.

Something deep inside rose up and protested that thought. *She's nothing like your mother.*

He rubbed his chest, the ache in his heart, unexpected. It was true, she was nothing like his mother. The vindictive old witch would have kept at him until she'd drawn blood. Nadia retreated into silence.

Maybe she fights her own demons.

His stomach churned. Would he forget the painful lesson the women in his life had taught him? The Lady de Quinones carried many secrets close to her heart. Secrets she openly kept from him.

His conscious spoke up again. *Nothing like your ex- betrothed.*

His ex, Marla had seemed the perfect woman to help him rebuild the Cyrene line, but then she'd been overheard boasting about using him to get close to Prince Stefan. The day he'd gone to confront her, he'd found her in bed with a lover.

Shame heated his insides. He knew that Nadia was nothing like Marla, even with her own set of secrets.

He'd first sought her, not the other way around. But would these secrets make her reject him? Would he let her get away with that? He shook his head, unsure.

Gregor set his glass aside and checked the time. Crossing the room, he lifted a fresh bloom from his garden and plucked the petals from it. Opening the window, he tossed the petals into the air and watched them scatter in the breeze.

"I offer this gift in honor of Soira, goddess of the penetrating sight, of the triplet gods, Meren, Asha, and Naar, those who control the many aspects of life, and of Druj, god of death. Grant your blessings on this inferior servant that my instincts will be sharp, that I'll succeed in keeping Prince Reis safe, and that my sword will be true should any seek him harm."

He stepped back from the window, closing it, before turning to finish dressing while reviewing all the different ways attackers could come at them. With the open contract on the young prince, he and his men had to be on high alert. His prince was depending on him to keep his brother safe, and he wouldn't let him down. He shoved daggers in his boots, more up his sleeves, and slid his sword into the scabbard at his waist.

Satisfied he was as prepared as he could be, he mounted his horse and headed up the mountain to the palace.

When he arrived, ten men waited with weapons and mounts ready, the tiny gold dagger pinned to each uniform marking them as the most elite of the prince's personal guard. Their first priority was Prince Stefan and by extension, Prince Reis.

Gregor faced them and ten penetrating gazes locked on him. "Prince Stefan trusts us to keep his brother alive. Be vigilant. If attacked, protect Prince Reis first. Go after the enemy last."

As one, they pressed their fists over their hearts and chorused, "By the code."

Gregor led them to Prince Reis' rooms. Once there, he nodded to the guard at the door and knocked.

The prince opened the door himself, nearly tripping over his own large feet. Gregor suppressed a sigh. Having grown nearly a foot in the last year, Prince Reis was like a newborn colt. And from the size of his hands and feet, Gregor figured the boy would grow quite a bit taller than even Gregor's considerable height. The young prince had to have gotten it from his mother's side of the family for he looked nothing like his brother and father.

The prince swept his black hair out of his face, his odd colored eyes narrow. "You're late, Lord Cyrene."

Gregor raised a single brow and made a point to look at the door, and then the scowling young manservant standing behind him. "Your safety comes first, my prince. What if I had been an assassin?"

The prince's face flushed a soft pink. "Maro's life means no less than my own."

Gregor frowned. "Maro swore to put your safety before his own when he agreed to his position. He is trained to protect himself and you. You question his honor by refusing to let him do his job. If this has become a problem, then I'll speak to Stefan about finding a replacement."

Reis' face paled. "I just don't want him to be hurt or worse in my place."

"You are a royal prince," Gregor reminded him. "Every guard and knight sworn to your family puts his life on the line for you every single day and night. It is our honor to do so. Would you take our honor from us all?"

Reis frowned and shook his head. "I'm a bastard prince. Some would argue there is no honor in dying for one such as I."

"You are a prince of this realm," Gregor insisted, making a note to find out who had been saying such things in the prince's presence. "Those that matter consider serving you an honor."

The servant gave Reis a reassuring smile, gently took the door from Reis' hand, and bowed. "Welcome, Lord Cyrene. As you can no doubt see" —the servant glanced at the prince who gave him a chagrined smile— "Prince Reis is ready to be on his way."

Reis, his cheeks now a bright red, shrugged. "Thank you, Maro."

The servant nodded and held a cloak out to the prince, who took it and joined Gregor in the hall.

They made their way out of the palace through the kitchens, into the section of the outer bailey used for unloading goods.

Servants carried bags of stale bread and pails of the picked over carcasses of boar and fowl left from the last evening's dinner. They loaded the leavings into a covered wagon.

Gregor waved his men toward their horses and followed the prince toward a hunch-backed servant, who was securing the wagon's cloth covering, his long beard thrown over his shoulder like the tail end of a gray scarf.

"Good morn to you, Doron. Are we all set?" Reis asked.

The old man turned to his Reis with a wide smile. "Indeed we are, my prince." The man's smile faltered as he noticed Gregor standing behind the prince.

Reis gestured toward Gregor. "Lord Cyrene, you've met my father's gardener, Mr. Doron, yes?"

Gregor shook his head. "Not formally, no. Asha's blessing on you, Mr. Doron. Do you often accompany Prince Reis into Volos?"

"Actually, Doron started all of this, with father's permission, of course," Reis said. "I join him on the seventh day with fresh food I acquire with my own allowance."

The older man flushed at the prince's mention of his good deeds. "Just didn't seem right to do toss so much perfectly edible food. Dieuroi Mavros, Asha bless him, agreed and is generous enough to allow it. Ain't nothing to do with me."

Gregor suppressed a smile at the old man's discomfort. "Thinking of someone other than yourself is indeed commendable, Mr. Doron. I know others who would gladly join the king in contributing the leavings of their own table toward your cause should you wish to accept it."

The gardener's face was all wrinkles and creases as he smiled widely at Gregor. "I thank you for all of Volos' hungry, my lord."

Gregor nodded and gestured toward his men and their waiting horses. "Shall we, my prince?"

After the gardener settled into the wagon with the reins in his hands, the Reis mounted his horse and, with Gregor and his men surrounding him, headed down the mountain into Volos.

As they passed the Emerald Mermaid Inn, Gregor looked for a glimpse of Nadia, then scowled and told himself to focus on keeping the prince alive. He knew she likely wouldn't even be in the inn either as she'd likely be working even now to help protect Reis.

They passed the busy market square with stalls covered in brightly covered awnings where vendors called out, waving plump fruits, silk scarves in the season's popular colors, and various other wares to catch the attention of those passing by. A man dressed in a bright array of mismatched clothing threw a selection of daggers into the air while kicking his pointy-toed shoes to the beat of the music being played by a more somberly dressed minstrel. The crowd clapped around them, a few coins landing at the pair's feet. The music stopped, and the crowd wandered away as Reis passed.

The fool, his face painted white with a wide smile painted in red around his mouth, started toward the prince, his daggers once again spinning into the air. "Your highness, please allow us the pleasure of entertaining you for a few moments."

Gregor gave the man a hard look, shaking his head and maneuvering the horse into the smiling man's path. "Not today, fool."

Reis frowned at Gregor, then gave the man a regretful smile. "Perhaps another day, kind sir. We've food to deliver to the hungry people of Volos."

The fool bowed. "May you be showered by Asha's blessings, my prince."

Reis nodded at the man, and they continued on past.

As they traveled closer to the harbor, the homes became smaller and the streets more cramped. They turned onto a narrow road lined with homes that became less tidy the farther they traveled from the main avenue.

A dirty square with a carved stone chalice in the center sat surrounded by unkempt homes, the thick smell of fish, and the sewage that flowed along the street to the harbor. Weeds pushed between the square's stone pavers, tripping the children running among a group of men and women in patched clothing, their laughter ringing off the stones. The women smiled at the young prince, and the men nodded as Reis' and his guard dismounted near the stone chalice.

When Mr. Doron pulled up in the wagon, voices rang out. "Good morn to you, Mr. Doron." The old man waved and smiled as the voices continued. "Asha's blessings on you, Mr. Doron."

A group of boys near the prince's age ventured near Gregor's men, and a stocky boy in front called out to him. "Good morn to you, Prince Reis. Any luck with your water experiments?"

A wide smile spread across the prince's face. "Sun shine on you, Tereus." Reis swung down from his horse, Gregor right behind him, and stepped toward the boy. "Master Himera said—"

Gregor placed a hand on the Reis's shoulder as two of his men moved to push the group of boys back. "I apologize, my prince, but I must remind you of the reason for the presence of myself and my men and ask that you allow me to make sure none are armed before they're allowed to approach you."

Reis flushed as Gregor pulled him farther away from his friends. Jaw clenched, the prince jerked from Gregor's hold. "That's unnecessary, Lord Cyrene. Tereus is my friend and wouldn't harm me."

Silence descended on the square as all eyes turned toward them. Gregor frowned, and silently cursed himself for embarrassing the boy before his friends. The prince shoved past the guards and approached the group of boys watching curiously.

Gregor followed, and leaned down, his voice lowered, as he said, "Someone wants you dead, my prince." He motioned for his men to surround the group of boys, scanning those once again too close to the his charge. "Your brother desires that you remain alive. I'm afraid that no one, not even a trusted friend, can be allowed near you without going through myself or one of my men."

Reis turned, his mismatched eyes narrow. "Stefan didn't mean for you to accost my friends, Lord Commander."

Gregor opened his mouth to reply, but movement over the prince's shoulder caught his attention. He stepped forward and shoved Reis to the side.

The ring of swords being drawn from their sheaths echoed behind him as his men surrounded the prince. The sharp steel of a dagger, held by one of the boys who'd been lurking at the back of the group, slid across Gregor's lower abdomen, leaving a trail of fire in its wake.

Gregor clenched his jaw and grabbed the hand holding the weapon, stopping it from doing any more damage.

The assailant's satisfied sneer turned to dismay when he realized he'd missed the prince. The boy lurched back, twisting his arm and jerking down to break Gregor's hold. Gregor lunged forward as the boy darted away, his fingers hooking into the loose pants around the urchin's ankle.

"Areisteo," Nadia called, pulling Gregor's attention from the would-be assassin.

He glanced over his shoulder to see Nadia, her gaze locked on the prince, while his men urged the boy back onto his horse.

Before he could think more about her odd behavior, a tearing sound brought his attention back to the urchin who'd attempted to kill Prince Reis. The boy jerked his leg, and the thin fabric of his pants tore, leaving Gregor holding nothing but a dirty rag. Shoving through the crowd, the would-be assassin fled past Nadia's friend, Pell, who reached for him and missed.

Trusting that his men would get Prince Reis back to the palace safely, Gregor chased the assailant down the narrow street toward the harbor. The boy jumped over a pile of stacked crates and dodged between fishermen hauling their catch to the market from the docks.

Ignoring the wound burning across his stomach, Gregor pushed himself to go faster. He vaulted over the crates and stumbled. The urchin dodged around a corner.

Cursing, he followed. As he came around the corner, he glimpsed the boy running down one arm of the piers which jutted out into the harbor like fingers. Then, with a glance back at Gregor, he hopped from tightly packed small fishing vessel to dock again and again until he reached the furthest arm of the piers before disappearing behind a large ship.

Sweat poured from Gregor's brow into his eyes as he determinedly followed along the shore until he came to the arm of the pier where the boy vanished. He slowed, chest heaving, and rubbed at the burning cut on his stomach.

Turning onto the last arm of the pier, he followed it toward the ship. He scanned the water, looking for a swimmer. Seeing no one, he peered into the shadows. Rows of barrels, waiting to be loaded, provided several places to hide. The sailors on the ship's deck went about their business undisturbed, so he assumed the boy hadn't boarded.

He passed the ship's gangplank to move to the end of the pier, looking carefully between each row of barrels. A hiss of air was his only warning as something hard came down on his head and pain exploded behind his eyes.

Gregor pitched forward over the edge of the pier and plunged into the cold water. Before he could do more than kick for the surface, the current caught him and spun him deeper into the water and out to sea.

His lungs burned as he tried to hold a breath he hadn't had time to take. He kicked harder, trying to free himself from the fast-moving current, but his arms wouldn't obey his command. Black spots danced before his eyes as he fought panic. Just as the black spots grew to cover his vision, slender arms wrapped around him and pulled him toward the surface.

****

Nadia motioned Pell and Jon down a street that circled around to the far side of the docks while she and Sarna followed Gregor. They'd been spread around the outside of the square when her nephew's retinue had arrived with the wagon of food. She had no doubt that Prince Reis, the spitting image of younger version of Diomere's King Delmar, was her lost nephew.

As soon as the assailant had lunged toward her nephew, they'd closed in on the group of boys, but somehow the would-be-assassin had managed to slip between Pell and Jon. Nadia ground her teeth and picked up her pace. She burst from between two buildings in time to see Gregor dart down the farthest arm of the pier. Jon and Pell, each leading their own teams, appeared from another street and joined them.

"Wait at the end of the closest piers," she ordered, and the two teams split, each heading toward the two closest pier arms.

She ran across the wood planks, Sarna and her own team on her heels. They entered the ship's shadows just as Gregor reached the end where the assailant jumped from behind one of the barrels, a chunk of driftwood held over his head, and swung it toward Gregor's head.

"Gregor!"

The hollow thump of wood hitting skull made her cringe.

Gregor fell forward with a splash and disappeared into the murky water. Nadia's heart stuttered.

The boy lowered the wood and swung around, brandishing the wood like a club. She lunged toward him, knocking his legs out from under him before he could swing the chunk of wood at her. Sarna and several members of their team jumped on top of the boy and knocked his head against the pier.

Sailors, hearing the commotion, moved to stare over the side of the ship.

Nadia glanced at Sarna as she pulled her boots off, then her pants. "Take my clothes and meet me on that deserted pier between those small fishing boats."

Sarna glanced up at the whistling sailors with a scowl and nodded. "I'll make sure this one makes it to Lord Cyrene's men."

Nadia turned away and jumped into the chilly water. She let the current sweep her out into the ocean until she was out of sight of the sailors. Reaching for her a'mi, she changed into her Mer form. She sucked water into her mouth and felt it rush through the gills at her neck, filling her with a fresh supply of oxygen. She burst forward with a powerful thrust of her tail, speeding along with the current, until Gregor's motionless body materialized in the murky water. Wrapping her arms around his chest, she pulled him toward the surface.

Nadia swam as fast as she could to the section of pier where Sarna and Jon waited. Using her glamour to keep from being seen in her Mer form, she swam just under the surface, one arm tight around Gregor's still chest. When she reached the dock, she focused on her a'mi, allowing Sarna and Jon to see them.

Sarna's eyes widened, filling with awe before she got hold of herself and forced her attention to the unconscious Gregor.

"Take his arm," Nadia said as she struggled to push his heavy body from the water.

Sarna grabbed Gregor's arms while Jon reached for his feet. Another pulse of her a'mi and Nadia had two human legs once again. She climbed up onto the dock while Jon began to pump the water from Gregor's lungs. Pulling on her pants, she dropped the glamour completely.

Dropping to her knees at Gregor's side, she covered Gregor's cold lips with her own and blew air into his lungs. "Come on, Gregor. Breathe."

Jon pressed on his chest again, and she blew air into his lungs twice more before he started to cough up the sea water he'd swallowed.

She slumped forward. "Thank the gods."

Gregor's eyes fluttered open, and he grimaced. Boots pounded down the pier, and she looked up to see a group of Gregor's soldiers running toward them.

The group reached her, and the leading soldier bent to check that Gregor was breathing. "What happened?"

"I saw a boy hit him over the head and push him into the sea over there," she said, pointing to the pier which stretched furthest out into the harbor. "I jumped in to pull him out before he drowned."

"Nadia," Gregor murmured.

Nadia jerked her attention back to Gregor. "When you said you planned to complicate my life, Lord Cyrene, I didn't know you'd also scare about ten years off me."

"You were worried," he slurred.

"Oh, stand up already."

His brow furrowed. "Can't move."

A knot formed in her stomach. "Pain?"

"Stomach," he said, his words more sigh than whisper as his eyes drifted shut.

"Open those gorgeous eyes, Gregor." Nadia shook his shoulder, fighting the panic threatening to choke her.

His lashes fluttered open, his gaze unfocused. The knot in her stomach grew bigger as she lifted his soggy shirt away from his skin.

"Gods-cursed assassin," the soldier, now kneeling next to her, muttered.

Nadia inhaled as she inspected the angry red cut oozing a dark yellow puss.

She flicked a glance at the soldier. "Do you have the knife?"

The man nodded at one of the other soldiers who pulled it from his belt. "I'm taking him to my sister." She shook her head as the soldier opened his mouth to protest. "You know as well as I do that this is probably poison. My sister is a gifted healer, personally assigned to the king and queen of Diomere, and right now she's staying at the Emerald Mermaid, which is much closer than the palace."

"Trust Lady Nadia, Captain," Gregor slurred.

The soldier nodded slowly. "It will be as you say, Commander."

"Let's move," she ordered and stepped back as a soldier slipped under each of Gregor's arms.

Gregor's head fell forward. Nadia gestured for Sarna to lead the way, while she walked backward in front of Gregor.

She reached up and lifted his chin, patting his cheek until he cracked his eyes open. "Talk to me, Gregor."

"I've dreamed" —he wheezed— "of you. You" —he gasped for more air— "haunt me."

Nadia moved his hair out of his face, doing her best to avoid the curious stares of the soldiers. "Do I?"

He moved his lips, and she bent closer. "What?"

"My beautiful mermaid," he sighed, then passed out.

Nadia's heart stopped. She met the Captain's confused stare, then bent and grabbed Gregor's legs.

"We have to hurry."

CHAPTER TWENTY-ONE

L ate that night, after Arriana pulled Gregor from the brink of death and put him into a healing sleep, Nadia stood on the muddy banks of the Gria River which flowed to the south of Volos.

Her guild members carried the last heavy crates from the decks of a barge they'd found waiting for Roland and loaded them onto three large carts they'd brought with them.

She glanced up at the night sky, its darkness moving from inky black to blue black, heralding the coming dawn. Impatient to return to Gregor's side, she motioned for the other two carts to leave.

Pell crossed over to her. "What about them?"

The barge dipped under her weight as she stepped onto the flat deck. The crew was tied together in the center of the deck, dark scowls on their faces.

She tossed a full coin pouch into the captain's lap. "No hard feelings, I hope, Captain. Give Roland our regards when you see him, won't you?"

The captain eyed the coin pouch in astonishment, then looked back up at Nadia's masked face. "Manhandlin' my men and myself warn't necessary, ma'am. I'd have sold it to you right enough."

Nadia shrugged. "Then you might not have taken my warning seriously. We aim to take over this territory."

The captain scowled. "Got a livin' to make. You lot keep your ill will for Roland."

Nadia tossed another heavy pouch into his lap. "Maybe avoid Volos ports for the next fortnight? Your men's lives might depend on it."

The grizzled old man gaped at the heavy coin filling his lap and nodded grimly. "A fortnight then, but not a day longer."

Nadia strolled forward and cut through the ropes holding them and said, "It's good doing business with you, Captain."

"I won't hold my breath. Roland's mean as a snake an' twice as slippery," he said with a scowl. "Either way, I'll expect payment when I show up with the next load."

"We'll be here," she promised, her gaze darting up toward the lightening sky. "You'll want to leave before Roland and his people get here. They aren't likely to be happy that their bar won't be restocked this week."

Nadia turned and swung up onto the bed of the last wagon. The driver snapped the reins, and the wagon lurched forward. The cart picked up speed as it hurdled away from the river.

She scowled at Pell. "Tell him to slow down. He'll overturn the cart around the first turn at this pace."

Pell stood to yell at the young driver and the cart hit what felt like a crater. He braced himself on the cart's rail. Heavy barrels shifted and, like weights on a scale, caused the wagon to lift on one side. A stack of heavy crates tilted toward her.

She jumped to the side as they crashed down. The horses panicked and bolted. The wagon tipped up onto two wheels.

Pell dove over the cart's side, his foot clipping a crate, sending it toppling toward Nadia.

Pain shot up her arm as she deflected it. Before she could jump over the side, a heavy barrel landed on her head. Her last thought was of Gregor as darkness took her.

****

Awareness seeped in first with the smell of damp dirt, followed by stinging pain in her wrists.

Something cold slid around her neck and she raised her head to get away from it as a pair of hands locked it in place.

"You Uncle Fernando sends his regards," a low voice whispered in her ear as her mind slowly cleared.

She pulled on her raised arms to ease the burning pain in her shoulders and her body swung. Her toes barely brushed the ground.

A chill moved down her back as she remembered the overturned wagon. Bumps rose on the exposed skin of her stomach. Why was she naked?

Her eyes popped open and she reached for her a'mi, only to have access to it blocked by a barrier linked to the thing around her neck. Her heart thundered in her chest as she took in her surroundings.

She hung from her tightly tied wrists in the middle of some type of cellar.

Roland stood leaning against the door, grinning. "Well, hello, Princess. Nice of you to join us at last."

A priest in the black robes of a royal questioner walked out from behind her, his hood pulled over his head so she couldn't see his face and his hands tucked into his sleeves. He nodded at Roland without breaking his stride toward the door.

"Take this thing off of me," she spat at his back as she recalled his whispered words. "I want nothing from my father or any of this brothers."

The questioner paused, then pushed the door open and left.

"The questioner assured me the slave collar would keep you docile," Roland said with a frown.

The fool didn't even realize that questioner had saved his life by using an a'mi suppressing collar used on a'mi slaves on the Mondami side of the gates. Panic buzzing inside her at the thought of one of them being around her neck, she ruthlessly shoved her useless emotions into a compartment in her mind and focused on her captor.

"I would thank you for the accommodations," she replied in her haughtiest voice, "but they leave much to be desired."

Roland pushed off the wall and leaned in until his mouth hovered in front of hers. "They're perfect for what I have in mind," he said, and reached a hand out to rake his fingernail between her naked breasts, leaving a burning, red scratch. "You owe me for that little stunt you pulled for the Shark. It'll cost me a pretty penny when the tavern keeper runs out of drink and his patrons go elsewhere. How else am I to get my tithe from him, hmm?"

"Good," she said through gritted teeth.

Roland reached up and squeezed one of her breasts until she cried out. "I'm going to enjoy taking my lost income out of your pretty little body."

She spit in his face. "I'll kill you first."

He wiped his face off on his sleeve, then reached out and yanked her head back by her braid and pressed her naked body against his. Pulling the dagger from his waist, he slid its sharp point along the scar on her cheek.

Blood dripped down her face.

"You're mine now, Princess. No one knows where you are. Your precious Shark can't save you," he said, rubbing his pants covered erection against her hip. "When I'm done with you, you'll beg me to stick my cock in your sweet little cunt."

She laughed in his face. "You think so?"

He brought the dagger to his mouth and licked her blood from its blade, then pressed the tip to her breast. With the precision of an artist, he dragged the blade, slicing a crude R deep into her right breast with its point.

Nadia cried out, her breast throbbing in pain.

"It's amazing what people will do to make the pain stop," he told her, then bent his head to whisper, "I own you and there is nothing" —he licked the blood dripping down her breast— "you can do about it."

Nadia jerked her body away from his slimy tongue.

He laughed and let her go with a stinging slap to her buttocks.

He picked up the lantern sitting in the corner and stopped at the door to look back at her.

"I'm going to have so much fun training you, princess," he said. "Open your legs willingly for me and perhaps I won't do any permanent damage."

The door closed behind him leaving her hanging in the dark. Fear filled her, sinking all the way down to her stomach.

To fight it, she focused on what she could remember. She remembered Pell jumping over the wagon's side. Had he gotten away? Was he hurt?

No, surely, if Roland had captured him, too, he'd have crowed about it. She closed her eyes and tilted her head back.

Though she feared what Roland had planned for her, she tried to relax enough to sleep, hoping the collar wouldn't stop her from dreamingsharing or that Gregor wasn't so deeply unconscious that they couldn't meet in their dreams.

Shoving the pain of her throbbing breast and screaming shoulders into a compartment in her mind, she inhaled a deep breath and willed herself to sleep.

Please be waiting, Gregor.

CHAPTER TWENTY-TWO

"Prime Guild. Don't forget, Gregor."

Gregor shifted away from the hot brick pressing into his stomach as the last remnants of his dream Nadia faded. A sense of urgency had him struggling to open his eyes.

"Just keep still a moment longer, my lord, I'm almost finished," Arri muttered.

He lifted heavy eyelids to see Nadia's sister bent over him, her hand pressed into his stomach.

"Why do I feel as though I just spent the last evening in Druj's grasp?" he asked.

"Because he nearly made off with your soul, my lord. It's lucky that Lareina saw your need and sent me here."

She lowered her voice to mutter, "Now if she could have only seen Nadia's need."

She pulled her hand away from his stomach.

The uncomfortable heat dissipated, but a sense of impending doom replaced it.

Before he could demand to be helped up, a plump woman bustled over with a steaming cup and slipped a hand behind his head, then held the cup to his lips.

"Drink, m'lord, it will help you regain your strength faster," the woman ordered, her gentle hands belying the firm order.

"Who're you and what is that foul smelling brew?" he demanded, pulling his mouth away from the cup.

The woman smiled down at him, her green eyes twinkling despite the tired smudges under them. "My name is Geeta, m'lord. I'm Nadia's cousin and a healer. Please drink."

Gregor choked down the drink, convinced Geeta's kindly facade was a cover for an evil witch intent on killing him with this vile poison. After the last of it finished abusing his taste buds, he collapsed back on the bed, his neck muscles unable to hold him up. The sense of urgency crawled up his back, adding to his misery. He needed to go, but where?

His fuzzy thoughts suddenly cleared. His weak muscles stopped quivering. He shot a startled glance at Geeta, who smiled and patted his shoulder.

"Thank you, Geeta. I feel much better," Gregor admitted.

He wanted to ask so many questions, but now that he wasn't distracted by his weakened body, something inside him was screaming that he needed to be somewhere now. He focused on Arri.

"Nadia's in trouble. What did you mean by "Nadia's need?""

Arriana gave him a strained smile. "It says much about your feelings that you jumped directly to the part about Nadia's latest folly."

"Oh, I'll ask for an explanation for it all, rest assured, but for now, why don't you tell me what Lady Trouble has got up to while I've been indisposed," he ordered.

"More than indisposed, m'lord," the petite woman said, giving him a hard look. "It took everything I had to stop that poison and remove it completely from your body. Especially with Nadia pacing and muttering behind me the whole time."

Gregor's heart warmed. "She was worried about me?"

"You two have got to be the two most blind, stubborn, dunderheaded coconuts I've ever met," Arriana said, rolling her eyes. "Of course she did. She kept on about finding a way to cross over into Mondami to hunt down a sorceress if you died. Something about having you brought back to life so she could kill you herself for putting her through this kind of stress."

Gregor's focus sharpened at the mention of the world of magic and the specific abilities of one of the A'mi. Could a sorceress really bring the dead back to life? And what of Nadia? Would she have really been able to cross over and find one?

His concern for Nadia, dampened for a fleeting moment by his obsession with the A'mi, surged to the forefront of his thoughts. His gaze darted around the chamber.

"Yet she isn't here, is she?" Gregor sighed, sure he'd fallen for the single most frustrating woman in all of Saimond.

Geeta spoke up from beside Arriana. "They were scheduled to go last night, but she refused to leave your side until she was sure you would live."

He ignored the surge of hope and focused on what the older woman hadn't said. "Go where? And she hasn't returned?"

"They went out to distract Prime Guild from Prince Reis. A simple plan, she assured me. Nothing would go wrong, she promised." Arri scowled. "Bah, I should've known better. It isn't clear why Pell was able to jump free of the cart and she wasn't before it overturned. I've given him a piece of my mind already."

An image of Nadia telling him to remember in his dream floated through his mind. He shook his head, then winced, as his head began to throb. Geeta's potion obviously wasn't a cure all.

Gregor held up his hand, halting Arri's rambling. "Are you saying that Prime Guild, that Roland, has your sister?"

Arriana nodded. "Pell said the man driving the wagon was driving too fast and hit a pothole, overturning the wagon, throwing him and Nadia. When he came to, Roland's people were arriving. He hid among the brush at the side of the road and watched them right the wagon and reload the crates and barrels. Roland himself unmasked Nadia and rode away with her."

Gregor jerked up and swung his legs over the side of the bed, pausing to let the room quit spinning. "I have to go get her."

Arriana and Geeta both pressed his shoulders back to the bed.

"You've just been at death's door, my lord. And while I agree that something needs to be done sooner rather than later, you'll do no one any good if you fall flat on your face," Geeta said, patting his shoulder.

Gregor pushed her away. "I'm fine. It was only a scratch, and whatever you gave me to combat the poison has worked." He pushed to his feet and took a deep breath to calm his roiling stomach. "How long has he had her?"

Arri slipped an arm around his back to help him balance. "All day, since first light. It's nearly last meal now."

Gregor cursed under his breath and jerked from Arriana's supporting hold. "I need to go to the palace and gather my men. I won't let her spend even one night in that monster's possession."

"There's no doubt you're meant to be her heartbonded, my lord. You're more than a match for my sister in stubbornness." Arriana shared a wry smile with Geeta.

Gregor whipped his head around at the mention of the heartbonded, then had to close his eyes against the dizziness which threatened to topple him.

"Once I have your sister back safe, you and I have much to discuss. You know more about the A'mi than any Sa'i I've ever met." He paused, considering whether to confide further in this woman he hardly knew. Acting on instinct, he continued. "Collecting knowledge about the A'mi is a hobby of mine. I would like to add what you know to my collection."

Arriana's brows lifted high on her forehead. "Sometimes the information we seek ends up being more than we bargained for." The tiny healer's gaze pinned him. "I'm not sure you're ready to hear what I have to say."

"Perhaps," he said, giving her a hard look. "But I still want to know all the same."

Geeta pulled clothes from the wardrobe and laid them on the bed. "Jon and Gordon found out which hole they've put her in and are even now putting together a plan to get her out."

"Take me to them," Gregor said.

CHAPTER TWENTY-THREE

B y dusk, Gregor sat in one of Roland's seedy taverns, a mug of ale on the table in front of him. He shifted in the hard chair, adrenaline keeping the fatigue away that hovered on the edges of his consciousness. After scratching the dirty stubble on his face, he hunched over his lukewarm ale.

A man sang off key at the top of his lungs near the hearth, his stomping foot pounding along with Gregor's head and the thoughts of what could have already happened to Nadia. He resisted the urge to howl his fury and rip Roland's head from his shoulders by clenching his hands around his mug.

Just when he'd decided he couldn't wait a moment longer, Roland and his two lieutenants rose from their table and crossed to a set of stairs that split, one part leading up to the second level and the other leading down to the basement. Roland said something to one of his lieutenants, who nodded as the Prime Guild leader descended the stairs to the basement. His remaining lieutenant leaned against the wall to keep watch, a sullen scowl on his face.

Gregor tamped down his impatience and waited until the lieutenant's bored gaze wandered to the cleavage of a passing waitress, then moved his hand to flick his ear. One of his men, a nightingale on his lap, stood and pulled the woman's legs up around his waist, then moved to the shadows under the upper staircase. Roland's lieutenant watched the pair, his scowl lifting into a hungry leer as he licked his lips when Gregor's man lifted the woman's skirt.

Signaling again, he sipped from his beer as another of his men tossed coins at the inn keeper and made his way toward the stairs.

The lieutenant's eyes darted between the man moving up the stairs and the man pumping into the nightingale, then with a grimace, he straightened and narrowed his eyes on Gregor's guy until he made it upstairs. The Prime Guild lieutenant returned to the show.

Gregor glanced at the inn keeper.

The man nodded and went toward the doors separating the kitchens from the bar room. "Kenny, go down and get another barrel. We're near out," he yelled.

One of Gregor's men, his build and looks similar to the inn keeper's son, pushed through the doors and headed for the stairs.

The lieutenant glanced over at him then back toward the moans coming from the shadows, then back up as the barrel toting man headed for the stairs down to the basement. Scowling, he said something to the Kenny look-alike, made a gesture for him to hurry, then darted a glance back at the fucking couple under the stairs.

Gregor signaled the last nightingale he'd hired. The woman pulled away from the group of Gregor's men she'd been entertaining and sauntered over to the flushed lieutenant.

The lieutenant's hungry gaze latched onto the nightingale's protruding breasts. She leaned in and pressed her lips to his ear. He darted a quick glance toward the stairs. The nightingale reached out and wrapped her fingers around the man's obvious arousal, jerking his attention away from the stairs. He moaned and shoved the woman deeper into the shadows.

Leaving coins on the table, Gregor pushed to his feet and wound his way around tables toward the stairs. When Gregor slipped past, the lieutenant stood, his back to the stairs and his hips jerking toward the face of the kneeling nightingale. Gregor descended the stairs on silent feet and ducked into a low-ceilinged basement lined with barrels of spirits and sacks of grain.

Across the room, Gregor's man leaned on a barrel and pointed toward a door obscured by more barrels.

"That door leads into a narrow hallway lined with two doors on each side," he told Gregor. "Roland's other lieutenant has his ear pressed to the last door on the right."

Another of his men descended the stairs behind him as the bard started a song which soon had the crowd upstairs singing along at the top of their lungs.

Sword in one hand, dagger in the other, Gregor turned toward the door and said, "Let's go."

The man on the barrel stood and eased the door open a crack, then peeked through. The other lieutenant, his ear pressed to the door's wood planks, stood with his back facing them.

Gregor held up three fingers, then pumped his fist. Once. Twice. The third time, they burst through the door into the narrow hallway, Gregor's dagger leaving his fingers before the second lieutenant could do more than jerk around. The knife burrowed deep into the man's thigh, eliciting a string of loud curse words.

Gregor, annoyed he hadn't hit the man in his heart as he'd intended, sprinted down the hall, jumped over the man writhing on the floor, and threw the door open.

Nadia, eyes squeezed shut, hung naked, except for a wide, gold collar, by her hands in the center of the room, dried blood on her face and dripping from numerous cuts and bite marks all over her body.

Roland stood in front of her, one hand tangled in her hair to hold her head in place, the other hand buried between her legs. He looked up at Gregor's loud entrance, a scowl on his face.

"I said don't—"

Gregor bared his teeth. "You'll pay for each cut, each bruise."

Nadia's eyes snapped open, blood shot and blazing with hate.

Roland jerked his hand from between her thighs and reached for his sword. Gregor met Nadia's dark stare, then glanced at Roland and back. Nadia blinked.

Gregor moved his free hand to his belt. "Now."

Nadia jerked to the side.

Gregor flung another dagger.

Roland jerked to the side, and it missed his chest to slice through the sleeve of his sword arm. Whirling around, the Prime Guild leader pulled his sword with his right hand and grabbed a hot iron from the brazier in the corner with his left.

"You don't really think you're going to get past all of Prime Guild with her?" Roland reached for a rope hanging from the ceiling and gave it a hard pull. "Because I can assure you, that won't happen."

Roland feinted his sword, and Gregor parried. But then, Roland stabbed the glowing hot iron toward Nadia's naked body. Gregor spun away, inserting himself between Nadia and the branding iron. Heat seared along his arm, followed by the smell of charred skin.

When Gregor advanced, Roland swung the iron again. Gregor brought his sword up to deflect it, tangling the branding end tangled in his sword's hilt. Roland yanked it from his hand, leaving him weaponless. So Gregor rushed the other man, dodged Roland's sword, and grabbed the shaft of the iron as close to Roland's own hand as possible.

Yanking the iron from Roland's hand, he earned more burns along both arms, but gained the upper hand. He deflected Roland's next swing with the iron, then hooked Roland's sword hilt and yanked it from the other man's hand.

Roland lurched forward before Gregor could pull back to swing again, grabbed his arm, and threw Gregor over his shoulder. Landing on his back, he used his momentum to roll over and jump to his feet. When his eyes landed on Roland, his heart sank.

Roland crouched in front of Nadia, Gregor's throwing dagger in his hand.

"Come any closer, and I'll bury this in her heart."

"Not if I have anything to say about it," Nadia muttered as she lifted her bare legs and locked them around Roland's neck.

Gregor jumped forward, catching Roland's hand before the man could slide the blade into Nadia's thigh.

Roland's face blanched white, then red as Nadia tightened her hold until the man struggled to breathe.

Gregor met her determined stare and squeezed Roland's wrist until the dagger dropped from numb fingers, then pulled back his fist and tunneled it into Roland's stomach. He jerked the gasping man away from Nadia's body and slammed him face down on the floor.

Jerking the man's arms up high behind him, he searched Roland's pockets for the key to Nadia's manacles. "Dieuroi Mavros won't take kindly to your mistreatment of anyone of noble blood. It would set a bad precedent, I'm afraid." He pulled the keys from Roland's pocket. "I'm going to tie you naked and ass up over a table in the Dieuroi's dungeon so the other prisoners can each have a go at you until they're satisfied," Gregor promised.

Shouts sounded in the hall, and Roland smiled. "You'll have to get through my men first."

Gregor met the man's cocky gaze and gave him a cold smile. "Do you really think I came alone?"

Roland's smile melted.

Gregor called one of his men into the room. "Take him to the palace dungeons. Make sure the other prisoners know how to welcome him."

The man pressed his sword tight against Roland's throat, hauled him to his feet, then dragged him from the room.

Gregor turned toward Nadia and stared into her dark eyes as he reached up to cut her wrists free, then lowered her to the ground, careful not to rub her cut skin against his clothing.

Her legs crumpled under her, unable to hold her weight.

Gregor caught her against his chest as she fell.

Knowing she'd hate him seeing her so weak, he sought a way to distract her. "How is it that you save my life one moment, then scare me right back to the grave the next?"

She wedged her bound wrists between their bodies and looked up with a scowl that did nothing to hide her wariness. "Get these cursed things off me and hand me your cloak."

He wiped blood from her face, revealing an already purpling bruise. Nadia flinched. Gregor forced himself to unclench his jaw and smile.

"No kiss for your hero, my darling damsel in distress?" he whispered in her ear.

A smile twitched on her lips, and he knew that though it might take time, she'd be fine as a fear he'd held deep inside relaxed.

"I'm not distressed, I'm pissed." She looked up at him, a flash of vulnerability dimming the fire he was used to seeing in her ebony gaze. "And I would scrub him from my skin first."

Gregor clenched his jaw as he pulled the ropes from her raw wrists. She immediately lifted her hands to the gold collar and clawed at the latch on the back until he gently moved her hands aside and unhooked the latch, then pulled it off her. She took it from him and studied where it latched.

"The questioner didn't have the a'mi to lock it with blood and power," she muttered as she showed him the symbol etched into the metal.

"It's an a'mi slave collar?" he asked, having read about them in a scroll about Mondami and the Jinn, a powerful species who had a thriving slave trade.

"Yes," she muttered. "And the reason I wasn't able to stop Roland from putting his vile hands on me."

First, he'd see to her every need, then he'd visit the dungeon and beat the life from Roland for the pain he'd caused her.

"One second," he said, then turned and stuck his head out the door to find his men waiting. "My cloak?"

It was passed along, then he stepped back inside, careful not to expose her to his men, and closed the door. He shook out the heavy fabric and held it out to her.

"Let's get you home," he said as she turned and let him drape it over her shoulders.

Once securely hidden within the deep folds of his cloak, she went to walk out the door and stumbled. Gregor cursed and swung her into his arms.

Nadia shoved at his chest. "I'm perfectly capable of walking out on my own two feet."

Gregor lowered his forehead to hers. "I know there's nothing I could have done to prevent this from happening, but some part of me sees that as a pitiful excuse. You needed me and I wasn't there. So, please, let me help you. Tell yourself you're humoring the idiot male if you have to, but please, let me help you," he softly begged.

Nadia's gaze softened as he spoke until only a soft frown marred her beautiful face. Without a word, she relaxed and pulled the cloak's hood over her head and face, then wrapped her arms around his neck.

When she laid her head on his chest, a swelling feeling filled his chest, making his heart pound. Neither said a word as he kissed her forehead and carried her out. He climbed the stairs to the inn's common room to find many of the members of Prime Guild surrounded by his men.

Roland's two lieutenants, one bleeding from the thigh wound inflicted by Gregor, were being held at sword point against the wall.

The inn keeper, his wife, the barmaids, and the nightingales huddled behind the bar.

"Innkeeper Gile, please accept my apologies for the interruption of your business tonight," he apologized.

"And your promise?" the innkeeper asked.

"I'll leave some of my people here for the week to make sure any members of Prime Guild that weren't captured here tonight know that this establishment no longer welcomes their patronage," he said, his gaze scanning the faces of Roland's men, who were kneeling with their hands on their heads as his people waited for their instructions. Resting his gaze on the two lieutenants, he continued. "For aiding in the abduction of a visiting royal, I'm going to make sure Roland, and those members of Prime Guild arrested tonight, spend the rest of their days in the Dieuroi's dungeon."

He adjusted his hold on Nadia, and she flinched. Jaw clenched, he mentally berated himself for not getting here sooner.

CHAPTER TWENTY-FOUR

B ack at the Emerald Mermaid, after a long soak in the tub, Nadia sat close to the hearth in an attempt to dispel the cold that went soul deep. She scrubbed until her skin was chafed bright pink, but could still feel Roland's hands on her, in her, each time she closed her eyes. She shuddered. When she'd arrived home, Gregor had personally carried her into her chamber and laid her on the bed. Then he reluctantly left her in Arriana's care.

She winced as Arriana pulled the comb through her damp hair, jolting her back to the present. Roland, the son of a Gazon Goat, had ripped some of her hair out at the roots, leaving her scalp bruised.

"He blames himself. As if he wasn't fighting for his own life only hours before." She glanced over her shoulder at her sister. "It makes no sense."

Arri parted Nadia's hair and began to braid. "He cares for you. And he's a man. I believe the combination creates an irrational need to protect."

She flinched when Arri reached over her shoulder, brushing her bruised jaw. She'd let Arri heal her enough that her clothes no longer irritated open cuts, but had made her leave the bruises. The dark circles under her sister's eyes told the story of what it had taken to save Gregor's life the day before.

"I ought to flay Pell alive for allowing Roland to make off with you," Arriana repeated for the fifth time.

Nadia shrugged. "And get himself killed in the process? Come now, Arri."

"It seems awfully convenient that you both were thrown from that wagon, yet only you were taken."

"Bah, you're ridiculous. He's a loyal friend, and I couldn't have done this without him." She met her sister's disgruntled gaze. "He followed me into exile. He's looked as hard for our nephew as I have." Her sister opened her mouth, and Nadia shook her head. "No, he's as much a victim as I."

A knock sounded and Nadia sighed. "Come."

Gregor opened the door to the bed chamber she kept at the Mermaid, a prettily wrapped package in his hand. His eyes noted each bruise visible on her face and neck, before sliding over the short silk robe she wore.

"I can come back when you're dressed," he said, devouring her with his gaze.

Arriana set the comb aside and walked to the door. "They're just legs and arms. She's not flashing her breasts and other lady parts." With a roll of her eyes, Arriana left the room, pulling the door closed firmly behind her.

Gregor smiled and shook his head. "Doesn't have much patience for our stuffy views, does she?"

Nadia pulled her hair over her shoulder and finished plaiting it into a loose braid. "In Diomere, women would parish from the heat if we were to stay wrapped in so much fabric from chin to ankle and wrist." When Gregor didn't reply, she glanced up to see him watching her, an odd look on his face. "What?"

"Do you realize how beautiful you are?"

"Once, perhaps, but those days are long past." She lifted a hand to the scar bisecting the right side of her face.

Gregor crossed to stand in front of her and pulled her hand away from her face. "It adds an edge of danger. I find it irresistible."

Nadia met his gaze, could see he meant it, and felt her heart soften. The fire flared, cracking one of the logs as her a'mi reacted to her emotions. Grabbing the poker, Gregor bent to rearrange the logs. Nadia focused inward to see the symbol for flame glowing brightly in her mind's eye. She cut the flow of a'mi, shutting down the link to her emotions as she'd learned when her abilities first developed. The flames died back down.

Gregor handed her the package and sat on the chaise beside her. "For you."

She pulled apart the paper, revealing the worn cover of a book. "The Battle at Lycia?" Warmth filled her stomach. "How did—?" She cut herself off before she mentioned the dreams.

"Your sister was grumbling about the piles of books stacking every surface in your chambers," he said, glancing toward a teetering stack near her elbow. "A love of literature is something we share." His gaze clouded in confusion. "My gut told me you'd enjoy this one."

She smoothed her fingers over the worn cover. And just like that, he unknowingly took possession of her heart. Fear held her frozen, the longing to grab hold of him and never let go an overwhelming yearning. Gods, if Lareina hadn't seen the need and sent Arri—.

"I thought I was going to lose you," she whispered. He trailed a finger over the fresh cut marring the scar, making her skin tingle. She closed her eyes as his finger moved from the scar to her lips, and over her chin.

"Arri told me you were worried for me," Gregor murmured. His soft lips touched the top of her scar and followed the same path as his fingers. "It'll take much more than a little poison to take me from you before I get to convince you that we belong together."

Though she knew she shouldn't, she longed to reach up, run her hands over his shirt. He was meant to be her heartbonded. Even now her a'mi urged her to complete the bonding. She resisted. He deserved to know all her secrets, for her to be open and honest with him before she asked him to accept a bond which could only end with death. What if her Mer form disgusted him? *You know better than that.*

His lips slid over hers, hot and firm. He kept the kiss shallow, tugging at her lower lip, easing the sting with his tongue, then sucking on her top lip. A low, soft moan filled the room, a sensually female sound only he could pull from her. Gregor broke the kiss and pulled her against his chest, resting his chin on her head. She listened to his heart pound in his chest, loving that he was as affected as her.

"Do you really think you'll ever find your nephew?"

"I'll never stop until I return him to Diomere and those responsible are made to pay."

"You believe he's alive. With someone here in Thuno," he said knowingly.

Nadia glanced up at him, then away. "I'm the closest I've ever been."

Gregor leaned back and studied her face, then picked up her hands. "Let me help you. All of Prince Stefan's resources will be at your disposal."

Nadia's pulse pounded a rapid staccato. She met his gaze, read the sincerity there. Had she ever met a man so unselfish? Her heart urged her to simply let go of the past and embrace the future. However, the voice of reason in her mind knew that she couldn't reward his heartfelt gesture with one of selfishness. And that's what it would be. Selfish.

Nadia squeezed Gregor's fingers. "I appreciate the offer more than you know, but this is my responsibility."

Disappointment flashed in his amber eyes. "So independent. I should count myself lucky that you aren't jumping to use my connection to Prince Stefan, too, but somehow, I don't. I need you to want my help."

Nadia's heart wept at the hurt in his voice, but she shook her head. "I have to do this myself."

CHAPTER TWENTY-FIVE

Gregor looked down at their joined hands, then back up at her. "I love you, you know." Her eyes widened. His heart raced as he told her what he'd realized as he sat in that seedy tavern waiting to rescue her. "Choose me over your secrets, Nadia. We'll find your nephew together."

She pressed her lips together, her gaze stricken. "I can't allow you to have anything to do with this, Gregor. I'm sorry."

He clenched his jaw against the knife of pain splintering his heart, resisting the urge to shake sense into her. Why wouldn't she let him in? His doubts rose up, threatening to choke him. She hadn't said she loved him, too. Was he seeing something that wasn't there?

"Is it the Shark?" he asked, his chest tight. "I know you feel something for me, so it can't be love that keeps you loyal to him. What does he have that I don't?"

Nadia's fathomless dark eyes narrowed on him.

"This has nothing to do with the Shark, Gregor. The only thing the Shark apparently has over you is the ability to trust what they know about someone's character," she snapped. "Would you assume a male royal was sleeping with the Shark just because they worked for Vromia Guild and didn't share all their secrets with you?"

You know she's nothing like your ex. Trust her, a voice deep inside him insisted.

He stood, unsure what to think and unable to stand her non-answers another minute. Damn her and her secrets.

His doubt grew, circling around inside his mind, until the small voice insisting she was essential to his future happiness fell silent. He bowed stiffly.

A single tear trailed down her cheek, but he steeled himself against it.

Turning, he left her sitting with his lonely declaration and her secrets. He moved down the hall, growing numb with each step until his heart felt encased in ice, his mind as still as a frozen pond.

Arriana stepped into the hall ahead of him. Her eyes widened, then narrowed.

Instead of stepping out of his way as he drew closer, she held her ground. "Don't let her push you away."

His heart throbbed, fighting to push the numbness aside, but he ignored it. "Good day, m'lady."

He stepped aside to go around her. She moved with him.

"My sister is a stubborn fool of a woman. She thinks she's protecting you by pushing you away." The tiny woman implored him with her big green eyes. "She's wrong. Don't let her do this."

The numbness thinned until the pain bruised his chest. "Protecting me from what?"

Arriana looked away. "It's not my place to say. I'm sorry." He clenched his jaw and made to step around her again. She grabbed his arm. "Please, Gregor. She's trying to protect you. It's what she does and how I know she really cares for you."

He stopped, spine rigid, the last of the numbness around his heart melting until the pain radiated out from his chest. "She doesn't trust me to take care of myself, Arriana." He pinned Arri with a hard look. "Give me one reason why I shouldn't walk out of here and never give her another thought."

Arriana gave him a sad smile. "Because you love her. You're meant to be her heartbonded."

Gregor clenched his jaw. "Yes, which makes the fact that she doesn't love me back all the more difficult to bear."

He'd loved Nadia since the moment she'd decided to kiss him back in the forest behind Prime Guild's tavern. He'd been sure she returned his feelings, but undoubtedly, he'd been wrong. *What about the dreams?* Gregor ignored the thought. The dreams were figments of an overactive imagination, nothing else.

He frowned at Nadia's sister. "Whatever this heartbond is, it doesn't change the fact that she doesn't respect me enough to let me decide for myself and maybe even help her with whatever secret she's protecting me from."

Arriana opened her mouth to reply.

"Don't take it personal, m'lord," interrupted a derisive male voice. "The Lady Nadia trusts very few with all of her secrets," Pell said, a smirk on his face when they turned to face him.

Gregor studied the shorter man. His inquiries had been unable to confirm that Pell was the Shark, but his continued presence around Nadia left him little doubt.

Gregor bared his teeth in a smile that didn't reach his eyes. "I'm sure she has her reasons—, Mr. Pell, isn't it?"

Pell scowled. "Pell de Argustanos, Lieutenant in Diomere's royal army and humble companion to Lady de Quinones until such time as she finds the means to reverse her banishment." He clasped his hands behind his back. "The lady is daughter to one of the highest ranked nobles in Diomere, sister to the queen, and holds the rank of Capitán in Diomere's royal navy. When she finds her nephew, she'll return to her home and position, at which time she'll be expected to form a high-ranking match to help strengthen her family's position in society. A foreigner wouldn't be accepted unless he was royal. I wouldn't take it personally. None of us do."

Arriana snorted under her breath, and Pell shot her a withering look.

"Being seen as inferior is always personal. Anyone who says otherwise is a liar or a fool." Gregor gave the other man a curt nod, and then bowed to Arriana. "Lady Quinones, I won't keep you from caring for your sister any longer. Please, if there's anything else I can do for you, don't hesitate to send word." He met her searching gaze. "We still have much to discuss, you and I."

Arriana nodded, a small smile on her face. He turned on his heel to leave, Pell's glare burning into his back.

CHAPTER TWENTY-SIX

After a sleepless night spent vacillating between her feelings for Gregor and the danger to her nephew, Nadia threw herself into putting together a plan to keep Reis safe until his parents arrived. She knew convincing her nephew would be her biggest hurdle.

That evening found her slipping up the stairs of the palace, thankful that the gate made it so her glamour could be counted on to hide her from the guards patrolling the halls.

She'd already made sure Gregor remained at his city home. The thought of him formed a lump in her throat. She'd hurt him even though she'd been saving him from an impossible choice. The pain in his eyes had gutted her.

She paused and silently inhaled, forcing the painful memory into its box and shutting the lid tightly. She'd let herself wallow in misery later.

A guard stood before Reis' door, a bored expression on his face as he flipped a coin between his fingers. She smiled, thanking the gods for sending fortune her way. Positioning herself near the door, she reached out and waited for the guard to flip the coin back to his first knuckle, then flicked it out of his hand. He grabbed for it, brushing her fingertips before she could pull them out of the way. Nadia held her breath. The guard stepped forward to chase down his coin, seemingly unaware it had been anything other than an accident. She sighed and silently lifted the latch to slip into Reis' receiving chamber.

Pushing the door closed, she stopped and listened, letting her eyes adjust to the room lit by the glowing embers of a banked fire to her right. Two chairs sat near the hearth, a table between them. To her left, a desk sat against the wall near the black rectangle of an open door. Directly across from her was a set of doors which she assumed led to Reis' sleeping chamber.

A loud snort burst from the open door by the desk, followed by a long, drawn out snore.

Nadia shook her head and crossed the room to the closed doors. Stepping lightly, she pushed the door open, and soft light spilled over her. She slipped silently into the room and closed the door.

A large bed took up the center of the room, its covers pulled back, but still smooth. To the right, tall windows stretched from floor to ceiling on either side of the fireplace where her nephew, dressed in a thick black robe and fur slippers, sat in a chair before the fire. His long fingers held a stick of black charcoal, his hand moving in broad strokes over the page of a large journal. He lifted a charcoal-smudged finger to shove a lock of inky black hair out of his face in a gesture so familiar it brought tears to her eyes. How often had she seen Lareina perform the same gesture as she read?

She traced the sweep of his profile, seeing the perfect blend of Diomere's king and queen in the boy. "You remind me so much of your mother."

The prince jerked, dumping his journal to the floor in his haste to rise.

Nadia lifted the hood of her cloak from her face, and the boy paused midway and sank back into his chair.

"You saved Lord Cyrene's life," the prince said, eying her warily.

A knock sounded, and Nadia stepped behind the door as it opened. "My Prince, is all well?"

Prince Reis' gaze flicked to Nadia then away. "Yes, Maro. I nodded off, and my journal slipped from my lap."

"Can I get you anything, m'lord?"

"I'm fine. Get back to your bed."

The servant rubbed his eyes as he nodded. "Sleep well, my Prince."

The door closed, and Nadia moved forward to retrieve the journal from the floor. A sheet of paper slipped from between the pages. She reached for the sketch of a much younger King Delmar of Diomere.

Nadia sat back on her heels and studied the drawing. "You have his hair and eye-shape, though the mismatched colors are something very rare indeed," Nadia met her nephew's incredulous stare.

"You know who he is?"

Nadia frowned. "Of course. Don't you?"

Prince Reis opened his sketchbook. "I've dreamed of him and a pale-haired woman since I was little. I learned to sketch so that I could show my mother. When she saw this, she smiled sadly and told me it wasn't yet time. She disappeared soon after." He handed her several more sketches. "Who are they?"

"They are your parents. King Delmar and Queen Lareina of Diomere."

The boy wrinkled his forehead. "You're mistaken. I'm not your country's missing heir." He set the journal on a side table, stood, and crossed the room to pull a small trunk from under his bed. He opened the trunk and pulled out a tattered sketch book. He opened the book to a drawing of Jasara. "This is my mother. Dieuroi Mavros is my father."

Nadia pulled the updated painting of Diomere's royal family from her pocket. "You've been deceived." She handed the picture to the prince. "These are your parents, and that is your older sister, and apparently, Prince Stefan's betrothed."

The prince studied the small portrait and compared it to his sketches. "No, my father wouldn't have claimed me as his if I wasn't."

Nadia studied the stubborn set of his chin, so similar to his real father's. "Jasara was your nursemaid. When you were an infant, she used a'mi against your guard and vanished with you. I was that guard. I've been looking for you ever since."

"You're wrong," the prince insisted, his head bent to avoid her eyes as he gathered up his sketches. "I am the bastard son of the Dieuroi. My brother was ten years old when I was born. He'll verify that I have always lived in Thuno." Left unsaid was the fact that the man he believed was his father was mostly bedridden by his head illness and spent most of his time ranting madly at those around him.

"Ask him. I think the answers will surprise you," she said as she moved back to the door. He needed time to process what she'd told him. She paused to look back at her nephew. "Be careful in who you trust. Dieuroi Mavros has become much more paranoid since his illness began and would use you as a pawn to gain power over Diomere should he discover your real identity. You force those you tell to choose between loyalty to Thuno or the heir to a foreign kingdom."

Prince Reis, the wide-eyed uncertainty on his face making him appear very young, squared his shoulders and lifted his chin. "I am Prince Reis, the bastard prince of Thuno. I need not fear any other outcome to my inquiries."

Nadia nodded and lifted the hood of her cloak back over her head. "I'm quite certain you're my nephew. Humor your weary auntie and proceed with caution."

He remained silent as she slipped out of his room.

CHAPTER TWENTY-SEVEN

N adia marked her place and closed the book. After reading the last paragraph half a dozen times, she knew reading wasn't going to distract her from thoughts of Gregor. Neither waiting for her nephew's reply to what she'd told him, nor guild business, could keep her mind from obsessing over him the last two days. The memory of his declaration of love coupled with the hurt she'd caused had nearly sent her over to see him so many times, the consequences be damned.

Tilting her head back, she massaged her temples.

Focus on making your nephew safe first.

The door opened with a soft hiss. Nadia palmed a dagger, opening her eyes only a crack so it appeared they remained closed. Arri popped her head in, and Nadia slid the dagger back into its sheath.

Her sister rolled her eyes. "Because someone intent on your murder wouldn't be noticed by the twenty guild members lounging outside your door."

"It's the ones you trust who have the potential to be the most dangerous."

Arri shook her head. "Right." She held up a gold- edged card. "We've been invited by Prince Stefan to a dinner held in our honor for saving Gregor's life."

"Nothing from Prince Reis?"

"No, but I bet he's there. Gregor did nearly die while saving his life."

Nadia took the invitation and read it. "Tonight. Good. Gods willing, our nephew will have made his inquiries and given me some indication that he believes me."

"I don't doubt he will. I'm going to get ready. Remember, it's a formal occasion." Her sister gave her wrinkled salvar and dirty boots an arched look. "I'll order a bath ready and waiting for you at the Emerald Mermaid."

Nadia stuck her tongue out at her sister. Juvenile, yes, but also satisfying. Arriana rolled her eyes and left to start primping.

She placed her book on the teetering stack beside her chaise and stretched muscles stiff from that morning's workout. A bath did sound good.

With a sigh, she stood and followed her sister across the common area, stopping to speak with Sarna, Gordon, and the other guild members who didn't have families. Two of their youngest members moved around in the kitchen area, both having been assigned cooking duty for the evening meal. She laughed with them as they hassled the two young men, the cave echoing with laughter.

By the time she stepped through the stone wall into her rooms at the Mermaid, a bath waited. She'd just stepped out of the tub, hair dripping down her back, when someone knocked.

Wrapping a towel around her body, she squeezed the water from her hair. "I'm bathing," she yelled. "State your business."

Sarna's dry voice carried through the door. "Lady Quinones requests your presence in her chamber. Something about making sure you look presentable."

"Tell my sister to kiss my ass."

"I think I'll let you do that, m'lady."

She sighed and opened the door. "Did I ever say I was glad to have that little harpy here?" She pointed a finger as the other woman lifted a brow and opened her mouth to reply. "If you're going to say something sarcastic, then you can close your trap."

"Stupid question, sarcastic answer," Sarna said with a shrug.

Nadia scowled at her third. "What's that? You wish to go through this same torture and join us this evening?"

Sarna scowled. "You wouldn't."

Nadia smiled. "When we find my nephew, you'll assume command of Vromia Guild. Don't you think it prudent that you become familiar with the ruling class?"

"You had me memorize all their names and faces ages ago," the other woman said in a bored voice. "And I'm perfectly happy being your third. I'm still hoping you'll find a reason to stay."

Her thoughts turned to Gregor. "It isn't as easy a decision as I thought it'd be."

Sarna raised her eyebrows, but Nadia turned away from the question in the other woman's gaze and opened her armoire. "Tell my sister I'll be over as soon as I've finished dressing."

Her sister would, no doubt, dress in full Diomerean formal wear. Knowing she could do no less, she pulled a thigh-length tunic and matching salvar, both in black silk with gold embroidery at hem and cuff, and gold sandals from the armoire's depths.

She wrapped her wet hair in the towel and twisted it on top of her head, then pulled on the clothes. After wrapping a sheer black scarf with the same gold embroidery around her neck, she opened the door and went down the hall to the guest suite and her sister.

Arriana turned as she stepped through the door, her sister taking in her clothing with a nod. "Only you could make wearing salvar alluring."

Nadia shrugged and sat in the chair her sister had indicated. "Skirts are impractical. I conceded to them for the dinner with Gregor because you insisted, but this is my preferred method of official dress." She shot her sister a smug smile. "I'm glad you like it."

"I'm willing to admit that it might have its advantages," her sister said.

Nadia held a thin black dagger and sheath out for her sister to take. She hadn't bothered doing her own hair. Her sister would just redo it.

"This needs to be hidden in whatever you do so that's it's easy to get to." Nadia closed her eyes as her sister brushed out her hair.

When she finished, Nadia admired the elegant style that wrapped from one temple, around her head, and over the opposite shoulder. It hung in a loose reverse weave around the dagger hidden in the braid over her left breast.

She nodded. "You'll have to teach this one to Geeta. The dagger is much easier to get to."

Arriana raised a brow. "Because who cares about how beautiful it is."

Nadia shrugged and led them out of the chamber, biting back a smile as her sister sighed behind her. They made the trip up the mountain in comfortable silence, having already determined that if their nephew had told Prince Stefan of her visit, he'd have sent guards instead of an invitation to dinner.

The coach wound its way up the hill to the royal palace and its crown of spires, a god gazing down on the city of Volos from the heavens. They pulled through the massive front gate, the eyes of the square tower daring them to bring harm to those inside. Turning at the second gate, they wound around the massive palace grounds on a paved road in the same tan stone as the palace and its walls until they came to Prince Stefan's wing.

Servants in the crown prince's colors helped them out of the carriage and escorted them through a stone door carved with the royal crest. They were shown into a great room lined with stone pillars and dark and light marble inlaid floors.

Chandeliers dripping in sparkling crystals hung along the center of the room from the ceiling's arched peaks, bathing the room in a golden glow. Tables surrounded by cushioned chairs lined the room where Stefan, Reis, and many of the crown prince's retinue, including Gregor, gathered in small groups chatting to one another.

When they were announced, conversation stopped and all eyes turned to them. Nadia couldn't help but look up at Gregor as he crossed toward her behind Prince Stefan and Prince Reis.

His cool gaze heated as it moved from her head, lingering on her breasts and hips, before traveling back up to her face. Desire shot through her body, straight to her suddenly damp center, and she shifted. Gregor smiled, as if knowing exactly how he affected her. She forced herself to look away as Prince Stefan stopped in front of them.

She met Prince Reis' troubled eyes before her attention moved to the smiling crown prince. "Welcome to you both," he said cheerfully, his sharp gaze missing nothing. "You honor us with your presence."

Nadia bowed. "My sister is the healer responsible, your highness. I simply got him to her as fast as possible."

Prince Stefan turned his smile onto her sister, who blushed, as he pressed a gentle kiss to the back of her hand. "You have my unending gratitude, Lady Quinones. Gregor and I have been friends since we were boys, and I would have been heartbroken to lose him. Thank you."

"I only did what any person of my profession would. I'm just happy that I happened to be visiting when it happened," Arri said demurely.

"Seeing as how it's my life you saved, I couldn't agree more," Gregor said, from behind the prince.

Nadia couldn't help the skip of her heart at the sound of that quiet voice.

He moved closer, until he stood next to Prince Stefan. Turning his attention to Arri, he bowed. "Thank you, m'lady."

"You are quite welcome, Gregor."

He turned a smoldering gaze to Nadia and stepped forward. Lifting her hand, he bowed and turned her hand over to press a warm kiss to the underside of her wrist. She jerked as she felt his tongue flick against her skin. A shiver moved up her body. Their eyes locked.

"Your quick acting saved my life as much as your sister's healing abilities, Lady de Quinones. For this I am eternally grateful," he said, his voice low.

"I could do nothing less, m'lord."

"Couldn't you?" he asked, his smile causing her muscles to quiver low in her stomach.

Dinner was announced and Gregor tucked her hand into the crook of his arm to lead her into the dining room behind Stefan. His elbow brushed her breast and desire arched through her body.

Nadia blushed and then clenched her jaw at his knowing expression. She attempted to pull her arm from his, but he refused to release her, instead closing his other hand over hers and rubbing his thumb over the inside of her wrist. Her thighs clenched even as she fumed at his high-handedness.

Gregor led her to a chair to Stefan's right, keeping hold of her hand as he took the seat next to her. Reis escorted Arri to seats on Prince Stefan's right. The rest of the courtiers sat by rank around the long table, their conversation filling the room.

A servant set a tureen holding a fragrant broth with mushrooms floating in it between her and Gregor, ladled a serving into the small bread bowls sitting on the silver trencher in front of each of them, then bowed and left.

Nadia tugged on her hand and shot Gregor an annoyed look when he wouldn't release her. Holding his gaze, she picked up her spoon with her left hand and dipped it into her bowl. Gregor's eyes followed the spoon as she lifted it to her mouth, then heated as she slipped it between her lips. Muscles low in her stomach quivered, and she looked away from the desire so clear on his face.

Stefan glanced between her and Gregor, his brow lifted. "Gregor has shared a little of what brought you to my country. Have you had any luck with your search?"

She smiled, trying to ignore that Gregor held her hand pressed to his thigh. "It's going well."

"I'd like to offer you my assistance. My country is unaware that such a treasure has been hidden under our noses and would be honored to assist in returning it to you."

Nadia shook her head. "That is a generous offer, your highness. But unnecessary."

Prince Stefan's brows lifted.

"It's nothing personal, your highness. I, too, offered my assistance and was turned down. It seems there really are people out there who don't wish to use us, even when the assistance is freely offered," Gregor said, the ease of his tone belying the hint of challenge in his narrow gaze.

Nadia faced Stefan and smiled, but she knew it didn't reach her eyes. The prince glanced between the two of them, his expression thoughtful.

Seeing her sister's discomfort, Arri leaned forward. "My sister tells me that Thuno produces the maple syrup that's used on meats and in porridge here. I've never tasted anything so divine. Sugar or honey is used to sweeten everything in Diomere, but I think my people would love this flavor cooked on their meats, especially bacon. Do you produce enough to export it?"

Prince Stefan smiled and pointed to a man farther down the table. "You'll want to speak with Lord Adula. His family owns our top producing sugar wood."

Nadia's attention strayed from the conversation and back to her trapped hand. She attempted to curl her fingers into a fist and pull her hand from Gregor's grasp, but he tightened his hold.

She lowered her head and looked up at him through her lashes, then bit her lip and slid her fingers closer to his groin. He pressed his hand over hers, halting her progress.

Nadia licked her bottom lip and dug her nails into his thigh. Gregor released a strangled breath and released her. She fluttered her fingers, grazing his erection, then pulled her hand back into her own lap.

Inhaling deeply, he leaned toward her and clamped a hand on the back of her neck and pressed his lips to her ear. "You're going to pay for that, love. I promise."

Her stomach fluttered. She clenched her thighs to ease the ache of desire pulsing in her core, avoiding his gaze as he sat back in his seat.

Tension buzzed between them as the soggy bread bowl was removed and a platter, holding two roasted fish covered in a sweet onion sauce, replaced it.

Nadia, normally possessed of a healthy appetite, picked at her fish, her focus the deep rumble of Gregor's voice as he spoke with Stefan and each brush of his arm as he reached for his wine.

The fish was followed by a pork and fruit pie topped with roasted chicken. And finally, the meal ended with a cherry pudding which had her sweets-loving sister's eyes fluttering in ecstasy.

The dining room doors were opened as Prince Stefan pushed back from the table and stood. Nadia shoved her seat back and followed before Gregor could once again confiscate her hand. They moved to the prince's drawing room with its gold damask walls and plush couches, where sweetmeats and spiced wine waited on a sideboard.

As the guests made their way from the dining room, servants moved among them with trays of wine. Prince Stefan took a glass and lifted it once everyone had been served. "Tonight's gathering is in honor of Lord Cyrene, who saved my brother's life, nearly losing his own. We also honor Lady de Quinones and her sister, who both played a part in saving Lord Cyrene's life. I truly appreciate all three of you. You have my heartfelt gratitude." The prince drank.

The other guests lifted their glasses and said, "Hear, hear."

The prince sat, and soon the room buzzed with conversation. Arri engaged Prince Stefan and Gregor in conversation, leaving Nadia free to speak with their nephew.

"Prince Reis, would you care to join me for a game of draughts or chess?" she asked, gesturing toward the small table across the room inlaid with black and ivory tiles.

Her nephew glanced at the table then back at her. "I'd be honored, Lady de Quinones."

From the corner of her eye, she noticed Gregor's head turn, his gaze following them to the game table. Nadia took her seat as Reis took the gold and silver disks from the table's single drawer. Handing her the silver bag, Reis kept his attention on the gold disks as he placed each on its appropriate square. Nadia did the same, then looked up to meet the startling dual-colored eyes of her nephew, his brow wrinkled.

"You really believe I'm—"

"The Crown Prince of Diomere, His Royal Highness Areisteo de Amadeus y Quinones, Infante de Isere," Nadia interrupted, her voice low enough that only he could hear.

Her nephew dropped his gaze, but Nadia knew he wasn't looking at the game pieces. "My brother told me that my mother disappeared after announcing her pregnancy, then reappeared after I was born. My age and the time she was gone were right, so no one really questioned her claims."

He looked up, his brows lowered over eyes flashing with anger. "All this time, being treated as if I wasn't worthy by Thuno's nobility, believing myself my fa" —he glanced up at Nadia— "Dieuroi Mavros' bastard."

Nadia reached out and moved one of her silver disks on the board. "Your mother believes fate stepped in, robbed you of knowledge of your birthright, in order to prepare you for a difficult rule. On the night you were taken, she saw you sitting upon Diomere's throne with sharks circling the island."

Following her lead, Reis moved one of his gold disks, a frown pulling down the corners of his mouth. "I was taught that the gates no longer exist," the prince said. Nadia moved her next silver disk, then looked up at him. Reis sighed. "Another lie." He ran a hand through his black hair. "I'm not Sa'i, am I?"

Nadia called her a'mi, focusing on air, and a soft breeze ruffled her nephew's hair. He jerked his gaze up to hers.

Nodding toward the table, she used the air to move her next disk without a finger touching it. "The royal family has long been the keeper of the last gate between the worlds of the Sa'i and the A'mi." She crossed her arms and muttered. "Though, apparently, the other gates still exist."

Her nephew took his turn. "I should tell my brother, er, I mean, Prince Stefan." His shoulders drooped. "I'll miss not having Stefan as my brother."

Nadia studied the board, then moved one of her disks out of the path of Reis' gold ones. "The bond you've developed with Thuno's heir is one that may come in useful if what my sister saw comes to pass."

"So you're my aunt and the captain of my guard, like Lord Cyrene is lord commander of Stefan's guard?"

Uncomfortable at the comparison with Gregor, Nadia shook her head. "Not anymore. It's my fault that you were taken and my responsibility to see you returned to Diomere."

"If fate decreed this to be my life's course, there isn't really anything you could have done to stop Jasara from taking me, could you have?" he asked, tilting his head as was his mother's habit.

Nadia smiled. "You're every bit as smart as your mother. She'll be so excited to teach you of our history and your place in it."

"She's missed me, then?" the prince asked. And his gaze was so hopeful that Nadia vowed to hunt Jasara down and make her pay for ever letting this precious boy miss out on a mother's love.

"Very much. She writes me for updates every month and prays daily to the gods for your safe return."

"And my father?"

"He has aged greatly since you were taken," she told him, repeating what Lareina told her in her letters. "They both want you back and safe in their care."

The prince leaned back. "Then let us go tell my brother. He will help me find the first ship headed to Diomere."

"No."

He lifted a brow.

"He'll be forced to choose between loyalty to his king and loyalty to the heir of another nation. He'll be honor bound to tell his father," she said.

"You really think Dieuroi Mavros will harm me if he discovers who I really am?"

Nadia nodded. "With Stefan's engagement to your sister official, the Dieuroi sees his son ruling both nations. I don't believe a king who refers to himself as god king, will allow an opportunity to gain power over Diomere's valuable shipping trade just sail away with the next tide. Do you?" she said, maneuvering one of her silver disks to jump one of his gold ones.

Reis' shoulders sagged. "You're right. Dieuroi Mavros covets the combined power of a marriage between Thuno and Diomere. And he is much more volatile even in his lucid moments." He leaned forward to study the board, picking up one of his disks and jumping one of hers. "What would you suggest we do instead?"

Gregor, who'd been sitting with Stefan and Arri, stood and crossed toward her.

Nadia smiled, shot Reis a triumphant look, and jumped two of his gold disks with hers. Turning her head so Gregor couldn't see her quiet response, she said, "We make you disappear."

Gregor pressed his palm against Nadia's back and leaned over her shoulder. "She's making your gold disappear faster than usual, my prince," Gregor said, looking down at the game board. "You two seem to be having a serious conversation. A strategy I'll have to remember."

He smiled at Nadia. "His highness usually has Druj's favor when we play this game."

Nadia smirked at him. "Either you let him win, or you aren't as good at strategy as I first thought."

"Lord Cyrene doesn't let me win." Reis frowned. "Do you, Gregor?"

Gregor held her gaze for a moment, then glanced over at Reis with a smile. "Rest easy, my prince. You've beaten me soundly with no help on my part." He studied the board again. "Stefan requests your presence. I can take your place here, though I can't say as I'll be able to do much better than you are."

Reis stood and bowed to Nadia. "It was a pleasure, Lady de Quinones. I hope you'll return soon and give me a chance to redeem myself."

"I would be happy to, your highness. Thank you for keeping me company."

Reis bowed again, then turned and crossed the room to join Prince Stefan and those sitting with him.

Gregor took Reis' deserted seat, studied the board, then moved a gold disk. "That must have been a heavy conversation," he said, his gaze jumping up to lock with hers.

Nadia focused on the board, then smiled. Picking up one of her silver disks, she jumped three of his, then looked up. "Or I'm just that good."

CHAPTER TWENTY-EIGHT

W hen they returned to the Emerald Mermaid later that night, Nadia ordered a runner to the port to purchase passage on the next ship to Diomere. Now that she had her nephew's cooperation, she was determined to reunite him with his parents before someone else tried to take his life. She knew another attempt could come at any time. She prayed Gregor would be able to keep her nephew safe until she could get him away from Thuno.

The servant returned to let them know that the next ship would leave at first light. Nadia called for the servants to bring Arri's trunks and ready a carriage.

"Lareina is due to arrive in six weeks' time for the betrothal ceremony with Madelena. Surely, we can hide our nephew until then," Arriana groused. "I bet she saw this in a vision and is even now making plans to come early."

Nadia shook her head. "We can't know for certain.

She didn't see that Areisteo would be taken, did she?"

They'd hastily tossed Arriana's belongings into her trunks.

"Careful." Arriana took the soft leather satchel Nadia was about to toss into one of the trunks. "That holds my herbs, tinctures, and ointments. If the glass vials break, their contents would ruin my clothes. I'll carry it with me."

Nadia rolled her eyes. "Why one person needs so many dresses, I'll never know. You're as bad as Zephyra."

"Says the woman who dresses like a man," her sister said in a bland voice. "You still own exactly three sets of black and three sets of brown salvar. Two of each in cotton, one of each in linen. Am I correct?"

Nadia scowled. "I had to add two each of wool to keep my legs and backside from growing icicles during Thuno's excruciatingly cold winters, and don't forget the silk salvar for formal occasions."

Arriana's face softened into a sad smile. "I'm not ready to leave. I've missed you so much."

Nadia stared hard at the books she was stacking inside a chest. "I don't want you to go, either."

They continued packing in silence until the trunks were full. They shared Nadia's bed the way they'd once done as children, talking long into the night, neither able to sleep.

Early the next morning, Nadia climbed in the carriage and sat beside her sister, one arm wrapped around her shoulders and the other holding a sack of blooms she'd picked from the garden.

"We'll be together again when Areisteo is returned to Diomere."

Arriana's eyes glistened with unshed tears. "No, our days of living together in the same home ended when we scattered to look for him. I think you'll find Thuno more difficult to leave than you would have only a fortnight ago."

Nadia frowned and ignored the part of her that agreed. "My goal has been the same for twelve years. That hasn't changed."

Arriana smiled sadly at her sister. "Hasn't it?"

They finished the drive in silence. When the carriage pulled to a stop, Arriana turned to take the footman's outstretched hand. Nadia shoved her chaotic feelings aside and stepped down out of the carriage to see her sister smiling at the reason for those feelings.

Her heart jerked in her chest, followed by a surge of irritation. Why had her heartbonded chosen this time to reveal himself? And why did he have to keep popping up everywhere she went?

Gregor looked up, a smile on his face. "Good morn, my lady."

"What brings you to the docks at this early hour, Lord Cyrene?" Nadia snapped.

Arriana laid a hand on Gregor's arm and smiled up at him. "Please forgive my sister, my lord. I'm afraid she's being forced to rethink certain of her goals, and it's put her in a foul mood."

Gregor lifted a dark brow. "Goals?"

Arriana winked. "Apparently, returning to Diomere may not hold quite the appeal that it once did."

Gregor studied Nadia's scowling face. "Indeed."

"My sister has recently developed a nasty habit of assuming more than she ought, my lord. If you'll excuse us, she has a ship she can't afford to miss, and we've still to ask the gods for their blessing."

Gregor's eyes widened. "Returning to Diomere so soon, Lady Quinones? I understood you were scheduled to stay another fortnight."

Nadia pushed her sister ahead of her toward the ship readying to leave for Diomere. "You were mistaken."

"Has something happened?" Gregor asked as he persisted on following them.

"It's none of your concern, Lord Cyrene."

Arriana shot her an annoyed look over her shoulder. "I'm perfectly capable of moving toward the ship on my own, Nadia. Do stop pushing."

"Don't, Arri."

"Don't what?" Gregor asked.

Nadia stopped, shot her sister a hard look, then turned to glare at Gregor. "Arriana has been summoned home, not that it's any of your business." She glanced around. "Surely you have someone else you can go harass."

Gregor studied her, his face inscrutable. "Why was she summoned back?"

Nadia inhaled loudly through her nose. Why wouldn't he just go away? Arriana stepped up beside her, a smile on her face, as if she found Nadia's predicament amusing.

Nadia squeezed the bridge of her nose. "Someone is sick. She's needed to heal them." She smiled tightly. "Happy now?" She ignored Gregor's narrowed gaze and whirled around to pull her sister to the waiting ship. "Let's go."

"Fair winds and safe travels, Lady Quinones," Gregor called. "We'll save that discussion until you return."

Her sister smiled over her shoulder. "Farewell, Gregor." Pulling against Nadia's hand, Arriana leaned toward him and whispered. "Heartbonded, Gregor. If you have any access to knowledge about the A'mi, look it up. Remember that nothing worth having ever comes easy."

CHAPTER TWENTY-NINE

Heartbonded. Gregor scoured his memory for any mention of the word before he'd acquired the Arenatou gate scroll. Some of the scrolls about the A'mi were historical in nature, some were children's tales warning what could happen if their powers were used for selfish reasons, but none spoke of a bond between hearts, of love. He shook his head knowing he'd never seen the term before.

Nadia and her sister knelt at the edge of the dock and tossed flowers into the water. She glanced over her shoulder. What thoughts lurked behind those beautiful eyes? Though tempted to move forward and badger both women for more information, he knew he'd only receive the sharp edge of Nadia's tongue.

He held her gaze, placed a hand over his heart, and bowed. She frowned, then turned back as her sister finished praying.

Difficult, but worth it, he reassured himself.

He needed to finish translating the scroll. Spinning on his heel, he returned to his carriage.

"Home, Mr. Martinos."

His coachman snapped the reins, and Gregor watched the scenery fly past. Though he was sure he'd never read anything about the heart-bonded before the scroll, he knew there had to be more out there. Arri seemed to think such a thing existed between him and Nadia, but wouldn't they have to be A'mi? He pinched the bridge of his nose, unsure about anything.

The carriage slowed as the gate of his family's two-story town estate appeared. The coachman guided the vehicle through tall, white pillars which stood sentinel against unwelcome guests, past towering hedges that grew in a thick fence of greenery, giving the estate absolute privacy. Sitting among colorful flowers like a kindly grandmother awaiting her guests, the home's warm tan bricks and white cased windows welcomed him home.

Gregor relaxed. Cyrene House, more than his family's country estate, held his fondest memories of childhood. Memories of the puppy his father had presented to him and his brother, of the days spent lazing in the thick grass with the pup's head on his chest, of the tree fort his father had helped the boys build, and his father's proud smile when he'd told his father that he'd been made commander of Prince Stefan's guard.

He frowned. His mother wasn't a part of any of those memories. It wasn't until he was older that he learned she preferred the country because of the lovers she'd taken after giving his father the required heir and a spare.

The carriage slowed to a halt behind Prince Stefan's carriage, members of the prince's guard standing in front of the door, a familiar presence since Gregor had set up an office for the prince to use when he needed an escape from the palace.

Gregor stepped out of the carriage, nodded to the guard, and entered his home. Hagnon, his steward, bowed as he stepped through the door.

"Good morn, m'lord." The steward lifted a tray with the morning's news sheet and reports. "The prince is in his office. He said he'd take tea with you when you arrive."

Gregor swept up the pile and gave the man a distracted glance. "Tell Stefan it'll be served in my study, Hagnon."

The older man nodded and turned toward the kitchens. Crossing the foyer to the wide staircase, he hurried up the carpeted stairs. They split halfway up, and he continued toward the west wing, which housed his suite. Pushing through the door, he crossed his large sitting room brightly lit by the sun shining through floor-to-ceiling windows, and stopped at the door to his study. He pulled a chain from his tunic, then over his head and inserted the key into the door's lock.

The door opened into a windowless room. He lit a lantern, its golden light bathing the books and scrolls organized neatly on the floor-to-ceiling bookshelves, in a golden glow. In the center of the room sat a long table covered in the various reference books he was using to complete the gate scroll translation. Against the back wall sat a mahogany wood desk, his copy of the Arenatou gate scroll and his partial translation spread across it.

A knock sounded at the door as he sat behind the desk. "Come."

His valet pushed the door open and carried the promised tea tray into the room, followed by Prince Stefan.

"Thank you, Jako."

The servant nodded, set the tray on the table, and left, pulling the door closed behind him.

Stefan started pouring tea into two of the cups. "Good, I caught you before you got lost in your translations."

"Just," Gregor muttered. "My lady's sister has dangled a carrot before me that is tied to the A'mi."

Stefan's brows climbed his forehead.

"And the allure to the Lady Nadia deepens. Beautiful, deadly, mysterious, and somehow tied to the A'mi. Should she prove to also have brains, one would be tempted to think she was created with you specifically in mind," the prince said, his voice incredulous.

Gregor kept his face carefully neutral, unwilling to give his sarcastic friend any more ammunition with which to harass him.

"Are you finished?" Gregor asked, eyebrow lifted.

The other man shrugged. "Just pointing out the obvious."

"She's not Marla."

Stefan nodded slowly, his frown telling Gregor his prince remained unconvinced as he finished his tea and stood. "Anyway, I'm headed back to the palace. You're welcome to join me in the great hall for dinner."

"As tempting as that sounds, I'm going to pass. I want to finish this translation tonight."

Stefan grimaced and jabbed his hand toward Gregor. "I'd rather stick toothpicks under my fingernails, personally, but duty calls."

Gregor nodded as the prince stalked out, muttering under his breath. Pulling the scroll toward him, he focused on the text which still needed translated.

The scroll held three paragraphs of text, the middle one being the longest. Pulling his desk lamp closer, he deciphered each foreign letter, wishing he could hear it spoken. Would it sound as beautiful as it appeared when written?

His mind jumped to Nadia. What would she think of his hobby? Diomere was one of the few places left in Saimond which passed down the story of the war between Saimond and Mondami as history rather than fairytale. Many of the scrolls he'd acquired had come from the island nation. Did their scholars still have the knowledge of the A'mi language? Would Nadia tell him if he asked? Would she even know?

Forcing his mind away from her, he burned through half the oil in his lamp translating the last lines of the scroll until he was finally able to sit back and read it in its entirety.

Of the same blood,
Each favoring a different element, Are the sacred five;
The Gate Keepers,
Each haunting the dreams of their heartbonded.

~*~

To Arenatou gate belongs air.
The heartbonded pair must bond the gate
To pass through and return and see
Air must touch air together.
Blood, heartbond, gatebond, elements, gates.
When all five are linked
Fully opened the two worlds will be.

~*~

Spirit links all
When element touches element
As one.

Gregor read it again. *Each haunting the dreams of their heartbonded.* Unbidden the erotic dreams of Nadia flooded his mind, heating his blood. Did Nadia have A'mi blood? Is that why Arri had told him to look for references to the heartbonded?

He remembered the feeling of being in Mer form in the dreams, his fish's tail powering him through the water as he chased Nadia. The ease with which he'd breathed underwater had been amazing, beyond anything he'd ever imagined.

He'd been drawn to the Mer since the day his father had acquired a painting of the exotic creatures when he was a small child. Had his own fantasies painted his dreams of Nadia, or were the dreams more than mere dreams? He rubbed his forehead, unsure, and read the first stanza again.

This seemed to imply that the gate keepers were of the same family. He'd always assumed they were chosen from among the peoples of the kingdom housing the gate. He pushed up from the desk and searched through his bookcases until he found the glass tube protecting the scroll he wanted. Pulling it from the glass, he unrolled it as he moved back to the desk. This scroll held knowledge of the five elements and their symbols. He skimmed until he came to the section he'd remembered.

Those of the same blood will typically share an affinity for one element, though in rare instances exceptions can exist.

So the Gate Keepers were a rare exception. He moved down to the symbols representing each element and compared them to those drawn on the pillars and arch which had decorated the edges of the scroll.

The unbroken circle, which represented spirit, had been sketched into the center of the gate under an arch with the words *Geto Inter Sokai*, Door Between Worlds. On the left column were the symbols for air and fire. On the right column were earth and water.

He sat back and rubbed his tired eyes. But what did it all mean? Nadia appeared in his mind's eye. What did any of it have to do with them and their tumultuous, almost relationship? He snorted. If you could call it a relationship.

Her body wanted him, of that he had no doubt. The heat of their kisses betrayed her efforts at remaining unaffected. However, she continued to push him away. All he could do was trust Arri, whom instinct told him he could trust despite the short time he'd known her. Nadia's sister had turned out to be an invaluable ally.

Unbidden, their conversation from the day before surfaced. What did Nadia think to protect him from? He scoured his mind for all their past encounters for any clues as to what it could be. He had to have missed something important.

There was her questionable relationship with the Shark. And he could admit that he'd been wrong to believe, even for a second, that she was the type to make love to one man while in a relationship with another. But the uncertainty still remained of exactly who the Shark was, the odd conversation about Prince Reis' mother, and her talk of being closer than ever to her nephew. The key to everything had to be finding her nephew, but who could he be?

Areisteo.

He paused. A name? Where had he heard it? When? The similarity to Reis' name didn't go unnoticed. It had been a woman's voice, hoarse and low. Jasara? A slender hand reaching for someone. Prince Reis? His head pounded, and he rubbed his brow.

He knew in his gut he was on the right track, but no matter how hard he tried, he couldn't remember any more. Could the bastard prince know something? He considered heading to the palace, but decided not to interrupt the young prince's evening. The morning would be soon enough.

Rubbing the back of his neck with cold fingers, he read the translated scroll again, scowling at its obscurity.

Why couldn't these things ever just say what they meant? And which element belonged to Thuno's Gate? The part about a heart-bonded pair bonding the gate sounded like rubbish written by a romantic. As if the key to controlling such powerful magic would be some type of match between two people who then had to consummate their mythical love under the gate's arch.

Shaking his head, Gregor stood. He placed the original scroll into an empty glass tube, labeled it, and slipped it onto the shelf designated to Arenatou.

As he snuffed out the lamps, he couldn't help but wonder if that romantic rubbish was exactly what Arri had been talking about.

CHAPTER THIRTY

E arly the next morning, Gregor's coach pulled up to the palace. He entered the great hall and saw the palace steward and Marshall Torin, their heads bent over a ledger.

Both men bowed as he approached, and he waved aside their formality. "Lestos, do you know if Prince Reis has come down for his morning bout of fresh air?"

"His guards escorted him to the palace gardens only moments ago, m'lord. Shall I send a servant with a message?" the steward asked, but Gregor had already turned toward the palace's expansive gardens.

"No need, Lestos," he replied as he walked away. "I'll find him myself."

He knew the young prince liked to wind his way through the garden's tall hedges toward the large fountain at the center.

A shiver of foreboding slithered down his back. The gardens were a perfect site for an ambush as the palace guards would hear the attack, but be unable to locate it very quickly. Anyone else who knew the prince's habits would know his destination and could be waiting anywhere along the path.

Gregor cursed. Hadn't he asked Prince Reis to vary his activities and keep his routine unpredictable? By the time he reached the garden's entrance, his mind had conjured up numerous nightmarish scenarios so bad that he was practically running. He forced himself to slow, acknowledging that he might be overreacting, and wound his way down the garden's path at a more moderate pace.

Prince Reis' voice, its tone calm as he asked one of his guards a question, carried to him as he neared the center so that when he broke from the path into the garden's center, he appeared completely at ease. The three guards with the prince each stood at one of the three entrances to the garden's center, which held a large fountain with a water nymph rising from the water with arms raised and face turned up to the morning sun. Reis sat on a bench, his journal in his lap, a replica of the statue staring up from the page. At the sight of Gregor, the guards came to attention, pulling Reis' gaze from his drawing.

Gregor bowed. "Good morning, my prince."

Reis smiled and gestured to the bench beside him. "Good morning, Gregor. What do I owe the pleasure of your company?"

Gregor lowered himself to the bench beside the prince, then signaled to the guards, who each moved out of the garden center into the paths leading to it. "I was hoping you could help me with something."

Reis raised his brow. "Of course."

"Have you heard the name Areisteo?" Gregor asked, gaze focused on the prince's expression. "From your mother, perhaps?"

The prince's face paled. "What? Why do you ask?"

Gregor bit back a satisfied smile. He'd guessed correctly.

"You know this person," he stated. "Do you know where he is?"

The prince sucked in his cheek, uncertainty written across his face.

Gregor leaned forward. "You know you can tell me anything. I'd give my life to keep you safe."

The young prince's agonized gaze jerked up to his. "I know, and that's why I can't tell either of you. It's safer."

"You're protecting us?" Gregor asked, his brow furrowed. "From what?"

Reis swept imaginary dust from his pants. "Divided loyalty."

Gregor narrowed his gaze on the boy. What were the chances that two people in his life were both protecting him from different things?

"My prince, you consider your brother and me to be somewhat intelligent, am I correct?"

"You're the two wisest people I know," the prince said.

"Then please, let us decide for ourselves what to do with the information you have," Gregor implored. "Trust us to know what is safe for us."

Reis stood and paced between the bench and the hedges surrounding the garden center. "If I tell you, it could start a war. People could die. People I love."

"We will think long and hard before we act on the information you give us," he vowed. "Your brother would not needlessly endanger the lives of the people he will one day be entrusted with."

Reis slowed, his shoulders lifting as he took a deep breath.

"I've wanted to tell Stefan all along. I love him like a brother. But—" Reis' eyes widened, then he coughed and stumbled forward.

Gregor jumped to his feet and caught Reis as he sank to the ground, blood bubbling from between his lips. One of the guards stood where the prince had been, a bloody dagger in his hand. The other two guards ran back into the garden center. Gregor pulled off his jacket, wadded it up, and wedged it under Reis' back between the ground and the wound.

The other two guards pulled their swords. Two more guards dressed in the Dieuroi's colors stepped from the paths behind Prince Reis' guards and ran them through before they could do more than step forward.

Gregor stood and faced one of his own men. "Traitor."

The guard shrugged. "Our mad king has offered a handsome reward for the bastard's death."

"You won't live long enough to collect your reward," Gregor promised, pulling his sword free of its scabbard.

The guard lifted both brows, a smug smile on his face. "Those are big words from a man who's outnumbered three to one."

Gregor pulled his hands from his waist and with a flick of his wrists, sent his dagger into the throat of one of the traitors while lunging toward the other and running him through with his sword. Both men sank to the ground. The first guard's smile melted from his face.

Gregor smiled. "Problem solved."

The traitor lunged forward, slashing at Gregor's midsection. Gregor stepped back, and the other man's sword only met air. They circled the fountain. Seeing his opportunity, he swung his sword high, forcing his opponent to block. Then he stepped into the other man's embrace and punched him in the temple with his free hand. Pain exploded across his knuckles, but the guard released his sword and stumbled back. Gregor snagged the other man's sword in his throbbing hand and tossed it behind him when his hand wouldn't close around it. Shouts came from the direction of the palace as the guards picked up on the sounds of clashing swords.

Focused on the traitor who unsteadily waved the bloody dagger used on Reis, Gregor slashed at the man, opening his arm from wrist to elbow, then slashed across the man's thigh. The guard cried out, limping around the fountain back toward the bleeding prince. Unwilling to prolong the man's death any longer, Gregor lunged forward and shoved his sword, hilt deep in the man's stomach, jerking his blade up and twisting.

The king's men burst into the garden center, swords drawn.

Gregor jerked his sword free and cleaned it against the dead man's clothes before turning away.

"Clean that up," he ordered, then knelt by Prince Reis and lifted his gently into his arms. "Someone run ahead and have the healer summoned to Prince Reis' suite."

One of the guards turned and ran out of the garden center. Gregor followed behind, the injured prince in his arms. He prayed to each of the gods, even Druj, to keep the boy alive for Stefan and Nadia's sake. Reis might well be the key needed to discover where Diomere's heir was hidden. The prince gasped for breath, and Gregor walked faster. If only Arri hadn't already left for Diomere.

CHAPTER THIRTY-ONE

"Another assassin picked up the contract. They ambushed the prince while he and Marquess Cyrene were in the palace gardens. Lord Cyrene killed the assassins, then carried the injured Prince Reis out of the garden himself," Sarna said, while Nadia, who'd been preparing for bed in hopes of dreamsharing with Gregor again, paced before the hearth in her sitting room.

She closed her eyes, relieved that Gregor hadn't been hurt. Then guilt washed over her as she realized she'd thought of her potential heartbond before her nephew.

"And Prince Reis?" Pell asked.

"Alive, for now. The royal healer was sent to his rooms," Sarna answered.

Nadia whirled around, pinning the other woman with a hard stare. "Was the weapon poisoned, as before?"

"I'm unsure. They are allowing only the prince's manservant to assist the healer. He is keeping his own council."

Nadia's eyes widened. "Go. Send word to Lord Cyrene that Geeta is available to assist the healer if she is needed."

Sarna nodded, turned, and left the room.

Nadia ran her hands over her head, a feeling of helplessness washing over her.

"I shouldn't have waited," she whispered, shooting Pell an agonized look. "Lareina will never forgive me if he dies."

Pell stepped in front of her and clasped her shoulders. "You know that isn't true. Your sister loves you and has never blamed you for her son's abduction."

She inhaled a deep breath, a part of her knowing he was right. She pressed her lips together, then met her friend's gaze.

"I won't forgive myself," she said, then titled her head back to stare up at the ceiling as she decided her next step.

"As soon as he's healed enough to travel—" she said, determined to keep something like this from happening again. "—we're getting our prince out of that palace. We can hide him in the Gate Keeper's Palace until Lareina arrives."

"Are you returning to Diomere with him?" Pell asked, those pale eyes unblinking as they focused on her.

"No. Yes." She dropped her chin and met his gaze. "I may not have a choice."

Disappointment flashed across his face before he blanked his expression and Pell dropped his hold on her shoulders, then folded his arms across his chest.

"Prince Stefan and Lord Cyrene will have tripled the guard on Prince Reis," Pell said. "How do you plan to get him out?"

Nadia inhaled, knowing her plan would look like a betrayal if Gregor discovered it.

"I'm going to create a distraction," she muttered, a plan already forming.

****

Gregor slid his aching body into bed that night, hoping for dreams of Nadia to distract him from his worries for Reis and his fears of failing Stefan. Moments after he drifted into sleep, he woke in their dream world to a night sky lit by a brightly glowing moon.

He turned his head to see Nadia beside him, her legs drawn up to her chest and her arms wrapped around them.

He sat up. "What's wrong, love?"

"I feel helpless," she said, turning her troubled gaze toward him.

Gregor wrapped his arms around her and pulled her into his lap. "Me too," he said, remembering his failure to keep Prince Reis from harm. "It's an unsettling feeling for people like us, isn't it?"

Nadia nodded, and he found the feel of her silky hair against his chest soothing. She didn't tell him that he shouldn't expect to be able to fix everything, that only the gods were infallible. He appreciated that she understood him so well.

"I wish we could've met before my exile."

He looked down into her upturned face. "Why?"

She lifted her hand to caress his chin, a sad smile on her face. "Because I didn't have nearly so many secrets, so many obligations to pull me away from you back then."

"Why can't you tell me your secrets?"

She leaned up and pressed her forehead to his, gazing deep into his eyes. "I'm protecting you."

"From whom?" he asked, his mind growing heavy, almost as if he were awake and only just now drifting into sleep.

She frowned. "From me."

As the darkness closed over him, her statement echoed over and over in his mind as if she'd uttered it into an endless cave.

I'm protecting you. From me.

Gregor woke feeling restless, the dream and Nadia's words echoing in his mind. Pulling himself out of bed, he sent his valet for his breakfast and dressed while turning over dreams that seemed disturbingly real despite the exotic location.

His valet arrived with his breakfast and a summons from Stefan. Gregor read the unusually curt missive, his stomach clenching. Ignoring his breakfast, he called for his carriage to be brought around, praying to all five gods that Prince Reis was well.

Stomach full of knots, Gregor arrived at Prince Stefan's reception chamber a short time later and nodded at the guard. "Sergeant Zaan. Everything was quiet overnight?"

"Yes, m'lord. Lady de Quinones' healer, Geeta, arrived early this morning to lend her expertise. Last report had the young prince resting comfortably."

Gregor nodded. The guard opened the door to the small antechamber where Stefan's steward sat penning letters.

At Gregor's appearance, the man stood and bowed. "Good morning, Lord Cyrene. His Highness will see you next. Can I get you a drink while you wait?"

The door to Stefan's office opened before he could answer. Three men in the royal Questioner's black robes, their faces hidden in deep hoods, strolled out in silence, and the steward showed them out.

Stefan stood at the door to his office, watching the men with a scowl on his face. He glanced at Gregor and waved him inside.

"Seems a little early to stomach such morbid visitors," Gregor said, closing the door. Stefan moved to stand behind his desk, the scowl not leaving his face. Another knot twisted Gregor's stomach when the other man didn't respond. "Stefan, what's wrong?"

"Tell me about Lady de Quinones."

Gregor's brow wrinkled. "What do you want to know?"

Stefan began to pace. "Everything. How well do you know her? What led her to believe her nephew was here?"

Gregor watched the prince, his shoulders tense. "Her nephew was taken by a distant cousin. Nadia followed the woman's trail, which led her here."

"It's come to my attention that she recently found her nephew's remains."

Last night's dream and Nadia's sadness came to Gregor's mind.

Stefan paced faster. "She blames my father and plans to take her anger out on my brother and me," Stefan growled, his face flushing bright red. "How dare she throw my friendship in my face. I held a dinner in her and her sister's honor, publicly declared my appreciation, and this is how she thanks me? By plotting to harm me and my brother in some twisted act of revenge?"

Gregor jerked his attention back to his prince. "Nadia wouldn't hurt a child, nor would she harm you for something you had no part in."

Stefan stopped pacing to glare at Gregor. "You'll excuse me if I don't trust your judgment of women."

Gregor flinched, and Stefan's expression softened into an apologetic frown.

"That was low. Sorry," Stefan muttered, then thrust a hand through his hair. "Though I trust you, this is a serious accusation. Find out whether these remains really were discovered or not. I'll give your lady the benefit of the doubt, for your sake, but I need proof."

"You honor me, highness," Gregor said.

As he walked out, Nadia's parting words from last night's dream echoed through his mind, sending a shiver of unease through him.

I'm protecting you.

From me.

CHAPTER THIRTY-TWO

N adia pulled her cloak tight around her face and stopped in a dark alcove near a bust of one of Thuno's past kings.

Two of Prince Stefan's guards moved down the hall, their sharp eyes passing over her glamoured form. It was a relief to know she could actually rely on her Mer abilities. Only her heartbonded, and those related to her by blood, could see through the glamour when it worked correctly.

Her heartbonded. She rubbed her chest over the ache in her heart, wishing she'd not been such a bad-tempered harpy the last time she'd seen him.

Her sister was right. The need she'd felt to return to Diomere had dimmed. Sure, she still missed her sisters, but Gregor had slipped his way past all the walls she'd put up around her heart. No matter how snarky she was, he refused to give up on her.

Shame filled her, and she silently thumped her forehead against the wall. How many of the A'mi would give anything to find their heartbonded? And here she'd been fighting against such a rare, priceless gift for a bunch of useless secrets.

She lifted her chin. No more. Once she was sure her nephew was safely away from the palace, she'd find Gregor, and tell him everything.

Hadn't her nephew shown himself to be A'mi? Neither Prince Stefan nor Gregor hated the boy. They accepted him. Gregor would do the same for her. He was different than most Thunoans. Special. She pictured his striking face, pale eyes twinkling as he smirked at her in that way that said he found her amusing. She hated that look. She loved it, too. She loved him.

She loved him. And he loved her. He'd seen her in all her different personas. Spy, guild leader, innkeeper, and Diomerean royal. And he liked them all.

Her heart thundered in her chest. All her doubts clogged her throat until she couldn't draw a full breath.

"Just a minute. I thought I heard something," said one of the soldiers who'd passed by moments before.

Nadia realized she'd lost track of what she was supposed to be doing. Shoving her panic aside for later, she hugged the realization close to her heart and returned her focus to this most important mission. Her nephew was so close to being returned to her sister's loving arms. She couldn't afford to be distracted now.

"There's nothing down here," the other soldier said, though he dutifully helped his partner double check.

The soldiers peered into each of the hallway's shallow alcoves, once again passing her by. She waited until they'd reached the other end of the hall to move closer to her nephew's door and the single guard who stood to the right of it. The door opened. The guard's bored expression sharpened, and he reached out to hold the door open.

Her nephew's personal servant backed into the hallway, a covered tray in his hands. "Good eve, Sergeant. How fares the new babe?"

"He's a joy, Master Maro. A happier babe, I couldn't have asked for. The missus sends her heartfelt gratitude for the basket you brought from Prince Reis. The babe's eyes light up each time he hears the shaker, and the large loaves and delicious honey saved my wife much time in the kitchen this last week." The guard's face darkened. "How fares our young prince?"

"He lives, and is recovering quite well, thanks be to Asha," Maro said, a frown darkening his face. They both grew silent as the guard nodded, then the servant shook his head and forced a smile. "I'm happy the babe enjoys the shaker I chose for him. Give your wife my regards, won't you? She is a lovely lady."

Nadia eased forward as the conversation came to an end. When the servant moved out of the way, she darted through the door before the guard pulled it closed, being careful not to brush against him. She released the breath she'd been holding as the door latched.

Looking across the large sitting room, she found her nephew sitting before a fire. His pale face was much thinner than the last time she'd seen him. Geeta had told her that he'd come a hairbreadth away from losing his life, but it hadn't really sunk in until this moment.

"I owe the gods so many thanks for sparing your life."

Reis' head jerked up, and his gaze found her instantly, despite her glamour. That confirmation made something in her relax for the first time in over twelve years. Despite the overwhelming similarities between him and his parents, she'd still questioned that she'd really found him alive. Her eyes burned. She'd really found her nephew, the babe which had been stolen from under her nose.

He smiled, his tired eyes making him appear much older than his almost thirteen years. "As do I." He relaxed back into his chair. "What do I owe the pleasure of your company, m'lady?"

"Tia Nadia," she corrected him. The prince lifted a brow, and Nadia smiled, his resemblance to his royal father unmistakable. "Please call me Tia Nadia. It's how your mother referred to me in your presence when you were a babe."

Reis nodded. "Tia Nadia, then. What can I do for you?"

"It's time."

The smile melted from his face. "Already?"

"Geeta has given the okay for you to travel. We can't take a chance that the next attempt made on your life will be successful. Those hired to do the job will only grow more desperate as their deadline looms closer. Do you have a bag ready as I suggested?"

"Yes. I just need to add a couple of things to it." The prince stood and went into his room, calling out over his shoulder. "How are we getting out of the palace without being seen?"

"A summons from the Dieuroi will arrive any moment ordering you to join the festivities below," Nadia said, then pulled a set of commoner clothes from under her cloak. "Wear these under one of those overly dressy front button tunics the Thunoans like so much."

He handed over a small pack and took the clothes from her.

"When you reach the doors to the dining hall, I'll create a distraction. While everyone is focused on that, push the tunic from your shoulders and slip into the kitchens. Geeta's husband, Jon, a very tall, dark-skinned man with a Berezan accent, will be waiting for you in the cellars. Do you know where they are?"

A corner of the prince's mouth lifted. "My brother and I used to sneak down and steal one of the small barrels of the Dieuroi's rarest spirits. The only time we were caught was due to the lure of fruit pies the royal cook had left cooling in the kitchen. She nearly took off our hands before she realized who it was she attacked." He looked up, his gaze twinkling with remembered mirth. "I don't think either of us had ever laughed so hard. After that, we decided stealing pies was a much bigger challenge, and forgot about our father's spirits."

Nadia reached out and squeezed the prince's shoulder. "I'll forever owe Stefan a debt of gratitude for making sure your childhood bore good memories to temper the bad."

"I'm going to miss learning from him, the advice he gives, and the brother he's been to me," her nephew said in a low, sorrow-filled voice.

Nadia laid a hand on his shoulder and squeezed.

"You can honor him the most by using the things he taught you to be the kind of king that he'd be proud to ally with," she said, understanding that sibling bond and how much he'd really miss it.

A knock sounded at the door. Nadia returned to the corner of the room.

Maro entered, frowning. "The King has ordered you to join the festivities below. Should I let him know you've already eaten?"

"No, I'll go," Reis said, crossing the room toward the door to his sleeping chamber. "It's better not to risk his wrath any more than I already have." Reis paused before he disappeared through the door. "Let them know I'll arrive shortly."

The servant quickly penned a response, pressed her nephew's seal into a blob of hot wax, and then returned to the door to hand it to the waiting messenger.

A few minutes later, Reis stepped out of his sleeping chamber dressed in a knee length, dark blue tunic edged in an ornate gold design which buttoned up the front from his neck to his waist. A gold embossed leather belt with a gold buckle and holding a jeweled dagger sat at his waist effectively hiding the coarse fabric of the plain trousers and shirt.

Reis placed a hand on his manservant's shoulder. "Thank you, Maro. For everything. You've been an amazing friend to me all these years."

The servant got a confused look on his face. "Is all well, my prince?"

Reis smiled softly. "Yes. I've just realized that I never know when I'll see someone I care about for the last time, and I wanted you to know how much your expert care has meant to me."

The servant's eyes glistened as he cleared his throat. "The pleasure has been all mine, Prince Reis."

Reis squeezed his servant's shoulder then moved to the door, his gaze darting toward Nadia then away. Maro pulled the door open and held it. Reis paused and Nadia slipped out ahead of him. He nodded to his manservant, and stepped through, closing the door behind him.

The guard stood at attention. At the sight of Prince Reis, he placed his hand over his heart, unaware that Nadia hurried past him and down the hall.

Reis followed at a slower pace, the guard marching a step behind. The other two guards fell into step on either side of the prince.

Nadia sent up a prayer that the gods would protect her nephew until he was safe in their care. She ran down the stairs, throwing one side of her cloak back so it revealed a gown of deep sapphire cut in the Thunoan style, while still hiding Reis' pack in her other hand. Geeta had lightened her black hair to a reddish-brown and pulled it up into an intricate sweep of curls. Her scar was hidden so that she looked nothing like herself.

Despite her disguise, she knew Gregor would recognize her. Their bond would assure it.

She slowed to a walk, thankful for the soft slippers which let her pass undetected. When she reached the wide-open doors leading into the dining hall, she stopped and waited.

Thunoan courtiers streamed past her into the large room lined with tables. When Reis appeared at the end of the hall, Nadia straightened and noted who approached the dining hall doors. The short, round figure of Lord Victor Pajari appeared. Nadia smiled grimly. She couldn't have asked for a better distraction.

Dropping her glamour, Nadia stepped away from the wall catching the cocky lord's eye. She gave him a demure smile.

He smirked, then crossed toward her. "Good eve, m'lady. I am Lord Victor Pajari, Earl of Juktas. Please tell me the name that belongs to one of such beauty."

Turning so the hand holding Reis' pack was on the opposite side of her body from the noble, Nadia bit her lip, and looked up at the man through her lashes as she held out her hand.

"My name is Sharis Zakros," she said, voice demure. "I'm a widowed cousin of the Earl of Zakros, and am here as chaperone for Earl Zakros' daughter."

Lord Pajari smiled as he brought her hand to his lips.

"My deepest condolences on your loss, m'lady," he said, then stepped closer so that his chest brushed her breast as he pulled her fingertips to his lips.

Nadia saw Reis over Pajari's shoulder, steps from entering the dining hall.

Yanking her hand from the man's hold, she screamed, "How dare you touch me without my permission."

She used his encroachment into her personal space to hook her foot behind his, then shoved the overbearing man, who stumbled backward, his expression one of surprised alarm as he fell to his backside.

She stepped backwards, hand pressed to her throat, and looked around frantically.

"Someone, please, help me," she said, her eyes beseeching those who'd turned at the commotion. "This man accosted my person, and attempted to take liberties I didn't allow."

Reis met her gaze and nodded. "Guards, take Lord Pajari into custody until we can clear this up."

The red-faced Lord Pajari climbed to his feet. "Why, you little trollop, I did no such thing."

Nadia wailed and feigned panic. "Oh stop his vile tongue from addressing me." She forced tears to well from her eyes and sagged against the nearest noble. "I feel faint. Please, m'lord, don't let him near me. I can't stand the sight of him. He sought to damage my honor."

A crowd of courtiers waiting to enter the dining hall whispered behind their hands as more guards marched over and grabbed the noble by his arms.

Lord Pajari yanked against the guards' hold. "Unhand me. Do you have any idea who I am? How dare you take the word of some earl's lowborn relation over mine. Unhand me, I say."

The noble she leaned against patted her shoulder, then raised his voice to be heard over Pajari's protestations. "Everyone knows you take liberties not freely given you, Pajari. How can you think we wouldn't believe the young woman when you have a history of such behavior."

Other nobles voiced their agreement, while those who were friends with Lord Pajari stepped forward to argue on his behalf.

Nadia slipped from under the noble's hand and melted back into the crowd, while pulling her cloak closed around her body.

She scanned the crowd for her nephew, but didn't see him. Taking another step back, she pulled the hood up over her hair. When she reached the outside of the crowd, she turned and walked toward the palace's front doors. Had anyone been paying attention they would have seen her vanish into thin air. She slipped through the open door, past arriving nobles. She reached the drive lined with waiting carriages and stepped into the shadows to drop the glamour.

Stepping out of the shadow, she waved to an unmarked black carriage which moved out of line and pulled up before her. She nodded at the driver, then climbed in. Pell snapped the reins.

***

Gregor stepped out of his carriage outside the palace, just as the driver of another carriage snapped his reins making the horses lurch forward. The driver glanced back, a smirk on his face. Recognizing Pell, Gregor's gaze dropped to the hooded figure glimpsed through the carriage's window.

A whisper of unease twisted his stomach as the palace doors opened and raised voices carried toward him. He ran up the stairs into the palace, his heart a hammer in his chest. He halted in confusion as a crowd of wide-eyed spectators watched the red faced Lord Pajari argue with Lord Zakros, two of Reis' guards holding his arms.

"What in Druj's dark gaze is going on here?" he roared.

Everyone fell silent and turned toward him.

Lord Pajari yanked his arms from the guards' grasp and glared toward the Earl of Zakros. "This imbecile's relation accused me of besmirching her honor."

"For the last time, that young woman was no relation of mine." The haughty faced Earl sniffed.

Gregor glared at the guards. "Where is his highness, Prince Reis?"

Both guards jerked around. The crowd cleared to show the third guard on his knee beside Prince Reis' discarded silk tunic.

Gregor felt as though his heart was being squeezed in a tight fist.

Prince Stefan appeared at the door to the dining hall. "What is all this commotion?"

He met Stefan's curious gaze, unable to say anything. Stefan's face paled.

Gregor's shoulders sank. "I'm sorry, my prince. Your brother is gone."

Stefan's face flushed an alarming shade of red as he gritted out through clenched teeth.

"Arrest her," he ordered. "Now."

CHAPTER THIRTY-THREE

Nadia stepped into the gate cave, dressed once again in her usual male attire, her hair braided tightly down her back. She handed Reis' pack to Jon, who turned and headed toward the underground lake. Her nephew stood facing the gate, his hands slightly lifted into the air. Nadia tilted her head. He seemed taller, less frail.

"You feel it," she said and stepped up beside him.

He glanced over at her. "So this is what a'mi feels like? I've always felt hungry, but food never satisfied. I've always been sickly and weak. And since the fishing incident, I've felt as though I were growing weaker. That feeling is gone. I'm invigorated. For the first time, I feel strong."

"Yes, but this gate isn't fully open. The feeling may not last." She felt a pang in her chest, and halted her thoughts before they could turn to Gregor. "Your father is linked to the one in Diomere as you will be when you become king."

Reis turned fully toward her, his brows raised. "My father is the Gate Keeper?"

Nadia shook her head. "Only a temporary Guardian until the Gate Keepers return. He takes those that choose a'mi to Mondami."

"And you? Are you A'mi, as well?"

Nadia smiled, and turned toward the golden doors that lead to the lake. "Come."

As they walked, Reis ran his hands over the images of A'mi creatures on the tunnel walls. "These creatures really exist?"

"So I've been told. I've never actually been to Mondami, nor have I seen them for myself. However, since we exist, I have no doubt that so, too, do they."

Reis nodded. Nadia waved him along and soon the sound of the waterfall crashing into the lake echoed around them.

She turned the corner to find Jon and Geeta waiting. Reis gasped behind her, and she turned to see his wide eyes taking in the underground lake.

Jon and Geeta smiled at their prince's reaction, both happy to have the Diomerean heir in their safekeeping, at last.

She smiled at Reis over her shoulder. "Amazing isn't it?" She pointed at the two Mer, waiting with smiles on their faces. "Prince Areisteo, this is our cousin and healer, Geeta, and her heartbonded, Jon. They've been helping me search for you the last twelve years."

Geeta and Jon both placed their hands over their hearts and knelt to one knee.

Reis placed his own hand over his heart and nodded at each. "I am honored to have such loyal subjects. Thank you both for your sacrifices."

Geeta shook her head. "The honor is ours, your highness. We're so happy to finally have you safely with us."

"De celebration in Diomere will be loud enough to cross de Sai-mond Sea in all directions when you once again set foot on Diomere's shores," Jon said, a big smile on his face.

Both rose to their feet. "We've prepared one of the chambers of the gate palace to make his highness's stay here comfortable," Geeta said, then glance at Nadia. "We'll go fetch the evening meal as well as something to darken your hair back to its original color."

Nadia smiled her thanks, then turned her attention back to her wide-eyed nephew.

"I can't believe an entire hidden palace has been here and neither Stefan nor Dieuroi Mavros know anything of it," Reis said, his voice awed.

Nadia shrugged. "I think Thuno's last gate keeper probably had something to do with that. Diomere's royal family has a collection of histories passed down from past gate keepers. I asked your mother to research this gate in my last report. Hopefully, she can tell us more when she arrives for you." She turned back to the pool. "But first we need to teach you to call your true form at will."

"I'm not going to join my parents now?"

"No. I knew we needed to get you out of that palace before one of the attempts on your life was successful. You'll stay hidden in these caves until your parents arrive with your sister for the betrothal cer-emony. There is an underwater river which connects this lake to the Saimond Sea. It's the safest way to get you aboard the royal vessel when it arrives."

Reis stared at the lake. "We can breathe underwater for long periods of time?"

Nadia smiled softly. "I forget that you've only spent a few terrifying moments in your Mer form." She lifted her finger to his neck. "You'll have gills on either side of your neck, like a fish. They pull air from the water as it flows out, allowing you to breathe while submerged."

"And if I change back to my Sa'i form while I'm stuck down there?"

"Unless you're cut off from your a'mi, changing between forms is a conscious choice. The difficult part is making the change, but once made, you're stuck until you can focus enough to make the change back." Nadia sat, cross legged, on the cave floor at the water's edge. "Sit" —she patted the spot in front of her— "here facing me. I'll walk you through how it's done, then you can work on it while I let Geeta turn my hair back to its original color."

Reis sat facing her, his brow wrinkled. "You weren't afraid someone would recognize you despite your disguise?"

Nadia dipped her head. "Thankfully, Gregor wasn't there," she muttered.

"Lord Cyrene? What's he have to do with anything?"

Nadia inhaled loudly through her nose, her eyes closed. "I could murder Jasara for keeping you in such ignorance of your heritage." She looked up at her nephew. "Did you ever have your nursemaid come looking for you, wish that she wouldn't see you, and have her seemingly look right past you?"

"I was playing seek and find with the seamstress's children during one of my mo" —Reis blushed— "I mean, during one of Jasara's fittings. I willed the other children not to see me and they looked right at me under the table without seeing me. I jumped out of my hiding spot, nearly giving them a heart attack." Her nephew frowned. "I hadn't thought about that in ages."

"This is an ability that all Mer possess. We call it glamour. It's a survival tactic that keeps us from being prey to larger sea predators. And has helped us hide our secrets from non-Mer since our creation.

Only those that share our blood or our heartbonded can see through the glamour."

Her nephew's intelligent gaze sharpened. "Gregor is your heartbonded?"

Nadia nodded.

"What is a heartbond, exactly?" Reis asked.

"It's a bond created when one's a'mi recognizes our soul's other half. It's rare and much desired."

Reis tilted his head to the side. "Does one without a'mi recognize the bond?"

"Even those without a'mi feel it, though they feel it as an irresistible pull toward the one whose power has recognized them. They understand that the person is very important to them, though they don't realize why."

"Does Lord Cyrene know?"

Nadia looked away. "We aren't here to discuss that."

She took each of Reis' hands in her own, ignoring her nephew's frown.

"Making the change the first time is difficult because you have to figure out your version of focusing your a'mi," she said. "And that depends on the element in which your strength lies. Most picture it as a pool of light which they draw from, others see it as a shield of water, light, or stone that surrounds them. And then there are those who see it as a weapon or tool to which they hold an affinity. It is unique to the individual. Once you figure out the form your a'mi takes in your own mind, you will then be able to use it to figure out your specific gifts."

"Gifts?" he asked.

"While there are certain uses of a'mi which are universal among a people, like the Mer ability to shift forms and use glamour, each individual has a'mi unique to them depending on the element to which they have an affinity. Some, like Geeta and your Tia Arri, are healers, though within different elements. Because of this, Geeta's a'mi only affects the physical body, while Arri's ability affects the spirit and the physical body. Others are able to manipulate fire, water, air, earth, the mind, the body, and dreams to name a few."

"What is the form your a'mi takes? What are your unique abilities?"

Nadia smiled at the eager curiosity lighting up her nephew's face. "I, along with my sisters, am able to draw from all five elements, though my strongest is water. I see my a'mi as two whirlpools on either side of a scale that shift size according to whether I'm using my a'mi to hurt or help. It helps me keep the dark and light sides of myself balanced. My specific abilities lean toward stealth and espionage, allowing me to spy using the water from the very air to see and hear."

"So the form my a'mi takes will represent something important to me?" Nadia nodded and the prince continued. "This sounds like it might take a while."

"Close your eyes," she ordered.

Reis inhaled a deep breath and released it slowly as he reluctantly obeyed her command.

"Inhale. Exhale. And again. Inhale. Exhale," she said, her voice lowering until she whispered the last.

Reis' shoulders relaxed.

"You're standing in a vast black landscape," she said. "You look around and notice darker shapes within the blackness. Focus on the shapes one at a time. How many do you see?"

Reis' eyes moved from side to side under his closed eyelids. "Four."

Nadia's brows lifted. Most Mer saw only one to two of the shapes which represented the five major elements with water being the predominant element. She and each of her sisters had seen all five, making them the strongest Mer born on either side of the gates since they were closed.

It couldn't be a coincidence that her nephew, the next ruler of Diomere, would be nearly as strong. Was it a sign that the gates between the two worlds would once again all be open? Were the gods making sure that Saimond had protectors in place to keep the past from potentially repeating itself?

Nadia shook her head, unhappy with the trajectory of her thoughts. "Continue to move your focus from shape to shape. Each one will elicit a different emotion. Do any of them draw you more than the others?"

"The first and fourth call to me equally," Reis said.

"Pull them toward you until the other two fade back into the surrounding darkness. Do the remaining two still call to you equally?"

"Yes."

Nadia frowned. "Are you sure? Try focusing on each for several seconds."

Reis yanked his hands from her grasp and reached forward, his eyes still closed. "One is an easel holding a large blank canvas and the other is a paint brush." His brows lifted. "Now it's a charcoal stick."

Nadia remembered the sketchpad she'd seen in his lap the first time she'd visited him. "Focus on the blank canvas. Take the charcoal stick and draw the first thing that comes to mind."

Reis lifted his hand and moved it through the air. The water of the lake began to swirl and Nadia new the second shape, which had turned into the charcoal stick, represented the water element.

The water rose into the air and began to form the image of a woman held between two cowled men. With each stroke of Reis' hands, the woman became more distinct, until Nadia recognized her own scarred face. She clenched her jaw, afraid she knew exactly what element the second shape had represented. His mother had passed on more than just the shape of her nose and mouth to her son.

The vision didn't stop there. The water began to form into the image of a man, wearing a cloak. When Reis got to the man's head, Nadia leaned toward the image, as first the chin then the lips, began to take shape.

In the middle of the upper lip, Reis' arm froze. The water collapsed.

Nadia jerked forward and caught Reis as he slumped to the side. She stood, Reis cradled in her arms, and ran toward the gate cave. She laid Reis on the pillows Geeta kept there for her own comfort.

Just as she'd ascertained that her nephew still breathed, Geeta and Jon ducked in from her sleeping cave. Their smiles melted when they noticed the unconscious prince.

Geeta set aside the tray of food she carried and hurried over. "What happened?"

"He used the lake's water to form his first vision."

Geeta jerked her gaze up to Nadia. "He can access two elements at once?"

Nadia nodded and sat back on her heels while Geeta returned her attention to the unconscious prince. As they watched, the prince's pale cheeks filled with color. His eyelids fluttered, then opened.

Dual colored eyes, one blue and the other green, locked on her. "You're in danger."

"Don't worry about me. The most important thing is that you're returned safely to your parents."

He pushed himself up to a sitting position, Geeta gently assisting him. "How was I able to see that?"

"You've inherited the visions from your mother, though hers don't manifest outside of her mind. The four shapes that appeared out of the dark landscape represent the four elements you can draw from. The two that called to you equally represent those which you are strongest. Water and Spirit. As you drew the vision in your mind, the water from the lake lifted into the air and formed the image you painted," she said, glancing at a stunned Geeta.

Reis frowned. "Does this happen with everyone?"

"No. Most Mer only see one shape. And that element is usually the water element. Some see two shapes. You've joined my sisters and me as those rare A'mi to have access to more than two of the elements. However, you're the only one that I know of to have more than one major element."

"What does it mean?"

Nadia placed her hand on his shoulder. "You'll be a very powerful monarch."

"Yet, I still don't know how to shift to my Mer form."

A loud knock sounded from her sleeping cave. Nadia stood and waved for Jon & Geeta to follow her.

"Stay here. You'll be comfortable here until I return." She stopped and looked at her nephew over her shoulder. "You'll be safe here. Don't do anything other than calling your true form. And don't step foot past this tapestry for any reason. Stay safe for your parents and Diomere, my prince."

Reis nodded, looking older than his twelve years as he reclined back onto the pillows.

"I'll go get the hair dye," Geeta said as they left the gate cave and locked the door behind them.

"Meet me in my bathing chamber in the Inn," she said.

Geeta nodded as they stepped through the opening and made sure the door was completely covered by the tapestry. She sat on her chaise and picked up one of Vromia Guild's expense reports from a pile on the table, then nodded at Jon and Geeta who waited by the door that led into the main cave.

CHAPTER THIRTY-FOUR

J on opened the door revealing Pell on the other side. Nadia set the papers back on the table as the couple slipped past Pell and closed the door, leaving them alone.

"Our prince is comfortable?" Pell asked.

"Yes. We prepared a room in the Gate Keeper's palace and stocked the kitchens with food. Geeta will join him after she fixes my hair." Nadia turned toward the hidden door. "Would you like to meet him?"

Pell shook his head. "I've got business to attend to. Just leave the door unlocked and I'll slip in to meet him when I return.

Nadia shook her head. "No one gets in or out without me."

"After everything, you're choosing now not to trust me?" he said, his cheeks flushing red.

"You're not A'mi—" she started.

Pell stiffened. "So now I'm lumped in with all humans? I was a fool to think you weren't as sectarian as the rest of the A'mi elitists."

His acidic tone, heavy with disrespect, combined with the stress caused by her nephew's unexpected manifestation of power, pushed

Nadia past reason. She found herself sinking into that cold place in her mind. She smiled. Pell's glare became wary as he stepped back and placed a hand on the sword at his waist.

"If you really believe that, then you know nothing," she said in a deadly soft voice. "We are childhood friends, true, but that does not mean I'll tolerate your disrespect. I am Capitán in the King's royal fleet and sister to our queen. You will remember your place, do I make myself clear?"

Pell clenched his jaw and nodded.

Nadia stood and opened the door. "Dismissed."

Pell spun on his heel and moved stiffly past her.

Jon, accompanied by Sarna, stepped aside as the fuming lieutenant growled for them to move.

"Grown men should be above such juvenile tantrums," Sarna muttered as he passed.

Pell kicked a barrel out of his path and stomped away. Nadia stepped out of her office and pulled the door firmly closed behind her. She glanced at Sarna, who took one look at her face and stepped back, gaze wary.

"One of these days he's going to push you too far. I'm not sure if I want to be here, or far away, when that time arrives," Sarna said.

Jon cautiously fell into step beside Nadia as she moved through the main cave toward the hidden entrance to her private apartment in the Emerald Mermaid. "Sarna has a report from one of our people in the palace."

Nodding her head, Nadia slipped behind a group of flat-topped stalagmites near the cavern's wall. She pulled a key from the hidden compartment in her wrist sheath, and inserted it into the keyhole of the steel banded wooden plank door, which she'd had installed into the stone. Once open, the door revealed the back of the stone wall into her private sitting room. She waved Jon and Sarna through, then closed, and locked, the door behind them. When the stone wall once again looked solid, she crossed to sit before the fireplace as Jon got the fire going.

She closed her eyes and tried to block out the sounds of movement around her. She always found it harder to leave that unfeeling place behind and reemerge into her more emotional self. Slowly, like Geeta's hot wax hand treatments, Nadia peeled back the coldness until one by one, her emotions returned.

Guilt swamped her. She hated that she'd been forced to treat Pell so harshly, but he knew how to push all of her buttons.

She opened her eyes. Jon and Sarna both visibly relaxed. Nadia waved for Sarna to give her report.

"Prince Reis has vanished. A woman claiming to be a relation of the Earl of Zakros' is believed to be involved." Sarna glanced up at Nadia's hair. "She is said to have reddish hair."

Nadia lifted a hand to her braid, and began to unravel it as Geeta appeared at the door, a basket of hair products in her hands.

"I'll be in there in a second," she said to Geeta's back as the older woman crossed to the door of her private bathing chamber.

Geeta nodded as she disappeared through the door.

"The Dieuroi must be overjoyed that someone has taken the boy off his hands," she said as she continued to finger comb her hair.

"Prince Stefan blamed his father and called him a superstitious old fool before storming out of the dining hall, the bastard prince's abandoned tunic in his hand," Sarna continued.

Nadia inwardly winced, sorry to cause Prince Stefan any heartache. *You could tell Gregor everything and ease the prince's worry.* She rubbed her chest over her heart, reminding herself of all the reasons, good reasons, she wasn't telling Gregor or Stefan what was actually going on. *Flimsy excuses. You still don't completely trust him not to disappoint you in some way.* She scowled and ignored the outspoken voice of her conscience.

"It's a testament of Prince Stefan's character that he cares so much for the wellbeing of his bastard half-brother," she murmured.

Shouting came from beyond the door that separated her private sitting room from her office. Jon and Sarna stepped between her and the door, swords in hand, as it was torn open. The king's soldiers, weapons drawn, filled the room. The soldiers parted, revealing a grim-faced Gregor.

Nadia stood, her stomach sinking as she pushed her unbound hair back over her shoulder, then raised her brows and forced a smirk. "An armed guard, Gregor? Really?"

He grabbed her shoulders and shoved his face into hers. "Tell me you didn't do this, Nadia. If you say you didn't, I'll figure out a way to convince Stefan of your innocence."

She widened her eyes. "Did what?"

Gregor gave her a long look, and she knew he didn't buy her contrived innocence. His gaze flicked to her hair and hardened.

He dropped his hands and stepped back, his jaw clenched. "Lady Nadia de Quinones, you are charged with the abduction of Prince Reis, bastard to his divine eminence, Dieuroi Mavros of Thuno. You will be taken into royal custody until such time as his royal highness has heard all evidence and is ready to declare your sentence."

She lifted a brow and crossed her arms. "What proof could you possibly have on which to base such allegations?"

Gregor's pale eyes met hers, lit with a blaze of fury, startling her into taking a step back. "The fact that you'd ask for proof rather than deny any involvement tells me everything," he said, clasping his hands behind his back. "Check her carefully for weapons. She's been well-trained in combat, and is much more dangerous than she looks."

She kept her gaze locked on Gregor's as guards surrounded her. With each weapon the guards took from her and piled on the floor, her dread grew. With her hair down and liberated of all weapons, she felt exposed. Her arms were pulled roughly behind her back and iron manacles placed snugly around each wrist.

"We're ready, m'lord."

"Take her to the Questioner's dungeon. Prince Stefan wants the location of his brother tonight," he said, his voice flat.

"And these two?" The guard gestured to Jon and Sarna.

"Let them go," he muttered. "She is the only one charged."

She glanced at Sarna, then shoved the part of the weapons pile with wrist sheath and hidden keys toward the other woman with her foot. "You and Pell share leadership."

She gave Jon an imploring look. "If anything happens to me, take Geeta back to Diomere."

Jon nodded, understanding that she spoke also of their prince.

As she gave orders, Gregor kept his unblinking stare on her. When she was finished, he ducked out the door, glancing back for only an instant. But it was enough.

In his eyes she saw hurt mixed with anger. And even though she'd known he'd see what she did as a betrayal, a part of her was disappointed that he thought she'd ever hurt a child.

As the guards dragged her away, she shoved the feelings down deep. She'd sacrifice her own happiness a million times over if it meant her sister's child was safe.

CHAPTER THIRTY-FIVE

N adia shifted on the cold stone floor, wincing as the manacles on her ankles rubbed the raw skin underneath. Focusing on her a'mi, she created a cushion of air between her skin and the metal. The guard outside the wooden door of her cell looked in at her.

Ignoring him, she blew her hair out of her face. She'd been locked in this cell for hours listening to the moans and rattling chains of other prisoners echoing down the stone hall that led away from her door.

She was bored. A shudder moved through her body. And cold. Pulling at the rough sack they'd forced over her head after stripping her of her own clothing, she glared down at her bare, exposed legs. The sorry excuse for clothing provided no comfort against the cold stones at her backside. Nor did it stop her skin from pebbling into a solid mass of gooseflesh.

She shivered again and hugged herself tighter.

With nothing to occupy her time, she kept seeing the hurt and anger in Gregor's eyes replay over and over in her mind. She reassured herself that she'd done the right thing. That Gregor would agree if he knew everything she did. *Tell him everything,* her internal voice insisted.

She shook her head.

The stomp of boots sounded down the hall. They moved closer then stopped outside her door. The guards muttered to each other, too low for her to hear, then the old guard left, and a new guard looked through the door's opening, and winked at her.

"Gordon?" Nadia smiled and studied the face which looked a good ten years younger without the wild growth of gray sprinkled beard covering his face.

"Geeta sent this," said the old guild man's familiar voice as he pushed a small glass vial through the bars.

She clasped his hand through the bars. "You look so handsome all cleaned up and dressed in the king's uniform. I almost didn't recognize you."

Gordon blushed. "That's the point, Lady Shark. Here, we haven't much time. Prince Stefan will be here shortly." He handed her quill, ink, and a small strip of paper.

Nadia nodded and peeled back the vial's wax seal. She smoothed open the strip of paper and read Geeta's neat script.

The little fish swims. What do I say about your prolonged absence? The Teniente has disappeared.

Her heart sank at the last part. She picked up the quill and quickly wrote a reply.

Tell the little fish the truth and the importance of making it safely to true kin. The taciturn woman is in charge.

She placed both scraps of paper back into the vial and replaced the seal, mashing the wax down the best she could. She slipped them back through the bars into Gordon's waiting hands.

The older man took the vial, quill, and ink and stuffed them into his tunic pockets. "You sure know how to get yourself into a right pickle, don't ya lass?" Gordon said, a smile softening his wry comment. "Sarna said there'll be a carriage waiting when you decide to get yourself out of here. She asked that you not hang around so long they actually succeed in offing you."

Nadia smiled, thankful for her friends. "Escaping is a last resort. If I disappear, it'll confirm my guilt. I can't do that to Gregor."

The older man's gaze softened. "If you don't eventually tell him the truth, someone else will do it for you, and then he'll believe you didn't consider him worth the truth. Some hurts are much harder to get over than others."

"I put him in an impossible position if I tell him," she said. "It would be selfish."

The older man reached through the bars and squeezed her hand. "You're taking the choice from him. Either you trust him or you don't. To see it any other way is selfish."

Voices echoed down the stairs and Gordon, with a final squeeze of her hand, moved away from the door. He'd no more than returned to his post when a group of soldiers in Prince Stefan's colors appeared at the other end of the hall.

Nadia jerked away from the door and quickly smoothed her hair neatly behind her ears. As the group got closer, she stood to her full height.

Keys rattled in the door's lock, then it was pulled open. Two guards marched in. They shoved her against the wall and patted her down for weapons. She clenched her jaw, as her cheek scraped roughly against cold stone.

Her a'mi stirred, reaching behind her as more booted feet entered her cell. And she knew he was there. The two guards, satisfied that she hadn't managed to magically pull a weapon from the air, roughly yanked her around. Prince Stefan, flanked by a blank faced Gregor and three more of his personal guard, studied her with a cold expression.

Nadia had eyes only for Gregor. A muscle pulsed in his cheek, but his expression remained bland. Nadia wanted to get him alone, and force him to tell her what he'd been told so she could explain... *Explain what? That you lied to him. Pretty sure he's figured that out.*

"You dared to enter my home and eat at my table, while all the time plotting against my family for something we had no part in? I must admit, Lady de Quinones, I wasn't expecting such a plot from Diomere," Prince Stefan said. "Especially from members of the very family to which I'm betrothed."

Nadia jerked her attention away from Gregor as the crown prince's words sank in. "Plot from Diomere? What are you talking about?"

Prince Stefan studied her face. "Tell me where my brother is" —his eyes darkened— "and he'd better be alive and unharmed, and I'll simply banish you from our shores rather than take your life."

"I didn't take your brother," she said, raising her chin as she finished the statement silently. *Areisteo is my nephew, not your brother.* And she wouldn't give him up just to save her own skin.

Prince Stefan turned to Gregor. "I'll leave her in your capable hands, Lord Cyrene. You've full use of the King's Questioner if that's what it takes. I want my brother safe in the palace by first light."

Gregor bowed as the prince and his guard filed out of the cell, and made their way out of the dungeon, leaving her alone with the man she loved. Once alone, Gregor turned and studied her in silence.

She met his gaze and smirked. "Did I not hear that Prince Reis was nearly killed not too long ago while safe in your palace? And now he's been abducted from right beneath your nose?"

Gregor lunged forward, pushing her against the wall, and wrapping his hand in a loose grip around her neck. "You, no doubt, had something to do with both." He ran a finger along the edge of her face. "So dangerously beautiful. We could have had something special, you and I. I know you felt it. I hope your attempt at revenge was worth it. Because it cost us both something much more precious."

"Revenge?" she asked, brows lowered in confusion. "Aside from making you pay for daring to treat me like this, I have no idea what you're going on about."

He lowered his head, his gaze drilling into hers. "Have you no honor? Do you realize what the royal Questioner is capable of? Even now, I would see you spared such treatment. Tell us where Reis is being held, Nadia."

She implored him to understand. "Your mad king wants him dead. You can't protect him, Gregor."

"You're one of the Dieuroi's assassins, aren't you?"

Nadia jerked her head back as if he'd slapped her, her heart sinking that he believed her so vile. "I would never harm a child."

Gregor's eyes narrowed on her. "Not even for revenge?"

"You really think me capable of killing a child for something so petty as revenge, Lord Cyrene?" Nadia snapped, anger heating her face. "What have I ever done to make you believe I would do such a thing? What revenge would warrant such an action?"

"For your nephew's murder," Gregor roared. "For the death of the child you've been trying to find for twelve years. The death you believe Thuno's royal family is responsible for."

She jerked back, having never heard him raise his voice before, and realized Gordon was right. She had to tell him the truth.

"He isn't dead." She sighed. "He's safe."

"If he's safe, then why did you kidnap Prince" — Gregor's jaw dropped— "you think Reis is your nephew," he whispered.

She looked away.

Gregor grabbed her shoulders and shook her once. "Do your delusions know no bounds? Dieuroi Mavros wouldn't have accepted the child as his if he hadn't been sure." He lowered his voice. "Your nephew is gone. When will you stop punishing yourself for something that was out of your control? It's time to move on and live your own life, Nadia. Does the idea of happiness scare you so much?"

A knot of disappointment filled her stomach. He didn't believe her. "Reis is my nephew. I know you were told about what happened when he changed, what he changed into. He is different like me. Surely, you've figured out that our dreams weren't just simple dreams."

Gregor jerked back as if burned. He opened his mouth then closed it, shaking his head. Without another word, he turned on his heel, and walked out of the cell without a backward glance.

Her mind raced. "Gregor," she called. He paused, but didn't look back. She clenched her fists at her side. "I want to call in the favor you owe me."

He stiffened. "I told you I wouldn't betray my prince."

"I'm not asking you to."

He finally looked back over his shoulder. Nadia crushed the spark of hope in her heart.

"For my favor, I ask that you think. Think about the dreams, all of our encounters, what my sister told you. Everything. You're right, we're connected. Use that connection and see that everything I did, I did for good reason. Trust your instincts," she implored him.

He studied her, his face carefully devoid of all emotion, then turned and addressed Gordon. "No one is to speak with the prisoner until I get back."

She rushed to the door and watched through the small barred window as his long strides took him farther from her. Did he go seek whether she could be telling the truth? She willed him to believe her.

At the stairs leading out of the dungeon, Gregor paused and looked back, his lips pressed into a thin line, his gaze inscrutable. He turned and ascended the stairs out of the dungeon without a word.

Pain, a freshly sharpened blade, punched deep into her heart. She slumped against the door. Gordon patted her fingers where they wrapped around the bars, but remained silent.

After only a short time, boots clattered on the stairs, and Nadia jerked her head up. She exhaled as three robed figures descended the stairs, fear a hard knot in her stomach. Were they here to collar her again?

She reached for her power.

The cowled men, dressed all in black, made their way down the damp corridor toward her cell. Each wore a heavy gold ring with a red carnelian stone. A shiver crept down Nadia's back. She knew the stone would be carved with the goddess, Asha's hands holding the tree of life, its roots spread deep into holy soil. These men were from Thuno's royal order of Questioners.

She backed away from the door. Reis' watery vision flashed in her mind. The cold stones of the wall brushing her back startled her from the tight hold of fear. She squared her shoulders, and stood to her full height. She would not cower. It was past time to make her escape.

Gordon stepped forward. "Lord Cyrene ordered no one save himself is to speak with the prisoner."

"Prince Stefan has ordered she be put to the Question. Let us in, then go. You're dismissed."

Gordon hesitated only a second, then turned to unlock the door, an apologetic look on his face.

The cowled men walked in.

She clenched her fists. Gregor hadn't believed her.

Inhaling past the crippling pain, she forced herself to focus on her a'mi. She called the symbol for earth as the Questioners surrounded her.

The ground had begun to tremble when the Questioner in front of her lowered his hood, revealing familiar dark blue eyes and blond hair.

She released the hold on her a'mi. "Pell! I knew you wouldn't desert me. Thank the gods. Let's get out of here."

He walked toward her in silence, but instead of reaching up to free her hands, he slid a slave collar around her neck. She shoved her power at the latch, managing to keep it from locking and separating her from her power.

Pell stepped back, blue eyes icy, and stared at her in silence.

"Pell?" she asked, her heart in her stomach.

He smiled, but it didn't soften his gaze. "I've been looking forward to this day since I volunteered for this never-ending mission," he said in a soft voice.

Her eyes began to burn. Betrayed. Again. She clenched her jaw against the sharp stab of the shattered pieces of her heart as she remembered Jasara's words the night the woman abducted her nephew.

"Remember this, dear cousin, even the weakest can overtake the strongest if they are cunning. Beware treachery from those you don't consider a threat."

"I can see you finally understand. Don't take it personal. My family has aspirations for advancement. Unfortunately, your vow to return your nephew to Diomere threatens that."

He lifted his hand and smoothed his thumb over her lower lip. "I'll admit I entertained the idea of sparing your life. We had such a good partnership; I just knew it would translate over into the bed chamber.

Alas, you really shouldn't have chosen your precious Lord Cyrene over me."

Nadia sneered. "It wasn't a difficult choice."

He backhanded her and her neck whipped sideways as fire bloomed along the side of her face. Blood trickled from the corner of her mouth.

She pulled her head back around and saw Gordon peeking through the bars of the door and glaring at the man they'd considered one of theirs. She reached for her a'mi, and the five symbols popped into her mind's eye.

"A choice you'll soon regret," Pell promised, bringing her attention back to him. "But first, I need your help accessing our dear prince's hiding place. Then I'm going to make sure neither of you are ever seen again."

Nadia cursed her decision to trust him with the discovery of the gate cave. "I won't let you hurt him." She focused on the symbol for earth, and punched her a'mi into the ground just as something hard connected with her temple.

As she lost her hold on her a'mi, Pell's voice echoed through the blackness closing over her head. "There's nothing you can do to stop me."

CHAPTER THIRTY-SIX

G regor walked into Stefan's receiving chamber and crossed to the sideboard to fix a drink. He'd spent the last half hour walking the gardens thinking about Nadia's claims. When it was clear that he was getting nowhere, he'd decided to come discuss it with Stefan, praying his closest friend would see things more clearly than he did.

He took a long pull from his glass then turned to face the prince. "I need you to listen impartially."

Brow lowering, Stefan sat aside the report and sat back. "Go ahead."

She has hidden Reis," he muttered. "However, if what she says is true then he's probably safer where she's stashed him than he would be here with us."

"Asha's tits, so we're doing this," Stefan said, then scrubbed his hands through his hair. "Fine, I'll humor you for a conversation but then you let me decide, you give me that trust."

Nodding, Gregor met his closest friend's grim gaze. "I've been dreaming of her. Strange dreams located on an island far out in the Saimond Sea." Stefan raised his brows, and Gregor continued. "The dreams start with us floating in the water, scaled fish tails where our legs should be. Then we swim to shore and our fins become legs."

"You've always had a special interest in the Mer," Stefan said.

"You're the only person I've ever told about those dreams," Gregor said, then drained his glass and set it aside. "Yet she knew about them."

"What are you saying?"

"I told you she's here looking for her nephew," he said, and Stefan nodded. "Well, she believes your brother is that child, the lost heir of Diomere. She knew about the incident during your fishing trip. Says Reis is like her."

Stefan, a frown pulling down the corners of his mouth, stood and began to pace. "So she risked my wrath and just abducted him? Why not come to me or you?"

"She claims he went willingly," Gregor said, flashes of conversation he'd had with Nadia, Arri, and Reis spilling across his memory. "They believe they're protecting us from something."

"War," Stefan muttered.

"Loyalty," Gregor said at the same time.

Stefan stopped pacing to stare out the large window which looked out over the palace gardens. "Reis came to me the other day. He asked about his mother and his birth. He hadn't realized that he wasn't born here."

The prince turned to face Gregor, his brow wrinkled. "Her version of things makes a weird sort of sense. I've always suspected Jasna lied about the pregnancy. And Reis looks nothing like anyone in my family." Stefan rubbed one hand along the back of his neck. "Unfortunately, my father's condition has significantly reduced his reliability for any kind of logical conversation. He's become more and more paranoid and unstable as his head pains worsen. I imagine Lady de Quinones fears that my father will try to use Reis as a political pawn, and that we'll be forced to choose between loyalty to Thuno or Diomere."

Gregor felt his stomach drop. "Then it's possible? He really could be Diomere's lost heir?" He jumped to his feet. "We need to bring Nadia in here, have her show us her proof. If she feels that we believe her and that we won't turn around and harm the boy, she'll let us see him."

Stefan nodded. "Do it."

Before Gregor could take more than a step toward the door, Stefan's steward knocked and stuck his head in. "I'm sorry, your highness, but one of the guards from the dungeons has an urgent message for Lord Cyrene."

"Show him in," Prince Stefan ordered.

The door opened wider, and the guard Gregor had left in front of Nadia's cell appeared, his face pale.

Gregor pinned the older man with a narrow-eyed gaze. "Why aren't you guarding Lady de Quinones' cell?"

"Three of Dieuroi Mavros' Questioners came and said they'd been ordered by Prince Stefan to discover where she'd taken Prince Reis. They knocked her out and dragged her from the dungeons."

Gregor swung around to face Stefan.

The prince frowned. "I didn't give any orders to anyone save you."

Gregor turned back to the guard. "What did this Questioner look like?"

"He had light colored hair," the guard said. "And she knew him. She called him Pell."

"He's the one that told me she found the body of Diomere's prince, and that she wanted revenge against my family," Stefan growled.

Gregor moved toward the door. "He came to Thuno with Nadia, and it sounds like he's playing both sides against the middle. I have to find her."

The guard stepped in front of him. "You'll want to talk to Sarna, m'lord."

"You're one of the Shark's people," Gregor said, giving the man a hard look.

The older man shrugged. "Retired guild. Lady Nadia and Geeta look in on me from time to time. Makes sure I have food." He glanced at Prince Stefan, who had his eyes closed as he pinched the bridge of his nose. "Taking a chance of being caught impersonating one of the Dieuroi's guards seemed a small thing after everything they've done for me."

Gregor nodded. "You'll take me to this Sarna."

"Yes, m'lord."

Gregor bowed to Prince Stefan. "By your leave, highness."

"Go," Stefan said. "Keep my brother and your lady safe."

Gregor waved the retired guild man ahead of him. "What's your name?"

"Gordon, m'lord."

They left the prince's suite and, after both stopped to retrieve their weapons, moved down the hall out of the prince's wing of the palace.

"Gordon, if we make it in time to keep Pell from harming Prince Reis and the Lady Nadia, I'll personally see to it that no charges are pressed against you for impersonating a royal guard."

"Appreciate it, m'lord."

They left the palace and jumped into Gregor's carriage as it was brought around. "The Emerald Mermaid, Mr. Martinos. As fast as possible."

The carriage lurched forward, throwing them back into their seats. They each braced against the walls of the conveyance as it raced out the palace gates and began the descent down the mountain into Volos.

Five minutes later, they pulled up to the Emerald Mermaid. Gregor jumped out, followed by Gordon, and pushed past the doorman.

The older man turned and led the way through the dining room, into the kitchens. Heads turned to follow them as they walked into a large storage closet. Gordon reached for an empty top shelf and pulled it down. A loud click sounded, and the whole section of shelves on the back wall pushed back. Gregor met the other man's sharp gaze.

"I recognize the way you look at the Lady Nadia. Don't make me regret trusting you," Gordon muttered gruffly.

Gregor nodded and followed the other man into a man-made tunnel lit to either side by lanterns hanging on hooks. After only a short time, the tunnel opened up into a giant cavern. Gregor stopped.

He stood in Vromia Guild's main headquarters. Lanterns hung from ropes anchored to the high ceiling by an intricate pulley system. The cave was divided into sections where guild members sat in various groups. The buzz of conversation ended as Gordon led him through the gathered men and women toward another tunnel.

The doll-like woman who'd been with Jon when he arrested Nadia stepped out of the tunnel, a frown pulling down the corners of her mouth and deep lines between her brows. "Why have you brought him here?"

Gregor stepped forward. "Sarna, I take it?" When she only nodded, he continued. "Since Nadia trusts you enough to put you in charge in her place" —he watched acknowledgment of his understanding of who exactly Nadia was cross her face— "then you must know a great deal about her and how different she really is."

The woman nodded once.

Gregor glanced at the curious attention they'd garnered from the other guild members. "Can we go someplace private to talk?"

"This way." She turned on her heel and disappeared into the smaller tunnel.

Gregor glanced at Gordon, who waved him on. "My part in this adventure is done. Go. Talk to her. If you need my assistance, I'll be out here keeping anyone from interrupting you."

Gregor nodded, and followed Sarna toward a round, wood plank door. He stepped through the door into a small cave crammed with full bookshelves. Immediately, some force surrounded him and pulled him across the cramped cave toward a chaise behind which hung a tapestry depicting two mermaids and a merman frolicking in the sea.

"She's here," he said, reaching to pull the tapestry aside. "I feel her."

Behind the tapestry, another wooden door stood ajar, leaking the sound of running water through the opening.

"Wait," Sarna called.

But the force pulling him wouldn't relent, and Gregor pushed the door open to step through into a cave pulsing with power from a glowing, stone gate. He recognized the words and symbols carved into it from the Arenatou scroll, though the creatures decorating it were different.

"Jon," Sarna whispered behind him, breaking his focus on Thuno's gate.

Looking away, he noticed water seeping under one set of firmly closed golden doors and flowing in a wide stream across the cave through a second set of gold doors that stood open, a man unconscious on the threshold. One of the gold slave collars on the ground next to him.

"Stop," Gregor said, hearing voices on the other side of the door as Sarna went to check on the fallen man who was beginning to stir.

Sarna nodded grimly, pulling a short sword from the scabbard at her hip. "We should probably go for backup."

Gregor shook his head, and reached for Jon's foot, pulling him behind the door so Sarna could kneel down and splash water on the big man's face. "I'm not leaving her in there another minute. And she obviously doesn't want word of this cave getting out."

Sarna leaned down to whisper in Jon's ear as the man's eyes fluttered open. He sat up, shaking off Sarna's helping hand and frowned at Gregor.

"I'm here to help Nadia. When you've regained your senses, grab a sword and join us," Gregor said in a low voice.

"Pell is de traitor," Jon mumbled groggily.

Gregor nodded and looked over at Sarna. "We're likely outnumbered."

"How are your fighting skills, fancy lord?" Sarna asked with a grim smile.

Gregor pulled his sword from its scabbard with a grim smile of his own and followed the growing river toward the open gold doors. "Let's find out, shall we?"

****

Nadia woke to someone's fist connecting with her stomach. Her breath rushed out of her as stars burst behind her eyelids, adding to the pain of her throbbing skull. She reached for her a'mi, the symbol for water wavering in her mind's eye. Gritting her teeth, she forced herself to focus through the pain. Finally, her strongest element answered her call, rushing toward her from a familiar underground lake.

"Wake up, Capitán. It seems you must be conscious for the doors to acknowledge your presence." The cold tone of Pell's voice brought back the last hours spent in the mad king's dungeon.

Opening her eyes, she found her hands pressed against the gate palace's golden doors. Her hold on the symbol wavered as the gold warmed under her palms. She tried yanking them back, but her pain racked body was no match for the two men in Questioner's robes who held her.

The lock clicked. Pell smiled, the collar in one hand, then pushed the doors open. She tried calling the fire symbol forward, but couldn't focus through her throbbing skull. Clenching her jaw, she focused on keeping the water symbol steady, praying it would be enough.

"Pell? Is Nadia wid you?" Jon's voice grew louder as he moved closer.

One of the Questioners yanked her head back by the hair, and pressed a dagger to her throat, which was free of the collar. *They had to remove it so you could access your a'mi to open the doors. Fools should have immediately put it back in place.*

The stockier questioner pulled a short sword and moved to the other side of the door. Water began to seep into the room from beneath the other set of golden doors behind her. Nadia could feel it reaching for her. Inhaling deeply, she directed it to flow silently toward the feet of the Questioner waiting to kill Jon.

Pell turned to face Jon, stepping so that the other man wouldn't see Nadia. "I couldn't very well have opened the doors without her," he said, voice heavy with sarcasm.

Jon's shadow, cast by a nearby lightbox, moved into her line of sight. She focused on the water, using her a'mi to slide it between the Questioner's soft bottomed shoe and the cave's stone floor.

Pulling back his sword, the Questioner tensed to jab it through Jon, but Nadia shoved her a'mi toward the water, thickening the layer under his feet so that he lost his balance. The Questioner's feet slipped from under him, and he landed on his back, pushing the door open so that Jon could see Nadia standing with the dagger at her throat.

Her friend froze in surprise beside Pell, giving the traitor a chance to knock him upside the temple with the hilt of the dagger he'd pulled from the long sleeve of his robe. Jon's eyes rolled up into his head, and the big man collapsed.

The fallen Questioner scrambled to his feet, his robe heavy with water, a scowl on the bony face no longer covered by the hood. The Questioner behind her snorted, his dagger inadvertently cutting deeper into her throat. Nadia ignored the blood she could feel dripping down her neck and called the water again, urging more of it to absorb into the wet fabric of the soaked Questioner's robe.

Pell sneered, but eyed the water. He glanced at her then at the Questioner holding her. "If she goes still or closes her eyes, knock her out, Consul. We can't replace the collar until we get through both sets of doors."

The hand in her hair tightened. "Yes, Director."

Pell stepped over him into the palace's entrance hall. "Let's go find our dear prince, shall we?"

"The attempts on Reis' life began before we figured out he was my nephew. You accepted the job behind my back."

Pell tilted his head back and laughed, his eyes finding hers, their manic glow chilling. "The mad king is such an easy scapegoat. I joined his Questioners almost as soon as we arrived. It wasn't hard to work my way up. After all, I grew up learning the most effective torture techniques."

"Once I became a director, it was simple to issue orders in the Dieu-roi's name," Pell boasted. "When you shared with me what Jon said happened with Prince Reis in that water, I looked into his background and suspected he was our long-lost prince. So I decided to take care of it."

His face darkened. "I didn't factor in Prince Stefan's devotion to his brother. But no matter, it ends today. Our prince shall finally die as he should have twelve years ago."

"You won't get away with this," she swore.

The Questioner holding her yanked her head back and slammed the handle of his dagger against her ear. "Shut up, bitch."

The sharp pain made her head ring, but somehow she retained a tenuous grip on her a'mi as tears streamed down her face. She squeezed her eyes closed, and the Questioner shook her by her hair.

"Keep them open or I'll do it again."

Her eyes popped open, her fingernails stabbing into her palms hard enough to draw blood, even as she steadied the wavering symbol in her mind's eye.

Pell smiled and turned to continue into the palace.

Pell's companion dragged her toward the closed doors of the gate palace's great hall, and she couldn't stop a small yelp from sliding out of her throat.

She bent her knees to ease the pressure against her throat. Her a'mi swirled inside her as she pulled it from deep inside, gathering it until the water symbol glowed.

Pell strode to the doors and yanked on the gold handles. When they didn't open, he stepped back and gestured toward the Questioner she'd felled with the water. "Open them."

Nadia channeled the pulsing a'mi into the water weighing down the man's robe. The liquid surged up the robe, as if alive with its own conscience, to flow up over the man's face and into his mouth and nose, filling his lungs. He coughed, then choked, his hands clawing at his throat, as she drowned him.

The Questioner holding her gasped, the press of the knife easing more as he watched his comrade drown.

Nadia clenched her jaw, and focused all of her will on holding the water symbol in her mind's eye. She wrapped her fingers around the wrist holding the knife and threw her head back, connecting with the man's nose. While her mind became one never-ending throb of pain, her body moved on instinct, twisting the man's wrist until it gave an audible pop, so that he released her hair with a scream of pain. She spun out of the stunned Questioner's arms, pulling water into a wide river around her feet.

She met Pell's narrow gaze and smiled.

***

Gregor eased his head around the door's edge and caught his breath. Nadia, hair sticking out around her head and blood dripping down her neck, stood surrounded by a wide river of fast-moving water while her eyes glowed with power. Pell and a bloody-faced man in the black robes of a royal Questioner faced her, their backs to Gregor. Another Questioner was sprawled out on the ground, his face stretched into an open-mouthed mask of death.

Gregor stepped into the palace's entrance hall, Sarna right behind him, and whispered, "She's magnificent."

Sarna's eyes widened as she whispered back. "Terrifying, more like."

Beautifully terrifying, Gregor thought as he eased forward slowly, not wanting to alert Pell and his bleeding companion of their presence. He knew the instant Nadia became aware of their presence, though she didn't betray them by word or gesture.

Her shoulders straightened and she focused on Pell. "You really thought you stood a chance against an A'mi?"

"But don't I? Even now, your injuries make calling your a'mi difficult. Isn't this why you've only managed to call water? It must be your strongest element. You can't focus enough to pull the other symbols forward can you?"

"How is it that you know so much?" she spit.

"It's amazing what you can learn from those A'mi with enough Sa'i blood to make them too weak to fight us," Pell said with smirk. "Poor Jasara would've done anything to free her daughter. Too bad her conscience wouldn't allow her to actually turn the prince over to us. The girl's screams for her mommy were so sweet."

At that moment, a robed figure pushed between Gregor and Sarna. "Stick your fingers in your ears now," a low female voice commanded, making both humans shudder as her power rolled over them, their hands releasing their swords and their arms jerking up to obey without either of their consent.

Their swords clattered to the ground, making Pell and his companions whirl around to face the robed woman.

Nadia narrowed her gaze on the woman, nodded, then pulled her hands up to cover her ears.

"And you'll pay a hundredfold for each of her screams," the woman called. Then she let out a screech so high pitched that it made Gregor, Nadia, and Sarna flinch.

Pell and his companions cried out and jerked their hands up to cover their ears, but it was too little too late. Blood dripped from busted eardrums. The one next to Pell swayed on his feet, his face screwed up into a mask of intense pain.

Pell sneered and lowered his arms to wipe his bloody palms on his robes. "Well that took care of that problem," he said in a raised voice.

Then without missing a beat, he shoved the companion closest to him onto Nadia's river of water and jumped onto the flailing man's chest.

The robed woman called for him to stop, but he only hesitated a moment before shaking off her command, the damage to his ears too great for much of her power to get through.

He jumped toward Nadia, and the two hit the ground in a tangled heap, Nadia's head bouncing off the hard ground. The river flowing around her stopped and spread out over the stone floor as she lost control of her a'mi.

His other companion rolled to his side, heaving water from his nose and mouth.

"No!" Gregor fought the power holding him. "Let me go."

The woman glanced over her shoulder, and he felt the power release him. He scooped his sword from the ground and rushed toward them.

Pell sat up, straddling Nadia, his dagger at her throat. "Stop." Pell glanced up at Gregor. "Doomed, I may be, but I'll take as many of you with me as I can before I die."

Suddenly, the water surrounding them surged upward, swirling around Nadia and Pell, tearing them apart. It rose into a whirling funnel, Pell and the Questioner trapped in its center, while Nadia's body flew toward Gregor, who landed on his back with her on top of him. Jon and Sarna pulled her off him as he struggled to catch his breath.

"I can't hold him much longer," Reis called, pulling Gregor's attention back to the funnel of water, and Prince Reis, who stood before the open great hall doors.

His gaze focused on the funnel, Prince Reis held his hand outstretched.

Nadia scrambled to her feet and made her unsteady way over to the pale faced Prince. "Gregor, when I release him, make sure he can't harm anyone else," she ordered.

Gregor stood and met her glossy-eyed gaze, then nodded.

Inhaling, she placed a hand on the prince's shoulder and closed her eyes. "I've got him."

Geeta appeared behind the prince and pressed her hand to Nadia's head. "And I have you."

Reis sagged. Gregor moved around behind the water funnel. The water stopped swirling and plunged to the ground, dropping a barely conscious Pell and his dead companion onto the hard surface.

Gregor reached down and hauled a coughing Pell up by the soaked robe hanging off one shoulder, baring the other man's back. Short sword pressed into the other man's bare skin, he noticed a pentagon shaped tattoo which had the letters VK inside it.

"Try anything and I won't hesitate to run you through," he promised the still gasping man.

"You have some explaining to do," he told the woman he recognized as his king's one time mistress. "Why are you even here?"

Jasna glanced at Nadia and then back to Gregor. "Her and her sisters are the key to getting my daughter back," the woman said, her gaze narrowing on Pell. "A vision told me I needed to come here."

Gregor met Jasna's tired green eyes. "If what he said is true, I can understand why you've done as you have. However, kidnapping the heir to one country and lying to the monarch of another is not something that I can allow to go unpunished if I find you here when I return.

Jasna nodded. "I've fulfilled my role here."

Nadia, attention focused on Pell's exposed tattoo, crossed to stand over the traitor. "Where did you get that tattoo?"

Pell glared up at her. "You already know the answer to that, Infanta."

Nadia clenched her jaw and looked away.

Gregor pulled Pell to stand, pushing the sword's blade harder into his back, causing Pell to flinch. "I've got to deliver this scum to the Dieuroi's dungeon."

Gregor met Nadia's tired gaze. "You're free to go as well, but I hope you'll be here when I'm finished." He looked around at the underground palace then back to her dark gaze. "You and I have much to discuss, starting with those dreams."

She gave him a wan smile. "I'll be here. Jon can show you a quicker way to the palace."

CHAPTER THIRTY-SEVEN

N adia pushed Geeta's hands away. "Don't. You took the worst of the pain away already."

"It's my job," Geeta insisted, lifting her hands toward Nadia's still aching head.

She met the other woman's tired gaze. "Stop, Geeta. How do you think I'll feel if I let you heal me, and you fall over dead as a result?"

Geeta sighed. "I just hate when I know you hurt, and I can help."

She reached over and squeezed her best friend's hand, then relaxed her head back against the pillows they'd scavenged from her chambers. After Gregor and Jon had left with Pell, they'd sent the water back to the underground lake, grabbed dry clothes from her chamber, dragged pillows and blankets into the gate cave, then collapsed in the nest they'd made at the base of the gate to recharge on the a'mi emanating from it.

She looked over at her sleeping nephew, sprawled across the gate cave's two wooden chairs in borrowed clothes about two sizes too big, his ass pressed up against the chair's back, his long legs hanging over either arm of that chair, his back stretching across to the other where his head and shoulders rested on the second cushioned seat.

"I'm still finding it hard to believe we've found him," she whispered to Geeta.

"Soon he'll be in Diomere where he belongs, thank the gods." The older woman looked at Nadia. "But will he be returning alone?"

Nadia closed her eyes, so afraid to hope despite Gregor's words before he'd left. A knock sounded from the round door of her chamber.

Reis sat up, face weary, as Geeta went to answer it.

Nadia's a'mi stirred as soon as Geeta opened the door, telling her exactly who was on the other side. She sat up slowly as Gregor stepped through the door, his gaze scanning her from her ratty hair down to her bare toes.

"You're well?"

She nodded, unable to look away, the a'mi pulsing off the gate seeming to grow stronger with his presence. "A few more moments here and I'll be good as new."

He looked up, studied the gate curiously, then focused back on her. "Good."

"Now that the threat to our Prince has been dealt with, I think it'll be safe for me to take him to my home for a good meal and sleep in a real bed," Geeta said, biting back a smile.

Nadia nodded, barely sparing a glance for the nephew she'd spent so much of her life hunting. The door closed with a soft click, and they were alone. Nadia curled her legs under her to stand.

"Don't."

She raised a brow, irritation pushing aside some of her uncertainty. She stood and realized her head no longer ached.

Gregor sighed. "You're going to make things difficult for the rest of our lives, aren't you?"

"Be careful what you wish for," she said, biting her lip.

Gregor crossed the cave to stand in front of her and took her hands. "I'm sorry I doubted you."

"I made it hard for you to do otherwise," she said. When he shook his head, and opened his mouth to protest, she lifted a hand to his cheek. "But if you need it, then I forgive you."

He released a breath. Hope swelled in her chest, and it was her turn to hold her breath.

He rested his forehead against hers. "The dreams were real. What we did. The secrets we shared." She nodded and he wrapped his arms around her. "I love you, Nadia de Quinones. Please tell me you feel the same."

Nadia closed her eyes and inhaled, trying to ease the pressure in her chest, knowing she had to tell him what loving her would really mean. "Before this goes any further, I need to tell you about heartbonding an A'mi."

She tried to pull away, but he tightened his arms. "No. Tell me what you think I need to know, but don't pull away."

She stiffened, saw the stubborn set of his chin, and huffed out a breath. "Fine, but we're going to discuss your highhanded tendencies in the very near future, Gregor."

She ignored his answering smile and settled into his arms.

"A heartbond is when one's a'mi recognizes its other half," she said. "They search out each other, first, in dreams. It's something coveted by most A'mi. You humans would call it true love. But it's more than that. A heartbonded couple are connected at the most basic level. The bond strengthens them both, but it also has two great weaknesses. If one dies, so too will the other follow."

Gregor frowned. "Even if one isn't A'mi?"

"Yes. If we complete the bond, my a'mi will fill us both. You'll become A'mi, manifesting your own abilities which I'll be able to access, as you'll be able to access mine."

His eyes widened. "And the other weakness?"

"Our connection to Mondami is what keeps those of us with a'mi alive. Without it, we enter a'mi starvation. Geeta, Jon, and I have been without that connection for years. Geeta is very close to succumbing, only the small amount of a'mi trickling through this gate is keeping her alive."

His arms tightened around her. "You have this access in Diomere?" he asked.

"The remaining active gate is located there."

He lifted his head to study the gate behind her. "Unless we figure out how to activate this gate, giving other, more dangerous, A'mi the chance to come through and possibly endanger the people of Thuno."

Nadia's heart clenched. She'd somehow found a man worth her trust. One who cared for the wellbeing of those around him. The last of her doubts faded. She shuddered as the last part of herself, which she'd held back, opened to him.

She forced herself to breathe past her suddenly pounding heart. "I love you, Gregor Cyrene."

A smile stretched across his face. She lifted her mouth to meet his in a kiss which sent desire shooting through her body.

He pulled back. "You won't regret it." He kissed her again before pulling her in tighter against his body.

The gate pulsed behind her, and she addressed his worry. "You love me, yet I'm A'mi. I think we can agree that good and bad exist everywhere. If it looks as though things will be the way they were before, the Gate Keepers will close the gate."

His smile faded. "How can we be sure the Gate Keeper will close it on our say?"

Following instinct, she threaded her fingers through his, and raised their clasped hands, pressing them against the gate's softly glowing pillar. A strong wind blew their hair back from their faces smelling of the dampness of fallen leaves, yet fresh and alive like green growing things.

The gate's voice filled their minds. *The Sankta Hogo-sha must take their places. Complete the key. Complete the bond.*

With each word it spoke she was filled with a surge of power so intense that, like a bolt of lightning in their blood, it bowed both their backs. Knowledge filled them both, their lives stretching before them.

Now he fully understood the heartbond, what he would gain, what he would lose.

When the gate released them, they fell to their knees on the pillows breathing hard.

He turned his head, his pale amber eyes glowing with an inner fire. "We're to be the Gate Keepers in Thuno."

She frowned. "Yes, but I'm unsure how we bond ourselves to the gate so we can control it."

Gregor pointed to the symbols carved into the gate. "Those are the symbols for the five elements."

Nadia jerked her gaze from the gate to Gregor. "You know of the five elements of a'mi?"

He met her gaze, a pink tinge coloring his cheeks. "My brother and I used to spy on Asha's priests when we were kids. One night, I saw them burning scrolls and books in some dark ceremony. I was appalled."

Glancing away, his cheeks heating, he swallowed, then admitted in a quiet voice, "My love of reading was second only to my love of pretending to go on A'mi adventures with my brother."

She grinned, imagining a young Gregor pretending to use a'mi.

Gregor just shook his head and continued, "After the priests left, I saved as many of the texts from the fire as I could. One of them, a scroll in a glass tube that hadn't broken when the priests threw it on the fire, contained a translated copy rolled inside the original. It was a story about a human king and the beautiful Mer princess who saved him from drowning. I used it and its translation to teach myself the A'mi language."

Nadia's brows climbed her forehead. "That's some hobby, Gregor."

He smiled wryly. "More like an obsession." He looked back up at the gate. "A scroll I recently acquired is about the Arenatou Gate. It tells of the five Gate Keepers, who each belong to an element. The Gate Keeper that belongs to Arenatou controls Air."

"My strongest element is Water," Nadia said and reached to trace the inverted triangle that represented her strongest element.

Gregor lifted his hand to hover behind hers. "For the Arenatou Gate, the scroll said Air must touch Air together." He glanced at her. "Do you think for Thuno's Gate Water must touch Water together?"

Nadia pulled her hand from the symbol as words bubbled up and out of her. "Do you accept my heartbond? As Keepers, we'll live a very long time. We'll watch friend and family die. We'll control the flow of peoples between Saimond and Mondami. Do you accept the gate's burden with me?"

He laced his fingers through hers, joining their hands.

"Forever," he swore.

This time when their lips met, her a'mi arrowed into him, tying them together in an unbreakable bond.

Before they could catch their breath, her a'mi urged her to lift their joined hands to the gate, over the symbol for water. Bright light burst from the columns, enveloping them in warmth. A thick cord of light shot from the gate, split in two, and attached to each of them, then split again to meet back up between them, creating a complete circuit.

The golden cord faded from sight, but she could still feel it there, connecting them on the most basic of levels.

I can't believe this is all real. I'm heartbonded to an A'mi, one of the mysterious Mer. She's so beautiful. I want to reach over and push that robe off her shoulders, to run my hands over her smooth as silk skin. To taste her.

Nadia blushed as Gregor's thoughts sounded clearly in her mind. She imagined his hands on her naked flesh and shivered. Nadia. His voice deepened, making her melt, as he too caught her thoughts.

Gregor turned and pulled her by their joined hands until they knelt on one of the pillows thigh to thigh, stomach to stomach, chest to chest. He reached up with his free hand and pulled the belt to her robe. It unraveled and he pushed it off her shoulders.

He shook his head once when she reached for his clothing. "I want to look."

Breasts swollen, pulse throbbing between her legs, Nadia gave Gregor what he wanted. His eyes shimmered more gold than brown as they lingered on her lips, her throat, the furled buds of her nipples, the glistening curls hiding her sex.

Biting back a moan, she watched his finger trace the path his eyes had just taken, until they fluttered over the pulse of desire.

"Gregor."

His gaze flicked to hers, then back down, a sensuous smile pulling up the corners of his mouth. He leaned forward and kissed her, his tongue stroking deep into her mouth as his fingers repeated the slow, teasing path over her other breast. Pulling back, his hands each moved to shape a breast, then without warning, he lowered his head and sucked one sensitive nipple into his mouth.

Her hands fisted in his hair as her back bowed, giving him even better access. He switched breasts and her body rocked into his, unable to remain still as the waves of pleasure washed over her.

Nadia felt her desire dripping down her thighs, sure she'd never been so wet.

He raised his head, his nostrils flaring, and she knew he could smell the heavy musk of her desire that surrounded them like a cloud.

Releasing his hand, she pushed his jacket off his shoulders and reached for the hem of his shirt. He lifted his arms. She pulled the shirt over his head and tossed it aside.

Gregor smoothed her hair behind her shoulders and let his smoldering gaze roam over her nakedness. "You're so beautiful." He ran the back of his hand over her stomach, between her breasts, and around to the back of her neck. "So soft. I want to taste every inch of your skin, leave my mark so you know who you belong to."

Breath catching, she laid her hand on his thigh and smoothed it up to his groin. She cupped him through his pants, making him jerk, then gently squeezed. "So long as you remember who it is you'll belong to. I will cut the fingers off any who dare lay a hand on what's mine, and gouge the eyes from any who dare stare too long."

Gregor laughed out loud then yanked on her neck, making her fall with him onto the pillows scattered around them.

Their mouths fused, tongues dueling in a battle as old as the gods. He kissed the corner of her mouth, her jaw, and her neck. He nipped her neck and returned to her mouth. She kissed him back, hot and wild, sending another wave of sensual heat through her blood. She was lost to him, rubbing and arching against him in wild abandon.

A groan burst from him, vibrating through her, sparking sensitive nerve endings until her moan joined his. He caressed down the curve of her waist, over the crease of her leg.

Nadia shivered and bit him gently on the neck. He groaned again. Ravenous, she kissed her way up his throat, along his jaw, to his mouth. His hand slipped between her thighs and cupped her sex. She moaned, sensation flooding every nerve ending in her body until it throbbed between her legs.

His finger entered her and she saw stars. Her back arched. Another finger joined the first and Nadia was sure her body was going to come apart. She ran her hand over the bulge at the front of his pants, feeling the heat emanating through the fabric.

She pulled at his waistband. "Need these off. Now."

He chuckled and flicked the swollen pearl of flesh between her legs, stealing the breath from her lungs. As pressure built low in her stomach, her hands found their way to his hair. He flicked her clit again. Her hands spasmed, clenching his hair in her fists as flames began to lick at her from inside. He curled the fingers inside her, stroking a spot that sent the flames higher.

She was a mindless mass of writhing flesh, an instrument he played to perfection. He stroked that spot again, the heel of his hand pressing against her clit. The pressure built until she wasn't sure if she wanted to pull away or press forward. He ground his hand on the little sensitive nub while vigorously stroking that spot inside until the pressure and flames erupted into a volcano of sensation that had her crying out his name.

She collapsed back on the pillows, spent.

Gregor pulled his hand from between her thighs and rolled away long enough to rid himself of his pants. He moved between her legs, his mouth lowering to one of her breasts and sucked the tight tip into his mouth. Nadia moaned as the pressure returned.

She lifted her hand and closed it around the erection brushing her hip.

He groaned. He laved her sensitive nipples. She smiled and moved her hand up and down his length, over the sensitive tip.

He lifted his head and pulled her hand from his erection. "Next time. Right now, I need to be inside you."

His words brought a fresh rush of moisture between her thighs. He nudged her legs apart, held both her hands above her head, and looked deep into her eyes as he slowly pushed inside her.

Nadia moaned at the stretching sensation, the pressure building with each inch he slid into her soaking channel until he pressed against her womb.

The love he felt for her shone from his gaze, pulsed along their bond, adding fuel to the blazing inferno inside her. A tear leaked down her cheek. This was a man who'd never do as her father had to her mother. Honor was in his blood. His brow creased in concern.

Nadia held his gaze. "I never dreamed I'd find someone like you. I love you."

He smiled and slowly eased out of her. "I've loved you since the night I kissed you in the forest behind that seedy tavern."

He covered her mouth with his and surged back into her. The pressure built as their tongues dueled and he pounded into her, his chest rubbing against her sensitive nipples with each thrust. She teetered on the edge of a cliff. Each thrust pushed her further toward the edge.

He ripped his mouth from hers. "So hot and tight. So good." His words came out in growl. "I look forward to doing this to you for the rest of our lives."

The breathless cry of her release as their bodies slid against each other only increased his pace until his every muscle stood out in sharp relief across his neck and shoulders.

He pounded into her once, twice more then with a groaned curse, threw his head back as he came in hot, thick spurts inside her. Their bond to the gate snapped fully into place with a surge of power so strong that both of them reached the peak again.

The gate's voice echoed through the bond. *It is done.*

EPILOGUE

N adia and Gregor stood behind Prince Stefan facing Diomere's royal family and Arriana on the pier. Dieuroi Mavros had woken with another of his headaches and sent his son to see the visiting monarchs off. The Siren, Diomere's royal vessel, finished its final preparations for departure after having spent a fortnight in port.

King Delmar, Queen Lareina, and Princess Madelena had arrived two days after Pell's arrest. The reunion between parents and son had been tearful and happy.

Prince Stefan and Princess Madelena delayed their official betrothal ceremony now that Prince Areisteo was found, and his close tie to Stefan solidified a friendship between the two countries. The princess would spend the next three months in Thuno getting to know Stefan with the option to return to Diomere if they both agreed they did not wish to make their betrothal official. Neither wished to marry someone they didn't know if it wasn't necessary.

Stefan turned to Reis and held out his hand. Reis grabbed it, and Stefan pulled him in for a hug. "You'll always be family and have a place here. Stay wary for those who would plot to end you before you can become king. May the gods keep you."

Reis squeezed him and stepped back. "You once told me that family is more than blood." He placed his hand over his heart. "I'll still consider you my brother even if you and Madelena don't decide to marry.

Stefan placed his hand over his heart and nodded. Prince Reis stepped back, and Stefan turned his head to a sad-faced Princess Madalena who was hugging her mother and father.

Stefan waited for her to reluctantly return to his side then nodded at the pale faced King Delmar, one king to another. "Though I am sorry for the circumstances around Reis' arrival in Thuno, I do not regret the years in which I called him brother. He is someone you can be proud to call son."

King Delmar returned the gesture of respect. "Thank you for taking such good care of him. Thuno will have Diomere's gratitude as long as I am king."

Stefan nodded and stepped back. "Godspeed to you all." With that Thuno's future king and his betrothed turned, and made their way back up the pier, the royal retinue swallowing them.

Nadia turned back to her family.

King Delmar coughed into his handkerchief, then nodded to her. "Thank you for working so tirelessly to find my son." Her king glanced around at those gathered, his lips twitching, then issued a decree for their benefit. "Know that you are welcome back to Diomere whenever you wish to return."

Inclining her head, knowing she too needed to keep up appearances, she replied, "Thank you, my king."

King Delmar nodded, then started coughing again.

Queen Lareina, after giving her husband a worried glance, and Arri stepped forward.

Lareina hugged Nadia. "Thank you from the bottom of our hearts." She stepped back and handed Nadia a sheaf of papers. "The information you requested as well as some I thought you might find useful, though I wish you were coming home."

Nadia met Gregor's loving gaze. "My home is with my heartbonded, sister."

"And there's your bond to the gate," her queen sister whispered as she stared sightlessly above their heads. "The time for the worlds to once again be open to each other is at hand. The gates call to their keepers."

Nadia met Arri's troubled gaze. If the Arenatou scroll Gregor had translated was correct, then the five sisters belonged to the gates and Arri, as the strongest of the five sisters in the Air element, would eventually end up in the desert country with her own heartbonded.

Nadia nodded, answering her sister's silent question. They'd chosen to keep this particular information between the two of them for now.

Nadia met the King's tired gaze. "There are those who would see the crown passed to a different branch of the royal family. Pell's family was promised a title." She looked at Reis. "Be wary. Your life isn't safe simply because you're finally going home."

Reis swallowed. "I'll not let my guard down."

"Such is the life of those in power." The king sighed. "I'll begin a quiet search for those who are plotting against my family."

Nadia nodded as the royal couple slowly ascended the plank to the ship, the king seeming to lean on the queen.

Nadia and Gregor exchanged a glance but remained silent.

Reis stepped forward and threw his arms around her. "Thank you, Tia Nadia. I'll miss you."

Nadia hugged him back, reminded of how young he was. "And I you. Remember what you learned while under Stefan's tutelage. Stay humble, yet strong."

She met his sapphire and emerald gaze.

"You'll be the strongest king Diomere has seen in an age," she told him. "With that strength comes responsibility. Take care of our people."

The boy nodded and turned to Gregor. "Gods keep you, Gregor. Thank you for saving my life even when I made it difficult. If either of you ever need anything, I will do everything I can to help."

Gregor smiled. "Spoken like a true royal heir. Gods keep you, my prince."

Reis nodded and made his way up onto the ship leaving Arriana standing before them, her big green eyes welling with tears.

She threw her arms around both Nadia and Gregor, her head barely reaching their shoulders. "I'm so happy you found each other. I only wish you weren't so far away from Diomere."

Nadia squeezed her back. "Are you sure you can't stay a little while?"

Arri's smile slipped and she glanced back at the ship. "King Delmar has been sick lately. Lareina only told me when I returned this last time. I've been unable to figure out what is causing it thus far. I have to go back."

Nadia gave her another squeeze. "Check for poison."

Arri nodded. "If it's poison then it's one I haven't seen before. I may have to return to the desert healers, and see if they can help. Gods willing I can figure it out before it's too late." She noticed their concerned gazes and shook her head. "But don't worry about that. I'm sure it's just some new illness I simply haven't had experience with before. Come, give me another hug. I hate saying goodbye."

"This isn't goodbye, sprite, but simply, see you later." Attempting to lighten the mood, she lightly pinched her sister's cheek. "When you return to the desert healers, be sure to stand on your toe tips as much as possible so they'll be more inclined to take you seriously. Being so cute must have its disadvantages with that stiff lot."

Her sister stepped back and slapped her arm. "Cheeky heifer."

Gregor laughed. "Gods be with you, Arri. I'll miss your refreshing frankness. Come visit us from time to time after you've taken care of your king. You'll always have a room in our home."

"Thank you," she said before turning and flitting up the gangplank.

Nadia clutched her fists, refusing to let the tears burning her eyes fall as the gangplank was hauled up and the ship sailed away from the pier.

Gregor wrapped an arm around her shoulders. "We'll see them again. I have a feeling the gods aren't done with us yet."

Keep reading for an excerpt from
Diomere's Healer, Book 2 of The Gate Keeper Chronicles

THE GATE KEEPER CHRONICLES

BOOK 2

Arriana's Story

Come back, handsome. I can't let you slip across the veil just yet.

Treves spun on his heel, searching for the female belonging to the musical voice. "Did you hear that?"

"She calls you back."

Treves met his sire's sad gaze. "She?"

"The One, my son."

Your boy called you Trev. Is that your name? It must be short for something. Trevor, perhaps? Hmmmm.

The woman laughed, a sound like a waterfall of soft musical notes that stirred something in Treves' heart.

No. Trevor is too boring. Trevelian? No, no. Much too pretentious.

She went silent again and Treves found himself straining to hear more.

I'm almost completely done mending the mess those dark fairies made of your insides. Won't you come back and tell me your name? Don't you think I deserve a reward for all my hard work?

She went silent again and Treves blinked, bringing his sire back into focus. "What do you mean by The One?"

This is going to hurt, big guy. I hope you're as strong as you look.

Treves turned and began moving closer to the voice, his question forgotten. A burning ache grew in his chest with each step he took away from his sire. Despite the pain now throbbing over his entire body, he couldn't resist the woman who called to a part of him no one had ever touched.

"The One who holds the key to your happiness, my son. The mother of your daughter and son. The one who can end the curse if you allow her." His sire whispered. "You only have to let her into your heart and have faith."

He turned at his sire's words, but a flash of pain consumed him as something jerked him out of the In-between and back into his body.

Time to wake up. Come on, love. Open those gorgeous golden eyes and ease your son's worry.

Treves lifted his heavy eyelids and met a pair of eyes the color of the purest emerald sparkling as if lit from within by the sun. "Juvelet," he whispered.

Her eyes widened, emphasizing the thick lashes and arched brows matching the auburn hair framing her fine-boned face.

She smiled. "Welcome back, handsome."

AVAILABLE ON AMAZON

To learn more or subscribe to Sabrina's newsletter for updates, visit:
https://www.sabrinaafish.com/d2

Made in the USA
Monee, IL
15 July 2025